THE DARK BRAIN
OF PIRANESI
and Other Essays

MARGUERITE

The Dark Brain
of Piranesi
and Other Essays

YOURCENAR

TRANSLATED BY RICHARD HOWARD
IN COLLABORATION WITH THE AUTHOR

*("Humanism and Occultism in Thomas Mann" translated
by Grace Frick in collaboration with the author)*

FARRAR · STRAUS · GIROUX
NEW YORK

CONTENTS

THE DARK BRAIN
OF PIRANESI
and Other Essays

Faces of History
in the
Historia Augusta

IF, OF ALL THE HISTORIES HUMAN MEMORY HAS RECORDED,
Rome's more than any other has made philosophers ponder,
poets dream, moralists preach, this is due in part to the genius
of a handful of Roman historians (and a couple of Greek
ones) who have forcefully helped perpetuate to our own day
and age the remembrance and renown of Rome. It is because
Plutarch shows us the conspirators assaulting the divine
Julius in the Senate that Caesar remains—and in spite of all
the political murders committed since—the exemplary image
of the dictator put to death. It is Tacitus who casts Tiberius
forever as the misanthropic tyrant, Nero as the failed artist.
It is because Suetonius's biographical series contains twelve
emperors that our library shelves and the façades of Renaissance palaces are almost obligatorily surmounted by twelve
busts of the Caesars.

But these great historians, several of whom were first and
foremost great stylists, all flourished, to use the customary
term, within the two centuries, more or less, between Caesar's youth and Hadrian's maturity. Dull Domitian, with

whom Suetonius ends his dodecastyle arcade, is the last Roman emperor to profit by a great portrait painter. After him, and during the three hundred and fifty-some years still to elapse till the Fall of Rome, we have none but mediocre witnesses, not only prejudiced (as invariably they are), but credulous, conventional, chaotic, frequently trivial to excess or superstitious to extravagance, working almost openly for propagandistic purposes, reflecting in their mind and in their language the end of a culture, yet absorbing because their very mediocrity confers a sort of veracity upon them, makes them the qualified interpreters of a disappearing world.

The *Historia Augusta*, that compilation in which six historiographers have marshaled twenty-eight portraits of emperors, as well as those of several pretenders and of several Caesars (the title here means: heirs presumptive) who died young, offers of these three hundred and fifty years a slice of life just less than two centuries thick. The work begins with Hadrian and his immediate successors, Antoninus and Marcus Aurelius, *i.e.*, in the palmiest days of the *Pax Romana*, at the apogee of a world unaware its end was so near. It concludes with the obscure Carinus, in the twilight of the third century. The very name and existence of the five chief authors (Spartianus, Capitolinus, Lampridius, Pollio, Vopiscus) is today a matter of controversy, and the dates assigned them vary, depending on scholars and specialists, from the middle of the second to the end of the fourth century. A good deal of the *Historia* compiles or epitomizes earlier biographies which have been lost, and has been abundantly interpolated in its turn. Like so many works from ancient times, it has reached us only through several rare copies, incomplete and erroneous, which are all that have rescued it from oblivion. And yet it is not possible for modern historians of Antiquity to ignore the *Historia Augusta*; the very ones who deny its validity are obliged to resort to it nonetheless. So sparse and meager are the second- and third-century documents which survive that it is this uncertain text, which eminent scholars have with some reason suspected of being almost a total imposture, which we must scrutinize, as best we can, for some semblance of the truth.

Authenticity is one thing, veracity another. Whatever the date, varying from the year 284 at the earliest and 395 at the latest, which can be assigned to the composition of the *Historia Augusta* as a whole, the significant question is one of its reliability, which will vary of course from compiler to compiler and from page to page. Verisimilitude itself is not always a decisive criterion for the reader, the concept of what is plausible depending, in historical matters, on the customs, prejudices, and ignorances of each period. Thus, for example, seventeenth-century scholars, steeped in Christian traditions, eagerly accepted any unflattering portrait of the pagan emperors, regarding them without distinction as infamous persecutors of the nascent Church; in reaction to them came the implicit confidence in human nature among learned men of the eighteenth century; then, later, the narrow-minded prudery of certain types of nineteenth-century historians, their curious respect for those in power (even those dead eighteen hundred years), or quite simply their lack of experience of life, often made these bookworms declare impossible or unlikely certain phenomena which a reader more accustomed to looking reality in the face will not hesitate to deem tenable or to believe true. The atrocities we have witnessed in our own century have taught us to read less skeptically the account of the crimes of emperors of the

Decadence; and as for the history of sexual morals, had not La Rochefoucauld already observed that Heliogabalus's debauchery would surprise us less if the secret history of our contemporaries were better known? In some cases, the *Historia Augusta*'s veracity is confirmed by other testimony of the period. In others, and with a singular frequency, the labors of modern historians have seconded the *Historia* after the fact. Hadrian's administrative and economic reforms are vouched for by too many epigraphical texts for us to suppose that Spartianus, or the biographer who assumes that name, would be satisfied to offer what has been seen as a purely imaginary portrait of that emperor's reign, imitated from the edifying model of Augustus's government. The countless medals and statues of Antinous recovered from the Renaissance to our own day abundantly confirm the brief mention by this same Spartianus of Hadrian's desperate grief at the favorite's death and the divine honors paid to his memory, which would otherwise have passed for the type of scandalous fabrication introduced into the biography of a sagacious ruler. That tale from the *Arabian Nights* which is the story of Heliogabalus as told by Lampridius seems less absurd today than it used to, by reason of our greater knowledge of the cults and customs of the East; we glimpse the meaning of what the chronicler denounced in ignorance. All in all, and in spite of the long list of forged documents, of inept assertions, and of confusions of names, dates, and events which can be instanced there, it is less in the statement of facts than in the interpretation made of the facts that error and mendacity often flourish in the *Historia Augusta*.

Nine times out of ten, mendacity is of course dictated by partisan hatred or by flattery of the reigning *princeps*. The portrait of Gallienus is merely a lampoon inspired by senatorial rancor; that of Claudius the Goth contains about as much truth as an electoral harangue of our own day, or as a funeral oration of the seventeenth century. And though such hatred and such adulation are particularly rife in the biography of those princes close in time to their portraitists, the emperors of the remoter past are similarly besmirched or whitewashed according to the political tendencies of the chroniclers and those of the present Augustus. Commodus was certainly a detestable ruler, but his life by Lampridius is no more than a rabid *post mortem* indictment which ultimately makes the reader want to side with this brute held up to public execration. The historians for the most part support the plutocratic and conservative group which the Senate had become; the best emperors, who made drastic cuts in senatorial sinecures, are excoriated; the worst, if they come from senatorial ranks or if the Senate has backed them, are exalted. But we must not look for too much consistency from the biographers of the *Historia Augusta*. Even more frequently than to prejudice, their efforts seem due to the puerility which uncritically welcomes the merest rumor, to the conformism which accepts any official version without turning a hair, and, at least with regard to the first part of the compilation, to the disparity in time.

For even in the most favorable hypothesis, the biographers of the *Historia Augusta* are separated from the Antonines, their great models, by an instance of some hundred and twenty-five years. Of course this was not the first time an ancient historian found himself so far, or even much farther, from the figures he was seeking to portray. But the ancient world in the time of Plutarch, say, was still homogeneous enough for the Greek biographer to produce, at nearly a hundred and fifty years' distance, an image of Caesar carved in virtually the same substance as Caesar. At the period when the *Historia Augusta* was compiled, on the contrary, the world had so altered as to render the great Antonines' way of life and of thought virtually impenetrable to biographers already on the road leading to the Byzantine Empire. A little closer in time, but more exotic, more rapidly distorted by popular superstition, the rulers of the Syrian dynasty vanish even more utterly beneath a forest of legends. Thereafter, chances of error due to remoteness in time gradually diminish with the emperors who devour one another during the rest of the third century, but models and painters alike sink into that magma of confusion, violence, and mendacity characteristic of all periods of crisis. From one end of the *Historia Augusta* to the other, everything sounds as if a small group of today's men of letters, more or less well informed but mediocre, and often no more than ordinarily conscientious, were to tell us first the history of Napoleon or of Louis XVIII by means of authentic documents seasoned with prefabricated anecdotes, anachronistically tinged by the passions of our own day and age, and then, shifting to figures and events of more recent vintage, were to offer about Jaurès, Hitler, Pétain, or De Gaulle a mass of worthless gossip mingled with some useful information, an avalanche of literature from Propaganda Bureaus and sensational revelations from the gossip columns.

The worst disadvantage of their constant mediocrity is that the biographers of the *Historia Augusta* never show us their man in his depths or at his heights—a serious matter when the man concerned is one who possesses heights and depths; still more serious, we perceive this defect only in cases where other documents of the period inform us that the man thus simplified, reduced, or enlarged was truly great. Spartianus has revealed in Hadrian the skillful and pragmatic administrator overlooked by those who prefer turning him into a sort of vague aesthete; he has also seen certain whimsical and irritating aspects of this complex man. But on the other hand, everything which concerns Hadrian the *littérateur*, the art lover, the traveler, the man endowed with universal curiosity, reaches us distorted by superstitions of another age or by a mediocrity of mind which is of all ages. Like so many of his contemporaries, Hadrian was certainly interested in divination by the stars, but when Spartianus shows us the astrologer-emperor noting on January 1 everything that would happen day by day throughout the year, he prematurely plunges us into the credulous world of the worst medieval chroniclers. Hadrian's literary tastes are discussed with the literalism of an ill-informed journalist, and the statesman himself, insofar as his innovations and reforms were inspired by a humanistic ideal the biographer no longer shares, is not always understood any better. In Capitolinus's hands, Antoninus Pius becomes a figure out of popular hagiography, the impeccable hero of a kind of imperial primer. If we did not have the *Meditations*, we should never divine the unique spiritual quality of the melancholy Marcus Aurelius in the conventional portrait this same Capitolinus draws of the good emperor and of Faustina's weak-minded husband.

The mediocrity which keeps the biographers from understanding the last representatives of the great Greco-Roman culture is equally detrimental to them when it comes to evaluating the singular figures of the Syrian dynasty, or even to assessing accurately the great military leaders of the late third century. Julia Domna's incestuous affair with her son Caracalla (whom the historian, moreover, erroneously supposes to be her stepson) too closely resembles Nero's episode with Agrippina for us not to suspect Spartianus of having sought to imitate the best models. Almost nothing is evident, in Lampridius's vague insults to Julia Soaemias and in his vague encomia of Julia Mammea, of the very special character of these frivolous Syrian ladies, scheming and ambitious but also pious, literary, devoted to the arts, worshipping Apollonius of Tyana or inviting Origen to their court; and once we subtract ritual motivations from the debauches of Heliogabalus, the voluptuous Eliacin of the Temple of Emesa is little more, in the *Historia Augusta*, than the crazed hero of a series of obscene anecdotes. It is not only political hatred which makes the portrait of Gallienus into a crude caricature: this cultivated man, devoted to the cause of religious tolerance, friend and protector of the great Plotinus, preserving certain bygone refinements in an age of anarchy, seems to have been even more misunderstood, if possible, than calumniated by his mediocre portraitist. The harsh Aurelian himself, crude promoter of the sect of the Invincible Sun, was perhaps made of finer clay than Vopiscus's clumsy sketch would suggest.

Even more characteristically, these biographers so unconcerned with true physiognomy, so eager to cast their heroes into the conventional mold of the good or bad *princeps*, are even more myopic in the presence of the great half-secret events which ultimately influenced history more than any palace revolution on the Palatine Hill. It would be impossible, reading the *Historia Augusta*, to guess that during these same two hundred years the Christian tide was gradually rising, and that the very moment this compilation is officially closed is just when Constantine assures the temporal triumph of this same Christianity channeled into the state religion. If, as certain scholars believe, the writing of the *Historia Augusta* was even later than we suppose, this incapacity to account for the Christian revolution is only all the more striking, and all the more typical of a certain kind of human behavior. These conservative and pagan biographers are ignorant of almost everything about the old order they revere, and seek to be equally ignorant of the new order being imposed upon them in spite of themselves, an order they oppose by a policy of silence, almost never uttering its name. Moreover, despite a long series of disasters always adjudged accidental or discreetly attributed to the follies or crimes of a prince or a pretender already dead, but never to the redhibitory defects of the state itself, despite the Empire's economic chaos, growing inflation, military anarchy within, and constantly increasing pressure of the barbarians on the borders, these historians seem not to have anticipated that great event whose approaching shadow nonetheless darkens the whole of the *Historia Augusta*: the death of Rome.

And yet, despite its fundamental mediocrity, or perhaps because of it, the *Historia Augusta* makes overwhelming reading; it enthralls us as much as, and sometimes more than, the work of historians worthier of trust and admiration. A dreadful odor of humanity rises from this book: the very fact that no powerful writer's personality has left its imprint upon it leaves us face to face with life itself, with that chaos of shapeless and violent episodes in which can be discerned, it is true, certain general laws, but laws which almost always remain invisible to protagonists and to witnesses. The historiographer wavers with the temperature of the mob, sometimes shares its unsavory and blasé curiosity, sometimes its hysteria. We have here what was whispered about Faustina's adulteries or Verus's brawls by lesser guests at Marcus

Aurelius's table, or what a third-century patrician whispered between two Senate sessions in favor of the "decent candidate" who had just bought himself many votes. No book ever reflected so well as this leaden and all-absorbing work the judgments of the man-in-the-street and the man-on-the-backstairs as to the history of the moment. We have here public opinion in the pure state—which is to say, impure.

From time to time, a detail is of a rightness which suffices to authenticate in and of itself: we see the swaying, effeminate gait of Heliogabalus; we hear his shrill laugh—the laugh of a badly brought up child that could drown out the actors' voices in the theater. We witness the murder of Caracalla, cut down by his guards as he gets off his horse to urinate at the roadside. The two brief biographies devoted to that dynasty of dandies, Aelius Caesar and his son Verus, transmit with an ineffable futility two slightly different aspects of the man of fashion as he figured in Rome between the years 130 and 150 of our era; add to this the few lines concerning Aelius Caesar in the biography of Hadrian and we shall see that Spartianus, or the anonymous author who borrows that name, has brushed in twice over the equivalent of a great Balzacian portrait, the glamorous sketch of a second-century Rastignac or Rubempré.

Sometimes even a certain poetry rises out of this mass of grim details, like mist from the bare ground: the senators' lugubrious imprecations over Commodus's corpse have the tragic grandeur of a crowd scene in Shakespeare; a strange beauty emerges from the few artless phrases in which Spartianus describes, on the eve of Septimus Severus's death, the emperor sacrificing in the Temple of Bellona in the tiny British town which is today's Carlisle in Cumberland, at the western end of Hadrian's Wall. The provincial victimiary, unfamiliar with Roman customs, had secured a pair of black bullocks, creatures of ill omen which the emperor refused to sacrifice and which, released by the temple servants, then followed him to his own doorstep, thereby adding a presage of death to one already disclosed. A glimpse of the Empire's quotidian life in the never-changing countryside is revealed by what in Spartianus is no more than a superstitious trait: these few words suffice to evoke a cold or rainy February day on the Scottish border, the emperor in military garb, his African complexion blanched by disease and the northern climate; the two placid bullocks, product and emblem of the earth itself, unwittingly escaping the bloody folly of sacrifice, ignorant of this human world and this alien man for whom they augur death, clambering free through the muddy alleyways of this little garrison town before returning to their wild hillsides.

But this poetry is a poetry we ourselves extract, as it is we ourselves who find—in the account of the young blond barbarian Maximian insolently detaching himself from the body of the troops on parade and caracoling under the emperor's eyes—a scene worthy of Tolstoy, a smell of sweat and leather, a clatter of hoofs across the morning earth sixteen centuries ago. In the same way, it is we ourselves who turn the quite fabulous description of the Suicide Tower built by Heliogabalus, with its gold daggers, its poisons in flasks of precious stones, its silk ropes for hanging, and its marble pavements for breaking skulls, into a fantasy in the style of Beckford's *Vathek*, a curious refinement of the gothic novel ... In each case, it is the modern reader's imagination which isolates and disengages from the huge mass of more or less fabricated anecdotes the tiny drop of poetry, or, what comes down to the same thing, the particle of intense and immediate reality.

.   .   .

The period's works of arts and its monuments constitute perhaps the best commentary on the *Historia Augusta*. The busts first of all, which confirm or occasionally contradict these imperial biographers: Hadrian's countenance at once judicious and dreamy, his nervous mouth and his features soon swollen by the advance of dropsy; the carefully barbered heads of Aelius and his son; the straight jaw and the hard, rectangular profile of Antoninus Pius; the benign Marcus Aurelius on the Capitol, who looks quite like the one in the *Historia*, and the weary, tormented head of a much older Marcus Aurelius in the British Museum, who instead resembles the author of the *Meditations*; Commodus's grotesque ringlets, Caracalla's face of an old trooper, and Heliogabalus's sly little muzzle, which, it must be admitted, corresponds better to Lampridius's young degenerate than to the mystic debauchee of the enthusiasts of historical fiction; the soft and pensive faces of the Syrian empresses, or the gnarled features of the Illyrian emperors, those "sabers"* who temporarily restored order throughout the Empire the way an officer on a night of rioting reasserts it in well-lighted public squares. Then we have the testimony of the coins: from first to last of the twenty-eight reigns described by the *Historia Augusta*, the imperial profiles gradually lose their modeling, their carefully differentiated surfaces, which were still those of ancient statuary, and end as those flat and ever more uncertain images scratched on gold coins thin as paper; even better than the *Historia*'s allusions to edicts forbidding the rise in prices, to sumptuary laws, and to public auctions of state property, they express the pangs of a dying economy. The Hellenized and neoclassical art of Hadrian's time, the

* *Manu ad ferrum.*

official and rather heavy art of Marcus Aurelius's abound in
the biographers' sense of these two wise emperors; the
obelisk on the Pincio corroborates in hieroglyphics Spartianus's account of the death of Antinous in Egypt; the
stuccos of the Pythagorean basilica at Porta Maggiore attest
to the poetic pagan piety which continued to inspire idealistic
souls between Hadrian and Alexander Severus, as it is
evoked, for instance, by Lampridius's description of the latter's private chapel. The civilized graces of Hadrian's villa, to
which Aurelian later relegated his captive Zenobia, the
enormous ruins of the Septizonium in which the already
orientalized court of the Severi gathered, Gallienus's pa-
vilion near the Via Labicana, meager vestiges of those
imperial pleasure houses in parks planted with rare flowering
plants, populated by tame beasts, which occupied a fifth of
the superficies of Rome, substantiate the drama by the
melancholy survival of its decor. The politics of prestige at
all costs and of pleasure at any, the mindless luxury of the
games and the megalomaniac processions are confirmed by
the gigantic carcasses of the monuments consecrated to public diversions and comforts, the Baths of Caracalla or
Diocletian, whose dimensions seem to grow and whose
ornamentation to proliferate by very reason of the Empire's
economic chaos, and doubtless served to keep it hidden. The
puffy and microcephalic athletes of the Baths of Caracalla
mosaics are indeed brothers to those gymnasts hired to
strangle Commodus and sought out by Heliogabalus for
other purposes. The horrible catalogues of the thousands of
African and Asian wild animals subjected to the terrors and
miseries of a long sea voyage and ultimately massacred to
afford the comfortably seated spectators an exciting afternoon—all this waste of the substance of the world is matched

not only in the Coliseum but in the provincial arenas of Italy and Spain, of Africa and Gaul; the frenzy for professional sport is still attested to by the vestiges of the Circus Maximus. But of all the constructions of the period, the Aurelian Walls indicate most tragically this mortal disease of Rome, whose temporary recoveries and inevitable relapses fill the *Historia Augusta*. These majestic walls, which are still for us the very emblem of the grandeur that was Rome, were the headlong product of the years of insecurity. Each of their vaults and guard towers proclaims that the old, open Rome, sure of itself and well defended on its frontiers, has ceased to exist; immediately useful and ultimately futile, like all defensive measures, they herald the sack by Alaric a little over a hundred years away.

Just as the abuses and weaknesses of third-century Rome were already to be discerned in the Rome of the Empire's great days, even in those of the Republic, many of the *Historia Augusta*'s defects are also imputable to the ancient historians of the major period; only by scrutinizing them closely do we note a difference due less to a change in method than to a cultural collapse. The same absence of system, the same incapacity to date an incident or a feature of behavior, and consequently the same tendency to offer as a man's characteristic what is often but an isolated action in the course of his life, the same mixture of serious political information and of anecdotes too intimate not to be fabricated in most cases, are to be encountered in Suetonius, too; but the latter's cold perspicacity, his realism equal to that of Holbein, ultimately makes these tiny juxtaposed chance touches into a convincing portrait, suggests rightly or wrongly a true likeness: there is a psychological truth in Suetonius, whatever defects there may be from the historical point of view. The chroniclers of the *Historia Augusta* are rarely capable of such successes. In every age, the great biographers of antiquity did not shrink from quoting uncritically or from altogether making up a speech or a celebrated phrase destined to epitomize a situation or a character: this is because history for a Livy or a Plutarch was an art at least as much as a science, and rather than a manner of recording events a means of advancing in the knowledge of mankind. The letters and decrees forged or corrupted by Vopiscus and Pollio, on the contrary, are simply fake documents and not psychological portraits.

The same is true of the exasperating moralism which encumbers the *Historia*; it also flaws the narrative by the greatest historians of Antiquity, thereby spoiling more than one authentic masterpiece. But if Tacitus, among others, is not free of the defect which consists in exaggeratedly blackening the guilty, idealizing the virtuous, even simplifying to excess the tumultuous array of human affairs, it seems that this anything but impartial man is nonetheless often fair. His genius as a great painter keeps him from falling into simplification or caricature; even when abusive, his indignation remains that of an honest man still inspired by the solid civic ideals of Antiquity. Spartianus, and all the more his four confrères, belongs on the contrary to a period in which this tradition of civic virtues, even the memory of a free man's morality, is eclipsed. Their furious tirades against luxury or the corruption of manners (often allied with love of obscene details) are borrowed from the banal repertoire of the period's rhetoricians and sophists. Superimposed upon this intemperate ethic, which puts the crime of eating expensive fruit out of season or relieving oneself in silver vessels on the same level as political assassination or fratricide, we notice of course an utter indifference to the real defects of the period: the cowardice of the mob, the universal servility with regard to the masters of the hour, the spasmodic but fierce persecution of Christian minorities, the pompous misery of a culture consisting of no more than a schoolboy's anthologies—all of which a few free minds were already denouncing and which the Christian historians (equally blind, it is true, to the sins of their own age) would have great sport indicting in centuries to come.

Gradually the eye learns to recognize in this chaos certain series of likely facts, certain recurrences of events—not precisely a plan, but certain schemas. In the second century, two emperors born in Andalusia, one of whom, at least, belonged in spirit to Greece as much as to Rome, afforded humanity almost a century's respite. This increasingly vast area from which the emperors would be drawn extends even more in the third century: Septimus Severus, a Carthaginian, succeeds Antoninus; the Syrians succeed the Punics; Philip, an Arab, presides in 248 at Rome's millennial ceremonies; Illyrians from the ranks, who know nothing of Rome but military discipline, temporarily reestablish the principle of authority in a world given over to anarchy, but without restoring a civilization to which they themselves are alien. The so-called attempts at liberalism come too late: citizenship is granted to every inhabitant of the Empire just when it ceases being a privilege and becomes a fiscal burden, and when Rome is no longer capable of assimilating these human masses it is no longer even governing. If the emperors' birthplaces are scattered, the sites of their death seem no less far-flung: Marcus Aurelius dies exhausted on the shores of the Danube, beneath the palisades of the city which will one day be Vienna; sickness carries off Septimus Severus at Eboracum, the future York; Alexander Severus is killed in a mutiny near Mainz; Maximian's head is stuck on a pike under the walls of Aquileia; two of the Gordians fall in Africa and the third on the Persian frontier; Valerian expires in Asia in Sapor's prisons; Aurelian is murdered on the road to Byzantium, Tacitus in Cappadocia, Probus in Illyria; the corpses of the Thirty Tyrants clog the roads of Germania and of Gaul; Rome is lost and won everywhere but in Rome.

The more lingering death of institutions is scarcely accounted for by the authors of the *Historia Augusta*. Form's survival conceals the disappearance of content; the jargon of Republican formulas, already virtually devoid of meaning under the first Caesars, is still employed alongside pompous protocols and servile adulation under the orientalized monarchy of the third century, thereby satisfying those for whom appearance counts more than reality, *i.e.*, virtually everyone. Adoption and election are no more than disguised forms of auction and *coup d'état*. The principle of dynastic succession founders in bloody incompetence among the Antonines with Commodus, among the Severi with Caracalla; the Syrian dynasty gives the world nothing but a young madman and a young sage, both promptly suppressed by troops to whom the vices of Heliogabalus are of no more advantage than the dim virtues of Alexander Severus. The dynasty of the three Gordians lasts six years. Gallienus rules eight, after the capture of his father Valerian by the Persians, but is murdered in his turn, along with his son Saloninus. The army, sole support of strong regimes, thereby becomes a principle of anarchy; increasingly composed of barbarian units, it acclimates Rome to barbarism at least as much as it defends the city against it. The fierce and minor intestine struggles which occupy the whole attention of these historians unfold against a setting of events too vast to be clearly perceived by contemporaries: the backlash of peoples once intimidated or conquered, the migrations soon to overturn the world's equilibrium, the thrust of new forms beneath the corruption or desiccation of cultures, the death of old myths and the birth of new dogmas. Seen from this point of view, the vices of a Heliogabalus and the brutal virtues of an Aurelian have little more than relative importance. Yet let us not too readily accept the bromides of those for whom history is no more than a series of events against which man can do nothing, as if it were not up to each of us to shoulder the wheel, to submit or to struggle: Heliogabalus, after all, did somewhat advance, and Aurelian somewhat postpone, the fall of Rome.

It is not for us, so myopic when it comes to evaluating our own civilization, its errors, its chances of survival, and the opinion of it the future will have, to be astonished that Romans of the third or fourth centuries were satisfied to the last by vague meditations on the vicissitudes of Fortune instead of interpreting more clearly the signs that their world was coming to an end. Nothing is more complex than the curve of a decadence. The incomplete graph the *Historia Augusta* furnishes is necessarily inconclusive: Hadrian's reign is still a peak, that of the lamentable Carinus is not a conclusion. Each period of dizzying decline is followed by a halt, even by a subsequent recovery, however temporary, which was invariably supposed to be a lasting one; each savior seemed to suffice for all. In the period when the *Historia Augusta* ends, with Carinus, Diocletian is already present; the savior Diocletian will be succeeded by the savior Constantine, the savior Theodosius; a hundred and fifty years will still manage to jolt past before the long list of Roman emperors comes to an end, pathetically enough, with the child of a secretary of Attila, characteristically decked out with the pompous name of Romulus Augustulus. Meanwhile, inurement to catastrophes has replaced the refusal to anticipate or to forestall them; more rudimentary forms of political life replace the vast, now useless imperial machine, more or less as, in the villas of the last patricians of Ostia, hurriedly dug cisterns replace the complicated systems of pipes no longer fed by water from aqueducts and public fountains. The closing of the great spectacle which lasted so many centuries will soon pass virtually unnoticed.

Better still: it is just when realities vanish that man's talent to satisfy himself with mere words functions at full tilt. Once Rome has vanished, its ghost will have a persistent life. The Greek empire of Byzantium having paradoxically inherited the title "Roman Empire," a more or less fictive millennial extension is added in the East to this interminable history: in the volumes Gibbon devotes to the decline and fall of the Roman Empire, the *Historia Augusta* furnishes substance for only the first few chapters; his work ends with Mohammed II's entry into Constantinople in 1453. Elsewhere, in Western Europe, the Holy Roman Empire having assumed the inheritance of the Caesars, the ancient game is played out down through the centuries with stakes more or less similar to those of the past and a singular resemblance in the temperament of the players. It is scarcely an exaggeration to show—beyond the deeds and actions of the popes and the Guelph or Ghibelline emperors of the Middle Ages—the chaotic adventures of the *Historia Augusta* extending down to our own days, to Hitler waging his last battles in Sicily or in Benevento like a Holy Roman emperor of the Middle Ages, or to Mussolini slaughtered in his attempted flight, then strung up by the heels in a Milan garage, dying in the twentieth the death of a third-century emperor. A decadence which thus spreads over more than eighteen hundred years is something else than a pathological process: it is the human condition itself, the very notion of politics and of the state which the *Historia Augusta* calls into question, that deplorable mass of ill-learned lessons, of ill-conducted experiments, of often avoidable and never-avoided mistakes of which it offers, it is true, a particularly fine specimen but which, in one form or another, tragically fill all of history.

To men of the late nineteenth century, the Roman decadence appeared under the aspect of rose-garlanded patricians leaning on cushions or on lovely girls, or again, as Verlaine imagined them, composing indolent acrostics as they watched the great white barbarians parade past. We are better informed as to the way in which a civilization ultimately ends. It is not by abuses, by vices, or by crimes which are perennial, and nothing proves that Aurelian's cruelty was any worse than Octavius's, or that venality in the Rome of Didius Julianus was greater than in that of Sulla. The evils by which a civilization dies are more specific, more complex, more deliberate, sometimes more difficult to discover or to define. But we have learned to recognize that gigantism which is merely the morbid mimetism of growth, that waste which makes a pretense of wealth in states already bankrupt, that plethora so quickly replaced by dearth at the first crisis, those entertainments for the people provided from the upper levels of the hierarchy, that atmosphere of inertia and panic, of authoritarianism and of anarchy, those pompous reaffirmations of a great past amid present mediocrity and immediate disorder, those reforms which are merely palliatives and those outbursts of virtue which are manifested only by purges, that craving for sensation which ends in the triumph of a politics of violence, those unacknowledged men of genius lost in the crowd of unscrupulous gangsters, of violent lunatics, of honest men who are inept and wise men who are helpless . . . The modern reader is at home in the *Historia Augusta.*

MOUNT DESERT ISLAND
1958

23

Agrippa d'Aubigné
and
Les Tragiques

ONE OF THE GREATEST but also one of the least read poets of
the French Renaissance, Agrippa d'Aubigné, was born near
Pons in Saintonge, in 1552, and died in Geneva in 1630. He
came from one of those families of the minor nobility which
more than all others have furnished France with specimens
of a type rare among us: that of the refractory writer set
against the grain of his age, obsessed by the chimera of an
uncompromising rectitude and an unblemished loyalty, allied
with a lost or persecuted cause. For Agrippa d'Aubigné (or
d'Aubigny, or d'Aubigni, or Daubigny—he was unconcerned by such orthographic trifles), the lost cause was to be
the Reformation.

When he was born, the first martyrs of a still young and
politically pure evangelism were being condemned to the
stake, and in the squares of Paris the flames burned bright
and clear. When he was eight and a half, he accompanied his
father through Amboise on a market day after one of the
stupidest brawls and one of the most hideous repressions in
French history; his father showed him the corpses of the

Huguenot rebels hanging from a gibbet and made him swear to avenge these honored leaders. When he was about twelve, he was captured with his tutor by Catholic troops and sentenced to the stake, from which he managed to escape the next day through the good offices of a defrocked monk; out of sheer bravado he danced a galliard to the music of his captors' violins. Such nonchalance was typical of a man it would be wrong to suppose glum or sullen. He took part in the festivities of the day; he personally frequented Henri III, whom he was later to insult in *Les Tragiques*; his play *Circé* was put on at the king's expense on the occasion of the scandalously extravagant wedding of the royal favorite, Anne de Joyeuse. Nor is there a necessary contradiction in all this between his life and his work: one can value as they deserve the elegances of a court and the literary tastes of its prince and still detest the figure he cuts in history. D'Aubigné loved women: his passion for Diane Salviati, a Catholic, inspired him to write many poems; married to Suzanne de Lezay, he was to mourn her death with convulsions of grief which ultimately brought on a hemorrhage; at seventy, sentenced for the fourth time to death *in absentia*, he married again—this time, an agreeable widow.

As brave soldier, as bold captain, and finally—belatedly— as no more than a field marshal, d'Aubigné played his part in those inexpiable civil wars known as the Wars of Religion, but without ever being numbered among the powerful leaders or the clever politicians of the Reformation party. War itself delighted him, as he himself contritely admits, and his autobiography shows how a young man might have regarded the miseries of the time as an exciting form of adventure. For years he followed the various fortunes of Henry of Navarre, though not setting much store by his legendary *bonhomie*; he judged severely a prince who was "subtler than he was wise"; nor did he ever forgive him his abjuration. "Neither pimp nor flatterer," d'Aubigné had to put up with the ingratitude typical of this first Bourbon, as did other loyal partisans with subsequent monarchs of the dynasty. One of his best sonnets describes, with that mixture of rage and pity characteristic of his work, the spaniel Citron, a fine curly-haired dog that was once Henry's particular pet, now abandoned to the streets and half-dead of hunger, bitter symbol of the payment reserved for old loyalties. In 1610, Ravaillac's knife impressed him as an instrument of God's wrath.

D'Aubigné lived to be old enough to see the Counter-Reformation definitively established in France with Louis XIII, who dedicated his kingdom to the Holy Virgin; having sought refuge in Switzerland, where the ardent evangelism he had known in his youth had long since coagulated into state Protestantism, he appeared in Geneva as a crotchety exile who, continuing to meddle in French affairs, risked embarrassing his co-religionists. His son, a worthless drunkard, returned to the more profitable fold of the Catholic faith; his indiscretions made the old man's last years into a sinister tragicomedy. His granddaughter was the shrewd and discreet Madame de Maintenon, devout promoter of the Revocation of the Edict of Nantes, a woman left unmoved by the dragooning of the soldiers of Louvois. In his descendants, this impassioned Huguenot was almost grotesquely hapless.

As for literary glory, his fortune has been equally mediocre or adverse. Few read his love poetry; his verses are well worth remembering, though they hardly exceed what we might expect of a gentleman of spirit and learning in one of the finest and most impassioned epochs of French lyricism. His *Aventures du Baron de Foeneste* no longer entertain us,

and perhaps never entertained anyone, and the political implications of his *Sancy* have turned savorless with age. His *His-
toire Universelle*, an ambitious title for a history of the
Europe of his day, had the honor of being burned by the
executioner upon publication, but these three folio volumes
retain their value as period documents without managing to
rank d'Aubigné among the great French historians; they are
consulted more than they are read, for all the interest or
dramatic beauty of certain passages in which Sainte-Beuve
rightly saw the equivalent of Shakespearean scenes. The
same is true of the narrative *Sa Vie*, of an occasionally admirable vigor and pace, but decidedly too helter-skelter and
incomplete to class d'Aubigné among the great memorialists.
There remains *Les Tragiques*, which suffices moreover to
win him a unique place in the history of French poetry.
Famous, frequently quoted in the anthologies, the work is
nonetheless rarely read through, and for this the responsibil-
ity is largely d'Aubigné's own.

Astonished by the sublimity of certain fragments—always
the same ones, which figure in almost all the textbooks—the
reader soon discovers, if he considers the work as a whole,
that the anthologists have shown taste in their selection and
above all in their cuts. One line more and almost invariably
the poet's inspiration falls short, giving way to repetition, to
confusion, and, what is worse, to rhetoric. Verbal pomposity,
that fatal defect of French poetry when it approaches politics
or high satire, is a redhibitory defect in d'Aubigné, as it will
be in Hugo. Further, the syntax of *Les Tragiques* is often
clumsy and obscure; platitudes or trivialities of an involun-
tarily comic nature, still savoring of the waning Middle Ages,
show through the pomp of an inopportune ornamentation
which creates the written equivalent of Baroque draperies

and festoons. Agrippa d'Aubigné had all the merits of the age, the vigor, the élan, the uninhibited realism, the passion for ideas, and the indefatigable curiosity about every aspect of the human adventure, whether found in the heat of the moment or sought in the remote ages of history. He also had all the defects of his period, and almost all the absurdities. This gentleman crammed with Greek, Latin, and Hebrew from his earliest youth, this soldier who versified all his life but devoted himself exclusively to letters only in old age, suffers from a superstitious respect for literature and learning. He also suffers, twice over, from that verbal indigestion typical of his times: as a Huguenot, he meditated upon his Bible; as a humanist, he greedily absorbed all the authors of Antiquity, not to mention a certain number of works of historical vulgarization which served up the ancient world in a sixteenth-century religious sauce. Thus the sixth canto of *Les Tragiques,* entitled "Vengeances," is inspired almost word for word by an edifying little volume published around 1581 and relating the dreadful deaths which Christian rancor supposed, rightly or wrongly, to have afflicted all of Christendom's persecutors. Agrippa d'Aubigné declaims, he rambles, he has retained all the bad habits of the schoolroom and all those of the pulpit instilled in him by his teachers. And yet the nine thousand lines of this uneven work, at once clumsy and learned, good yet not nearly good enough, remind us of those rocky mountain paths that occasionally lead to sublime points of view.

For *Les Tragiques* is a great poem, less a masterpiece than an admirable sketch of that great religious epic which it has not been given to France to produce and which would be located somewhere between Dante's and Milton's. The work's plan, as d'Aubigné drew it up, then covered it over, and often drowned it under a flood of indiscreet and monotonous rhetoric, reminds us more of the architecture of a Gothic portal than that of a Renaissance portico: the seven cantos of this long poem—"Les Misères," "Princes," "La Chambre dorée," "Les Feux," "Les Fers," "Vengeances," and "Jugement"—are organized in the manner of concentric voussoirs carved with real or allegorical episodes, clustered around the base of God's throne. The work's poetic unity, which would otherwise be nothing but a versified martyrology or a rhymed chronicle of the misdeeds of rulers and judges, results from this continual presence of Divine Justice, sometimes naïvely personified with the simplicity of a medieval image maker, sometimes abstract, absolute, source of all greatness and all good, prime mover of a nature itself quasi-divine but ceaselessly dishonored or, on the contrary, surpassed by man. The work's subject involved, in effect, the perpetual contrast between the outbursts of man's ferocity, which derive from nature, and his outbursts of heroism, which proceed from the same source. D'Aubigné tends to make *Les Tragiques* into a Last Judgment, where on the one hand tyrants, executioners, and liars are already shown in their loathsomeness as damned souls, and where on the other the victims pass with an almost objectionable serenity through the gates of suffering in order to enter heaven. In a country where more than elsewhere poets turn from the actual and the immediate, choosing to deal with a purified, distilled matter already overrefined by literary tradition, d'Aubigné's extraordinary audacity consists in having taken for his material the crude substance of his age. Even in its evasions and extravagances, by which it participates in the passions of the period, *Les Tragiques* represents the chaotic effort of a contemporary of the Wars of Religion to reevaluate the bloody events of his time, somehow to recompose them in eternal terms of justice and order.

The first canto, "Les Misères" (or at least the part of "Les Misères" which is still worth reading), is mainly a bucolic in reverse, depicting the agony of peasants oppressed by the instigators of civil war, villages destroyed and reverting to savagery, the cruelty of man depriving his wretched beasts of their pasturage. D'Aubigné transcribes in "Les Misères" that humble complaint which is soon drowned out, for the victors, by the clamor of *Te Deum* and which, even for the vanquished, is almost always smothered by the more glorious and more exciting fracas of arms; much more, he expresses the mute protest of the earth devastated by man's ingratitude. This country gentleman who has read his Virgil expresses an almost religious sentiment of the world's beauty, a sympathy not always self-evident for the tiller of the fields, and even a kind of tenderness, rare in any age but less exceptional than we might suppose in men of this harsh time, for the eternally molested creatures of field and forest. But homily and pedantic amplification of examples of famine and destruction in Israel encumber this depiction of French soil with their interchangeable rhetoric. The furious insults addressed to Catherine de Médicis and to the Cardinal of Lorraine overflow into the second canto of the poem, already engulfing in Juvenalian satire a writer overwhelmed by the matter of his work.

Attacking royal dissipations and extravagances in "Princes," this Huguenot (though he has nothing of the Puritan about him) seasons undeniable truths with a strong dose of pompous commonplaces and a few flagrant calumnies. Of course, one does not dispose of Henri III by banally comparing him to Heliogabalus or to Jeroboam; one does not account for Catherine de Médicis by making her into no more than an ogress determined to destroy France, a loathsome witch as adept in the lugubrious practices of sorcery as the three Weird Sisters evoked in the same period by *Macbeth*. And yet, like Titian's venomous portrait of *Paul III and His Nephews*, or like the grotesque images Goya was to paint of María-Luisa of Spain almost two centuries later, d'Aubigné's visionary portraits of the last Valois contain a considerable portion of truth too readily neglected by biographers eager to scour and disinfect their memory. His coarse Charles IX, at once sickly and savage, inured to agony and bloodshed by the daily carnage of the hunt, his plucked and painted Henri III, are likenesses attested to both by other witnesses and by fidelity to a certain human type which occurs in all periods. Even where his insults miss their mark, this painter outraged by royal corruption remains closer to psychological truth than we could ever come, by the very fact that he shares with his models the moral judgments and even the prejudices of the age. The sins for which Henri III so dramatically atoned during those flagellant processions which d'Aubigné mocks were assuredly the same as those the poet accuses him of, sins which appeared no less serious to the contrite king than to his Protestant detractor. A client of necromancers and astrologers, Catherine would doubtless have been less surprised to find herself accused of the crime of sorcery by d'Aubigné than acquitted of it by scholars who no longer believe in the powers of the Evil One.

Every prince who has ruled and reveled in the benefits of power in a period of public disasters is professionally responsible: the queen mother's conspiratorial activity, her taste for intrigue and compromise, are no doubt more deserving of d'Aubigné's reproaches than the praises of modern historians who disguise this short-term cunning as political genius, which is altogether a different thing; and whatever Henri III's royal virtues may have been, it is natural that the wild caprices and expenditures of this last Valois should have given rise to the grandiose insults of *Les Tragiques*, as to the low invective of the League's pamphlets. It is not only that anti-monarchist propaganda was used in the same way by the Protestant camp and the Catholic ultras, but that Huguenots and Capuchins were united in expressing on the subject of royal vices and misdeeds, real or supposed, the same point of view, which is quite simply the point of view of Christians.

"La Chambre dorée," which attacks the corruption and harshness of judges, remains medieval in its allegory and satire. God leaves His heaven to discover what is happening in the courts of justice, and what He finds in these palaces mortared with human bones and cemented with ashes is a troop of grotesques depicted with a truculence worthy of Bosch or Brueghel: snoring Stupidity; shabby Avarice concealing his gold pieces; Ignorance, which finds every cause simple and does not attempt judgment; rheumy Hypocrisy; insipid Vanity; Servility, which asks no better than to countersign any decree; Fear, which weakly assents; Buffoonery, which makes a joke of any crime; and finally Youth, set among this company of harpies as greedy, insolent, eager to serve the gods of the day and to pour out their bloody brew without giving the matter a thought. A series of harsh verses, though of a matchless realism and poetic daring, evokes a Spanish *auto-da-fé* literally taking place before God's eyes. The condemned, wearing the grotesque garments with which the Inquisition decks out its victims, *conspicuous heirs / of the robe, the reed, and the crown of thorns,* are offered a crucifix to reconcile them *in extremis,* thereby affording them, as we know, the mercy of being strangled instead of burned alive. The poet's indignation explodes at the image of this inert symbol of the Passion offered to men suffering in their own flesh the Passion of Christ. It is only natural that Elizabeth of England triumphing over Philip II should then be described as a divine Themis, a Celestial Virgin in whom the persecuted Huguenots put their hope, and natural, too, that the poet should pass over in silence the iniquities and legal barbarities committed in the reign of this Protestant princess, human and partisan nature being what they are.

In the next canto, "Les Feux," the most memorable perhaps of the poem's seven books, God continues to serve as witness to judiciary crimes, and the moving, the intolerable enumeration of heretics cast into the flames continues until the Absolute Being, outraged at having created the world, withdraws indignant into His heaven. But this naïve scenario counts for little compared to the dreadful detail of the agonies themselves, that long procession of victims, some of whom bear famous names (famous at least for specialists in sixteenth-century history), but the majority of whom are forever as forgotten in their martyrs' glory as if at the last moment they had abjured their faith and lived. Anne Dubourg, councillor to the parliament, burned alive in Paris; Thomas Cranmer, primate of England, burned at the stake in Oxford; William Gardiner, British merchant, his hands chopped off and then burned at the stake in Lisbon; Dame Philippa de Luns of Graveron, her tongue cut out and then burned at the stake in the place Maubert; but also a certain Thomas Haux, burned at Cockshall; one Ann Askew, burned at Lincoln; Thomas Norris, burned at Norwich; Florent Venot, executed in Paris; Louis de Marsac, burned at Lyons; Marguerite Le Riche, bookseller, burned at Paris; Giovanni Mollio, cobbler, strangled at Rome; Nicolas Croquet, merchant, hanged in the place de Grève; Etienne Brun, farmer, burned in Dauphiné; Claude Foucaud, tortured in the place de Grève; Marie, wife of the tailor Adrian, buried alive in Tournai; obscure victims chosen at random by the poet (or for the sake of the rhyme) among batches of those condemned whose names he himself does not know. Though believing that what he is writing is merely a work of edification, d'Aubigné ventures deep into the psychology of martyrdom: he has seen that exasperation, anger, the fierce desire to defy the judge's stupidity or the executioner's brutality to the end enter just as much as mystic fervor into the victim's incomprehensible courage. Nor is he unaware of the torturer's classic procedure: the art of reviling and degrading the victim until he no longer seems human, and is repugnant instead of pitiful. He knows that banal reaction which consists in "out-Heroding Herod," in the fear of not participating zealously enough in a partisan act of collective barbarism. For once, literature is beside the point: the lugubrious narrative of tortures on the one hand, of feats of endurance on the other, before which the imagination fails in either case, is of the same order as an account of a pogrom, a report from Buchenwald, or the testimony of a witness of Hiroshima.

In "Les Fers," finally, by an invention now distinctly Baroque and also suggesting the frescoed ceilings of the Renaissance, the Angels paint with their own hands on the heavenly vaults battle scenes of the Wars of Religion for the edification of the Almighty. Battle scenes which are all, of course, of Catholic excesses and bestialities, just as the martyrs of "Les Feux" were always those of the Reformation; yet within the narrow limits of his sympathies and his partisan indignations, d'Aubigné remains no less obsessed by the dreadful problem of man's cruelty to man. Too often we excuse the crimes of the past by attributing them to the *mores* of the period, which would supposedly have authorized them, even in the eyes of their victims. Agrippa d'Aubigné's reaction to the St. Bartholomew Massacre opposes this convenient attitude: his description of the carnage, with its habitual episodes of private vengeance cloaked by official fanaticism, of meaningless lynchings, of the licentious remarks exchanged by ladies of the court over the naked and abandoned corpses, testifies to an indignation as strong as that of at least some people today in the presence of the crimes of our own time, and it is equally and tragically futile. Confronting this sinister Parisian *fait-divers*, d'Aubigné expresses it in colors at once intense and fuliginous, accentuates it with great contrasts of light and shade which are those of a Tintoretto or a Caravaggio, his transalpine contemporaries. The preparations for the Massacre, the weddings of Marie de Clèves and of Marguerite de Valois which served as their prologue and perhaps as their signal, *these bloody beds, these traps, not bed but tombs, / where Hymen's torch is changed for that of Death,* this grim twilight, *where the sky smolders with blood and souls,* are seen not as we see our murders today, as a kind of gray and jerky newsreel, but in that grand style which remains that of the sixteenth century to the end.

In "Vengeances" d'Aubigné showed us the persecutors immediately punished by mortal accidents or serious diseases, contrary to both historical truth and the more mysterious ways of God's justice. Leaving aside this heap of fabricated anecdotes and their crude moralism, let us turn to what is, on the contrary, a grave meditation on invisible Justice, *i.e.,* to the poem's final canto, perhaps the finest of all, which is entitled "Jugement." It is marred by interminable theological digressions, but there is no reason to reject in d'Aubigné what we accept in Dante or Milton. Further, and despite the unbearable length of his discussion of the Resurrection of the Flesh, the poet here undertakes a great metaphysical theme, and "Jugement" is one of the rare testimonies from this age of dogmatic disputes which lucidly and fervently present a view not only religious but mystical, which offer a profound explanation of the nature of things. Whether or not the author sought it out, the influence of ancient philosophy circulates here at the heart of Christian thought: we recognize the d'Aubigné who at the age of seven translated Plato, the student who through his Stagirite glimpsed certain speculations of pre-Socratic wisdom. Above all, we perceive that the poet has dipped into the neo-Platonic treatise of the *Divine Pymander*, translated by his friend François de Candalle, and made his own that definition of God as universal principle, act, necessity, end, and renewal all in one. Here we are very far from that Huguenot fanaticism we uniformly attribute to d'Aubigné's partisan work, too easily forgetting that the Reformation was first of all one of the great liberal and intellectual movements of the Renaissance. The tone sometimes suggests Lucretius; this description of the Resurrection of the Flesh reminds us of the great austere art of Signorelli's frescoes:

> Here, at the branching of its roots, a tree
> Feels a living trunk, a breast emerge;
> Here, the water seethes and scatters wide,
> And from its depths first hair, then heads emerge . . .
> Like a swimmer rising from his deepest dive,
> All emerge from death as if from a dream.

What d'Aubigné wants to show, through the Christian dogma of the Resurrection of the Flesh, is the slow mingling of life and death, leading each creature to that perfect state in which eternity is gradually substituted for time:

> *Thus Change itself will not become our end:*
> *It turns us not to others but ourselves . . .*
> *The world has willed that Nature evermore*
> *Maintain herself, and in order not to die,*
> *Be born again from death and bloom anew . . .*
> *Perfect love and integral desire,*
> *For here the fruits and flowers know birth alone . . .*
> *Quite dazzled still, on reason still I stand,*
> *That I might see the world's great soul with mine*
> *And thereby know what none can ever know,*
> *What ear has never heard and eye not seen.*
> *My senses have no sense, my mind flies off . . .*
> *My ravished heart is dumb, I have no word;*
> *All dies, the wingèd soul resumes its place,*
> *And swoons ecstatic in its God's embrace.*

A great moment of universal mysticism is here conceived and experienced.

Les Tragiques was not published until 1616, more than thirty years after the end of the period it depicts, which is to say that it must have seemed superannuated upon publication, especially in France, where everything, even ideological conflict, is a matter of vogue. According to d'Aubigné, certain passages were composed during his youth, and a number in any case date from before the abjuration of Henri of Navarre; there is reason to believe that nothing was added after 1610. Whatever the case, d'Aubigné's vocabulary, his form, his rhythm, like his thought itself, are essentially those of a man of the sixteenth century. One of the reasons for his ultimate failure as an epic poet lies perhaps in the fact that the language he employed was not yet settled enough for the sustained great work he sought to achieve: he could not accomplish for epic what Corneille was to do for tragedy some years later; perhaps it was too early, as it was already too late, on the contrary, when Voltaire tried to write a sequel to *Les Tragiques* in *La Henriade.* We had to wait for Romanticism until d'Aubigné's work, like that of all sixteenth-century poets moreover, again compelled the attention of poetry lovers in France, and as a matter of fact this great chaotic book, this furious torrent of oratorical violence, already belongs in many of its aspects to pre-Romanticism. It is because this epic is in reality wholly lyrical, unique by its mixture of transcendance and impassioned realism, sublime above all by its sudden outbursts and its sudden halts, by those verses which abruptly explode like voices, rise and intersect as though in a Renaissance motet: *Man is a prey to man . . . Every home is exile . . . This spiny burden that we call the Truth . . . Our day's new ways demand another style: / Let us pluck the bitter fruit with which it teems . . .* Sometimes the implacable realism attains to a sort of stridency, as when the poet, glorifying Ann Askew's martyrdom, describes the unfortunate creature undergoing in silence the torture of the strappado, the tautened ropes "shrieking in her stead"; or when, by a dreadful foreshortening, he shows us Thomas Haux still alive but already half consumed by the flames, with "those bones that once were arms" signaling to his brothers to the end. Sometimes the image is impregnated with a kind of tender and indignant pity: *The ashes of those burned are precious seed . . . As the blood of fawns erodes the teeth of a trap . . .* or on the contrary with a grace which is the very flower of strength. No one would suspect that one of the most delicious lines in the French language:

Une rose d'automne est plus qu'une autre exquise
(An autumn rose is loveliest of all)

was written not by Ronsard to celebrate some aging beauty
but by d'Aubigné to glorify a belated martyr of the Reformation. The lengthily developed image of animals perishing
along with the lightning-struck oak is perhaps, in its imposing
simplicity, the only truly Homeric comparison in our literature; the prosopopoeia of earth and fire, of the waters and
trees in rebellion against the use made of them for torture
was partially adopted by the Hugo of *Les Contemplations*, in
the same audacious lyric impulse, and we might well imagine
that if *Les Tragiques* had not existed, Hugo would never
have produced that extraordinary mixture of epic narration,
lyric outbursts, and savage satire which constitutes *Les
Châtiments*. Certain verses already cited, the quintessence of
a metaphysical assertion of the identity of being, remind us
of a Mallarmé *avant la lettre*; others, where an apposition
of abstract terms is developed almost voluptuously into a
concrete image, herald the art of a Valéry; certain great
austere metaphors, isolated and almost abrupt, suggest before their time the lofty severities of a Vigny. *Les Tragiques*
reminds us of those monuments for which the richest materials have been gathered, heaped up at the work's base
without the imagined edifice's ever being finally completed,
and which, abandoned, agape, almost inexhaustible, have
served as quarries for subsequent generations.

But one reason which does little honor to human nature
may account more than any other for this great book's partial failure. Nothing, unfortunately, is more quickly outmoded than a martyr. As long as the cause for which they
have borne witness triumphs or at least survives, it makes use

of them, playing these bloody cards to take its tricks. But there comes, often quite soon, a moment when the faith they have served grows tepid, settles into a kind of conformism in its turn, prefers not to evoke too often these great and embarrassing examples. Further, each martyr drives out his predecessor; the deviations for which they were sacrificed are not reconciled but discarded; in the course of successive conflicts, thought or human fanaticism aligns itself otherwise. The September massacres, during the French Revolution, obliterate the memory of St. Bartholomew's Day; the mass executions of the Paris "Communards" in 1871 replace the Revolution's scaffolds; the dead of the Resistance sink in their turn into legend, overshadow, or oblivion. D'Aubigné's greatness consists in his having tried to imprison in poetry's resistant form not the groans but the fervent appeals to God offered by the martyrs of his cause; he spoke for voices reduced to silence; he also vented his fury on those he believed to have committed, or not to have prevented, injustice. Agrippa d'Aubigné could be neither the great captain nor the great politician his party required if it was to prevail in France, nor the great moderator who was even more necessary to his cause. This man of solid flesh and blood was not, himself, one of the saints or one of the martyrs. He was too prejudiced to be, as he would have wished, the definitive historian of the Reformation. But this poet, who in his childhood had promised his father to remember the hanged martyrs of Amboise, magnificently fulfilled the function of bearing witness.

CINTRA
1960

Ah,
Mon Beau Château...

SOME CHÂTEAUX ARE NYMPHS, indolently lounging beside their streams; some are versions of Narcissus, doubled in the still water of their moats, hostage to the reflections which cast upon stone ramparts a trembling wall of light. Chenonceaux belongs to both these categories. Smaller than most royal châteaux of the Loire, nestled within the idyllic landscape of a corner of Touraine, it does not evoke, like its great neighbors Amboise or Blois, the memory of decisive moments in the history of France. Nor is it, like Chambord, a vast hunting lodge born of a king's extravagant whim. Its almost discreet charm is that of a private residence, and as luck would have it, chiefly a residence of women. Finally, a sadder fortune has decreed that these successive chatelaines be almost always widows.

A widow superintended its construction; another imbued it with her legend; this stone trinket has provoked or sharpened the jealous passions of widows. A love-château, according to a certain touristic literature: more likely a château of worldly calculation and financial manipulation, and also of their collapse, a dwelling of carking care or of solitary old age, exposed to the litigations which follow the dissolution or downfall of reigns, encumbered with debts at least as much as it is enriched by memories, yet illuminated forever by the glow of some splendid festivities celebrated here between yesterday's uncertainties and tomorrow's. From this point of view at least, Chenonceaux is typical: it was always the misfortune of beautiful abodes to be, almost by definition, abodes of luxury as well, and as such especially subject to the unstable powers of money which we do not always recognize under their nobler or more picturesque guises from the past. Let us take advantage of this pretext—their juxtaposition in one and the same place—to examine these four or five masters, or in this case mistresses, of the house, each of whom represents the culmination of a society or a group, or its last stage before its decline; let us try to collect what we know to be true about these men or women. Everything has been said: we shall add no new facet to the history of their château, and of their own lives. Yet let us venture to reinvestigate the known facts—they are often less so than is supposed. "Diane de Poitiers!" recently exclaimed a young French novelist of talent and even a certain culture, "yes, that mistress of François I who publicly bathed naked in the Cher by torchlight . . ." Let us leave such pleasures to Technicolor and commit neither the error of the naïve reader, who is depressed by massacres and legal tortures and who congratulates himself upon living in the twentieth century, nor that of the reader of historical novels, who safely delights in the splendid crimes and scandals of the past; above all, let us not envy the past its stability . . . And let us even extinguish the floodlights projecting upon the walls and roofs of old residences a poetry which has its beauty but which is merely the reflection of today superimposed on yesterday, endowing things with a "lighting" they do not possess. In the course of this promenade without a *son et lumière,* perhaps we shall gain a better knowledge of these beings shut away in other compartments of time, and of this place itself, so often the object of passions or the stake of plots, and which today is scarcely more for the tourist than a noble witness to past splendors, a stopover, the goal of an excursion, a site where one can stretch one's legs and dream . . .

After an inglorious series of family disputes, of lean years and financial expedients repeated with grim monotony throughout the history of this fine estate, in 1512 a ruined gentleman sold his ancestral lands of Chenonceaux to one of his creditors, the rich bourgeois Thomas Bohier, who, by means of skillfully doctored contracts and barely legal distraints, had long since taken measures to be certain this ripe fruit would fall into his hands. At this period, the estate consisted of a considerable extent of woods and fields, a watchtower, sole vestige of a ruined manor house, and a mill beside the water.

Thomas Bohier and his wife, Catherine, she too from a family of rich Touraine bankers, both belonged to that small compact group of *généraux des finances* who were the farmers-general of the sixteenth century and whose members shared among themselves the cake of the kingdom's treasury. Catherine was the niece *"à la mode de Bretagne"* of the great Semblançay, who was ultimately hanged at Montfaucon for embezzlement and whose name remains known to poetry lovers thanks to an epigram by Marot celebrating his intrepidity on the gibbet. This powerful figure supported Thomas Bohier in his efforts to appropriate Chenonceaux. Thomas, for his part, possessed the generalship of finance in Normandy; he had accompanied two Kings of France on their Italian expeditions as master of accounts and treasurer-general of war: this astute banker was in high favor, being a man of resource in difficult times.

No doubt Catherine shared her husband's taste for luxury and for modern art, which in the sixteenth century was Italian art. Having possessed themselves of the premises, the Bohiers began at once by renovating the little watchtower in that almost medieval style of foliated windows, artificial catwalks, and decorative machicolation which in a sense was the graceful pseudo-Gothic of the Renaissance. It was between 1515 and 1522 that Catherine Bohier, during the long absences of her husband, whose functions kept him in Paris with the king, or with the army, supervised the building of the château proper. We do not know the name of the probably local master mason she employed for this undertaking, but we can readily imagine this woman who had been young in the days of Anne of Brittany and who perhaps still wore the starched coifs of the old court, riding on her mule or her caparisoned palfrey the six good leagues between Tours and Chenonceaux in order to oversee the construction of embankments and the rising foundations.

In 1521, Thomas Bohier left for the fourth time to rejoin the king's armies in Italy. If he took the time to visit his château still masked by scaffolding, what he saw did not differ in essentials from what is before our eyes today: a square dwelling with corner turrets and a still quite medieval moat, washed by the river onto which its southern façade backed. The new structure had been ingeniously set on the old mill's pilings, which, hollowed out, were destined to be turned into kitchens, cellars, slaughterhouses, boat sheds; in short, to supply that raw reality which is the servants' realm and into whose repellant detail the master does not venture. The nobler stories, their windows wide to the sun and air, their suites of rooms whose parquet and tiling were still to be laid, their straight staircases, an Italian invention replacing the medieval spirals, all testified to the amenity the Renaissance introduced into manners. They also proved that Thomas had not seen the splendid villas of the Lombard plain for nothing. This time the general of finance doubtless intended to bring from Italy all the furniture, tapestries, and hangings he could lay hands on.

Thomas was never to see Chenonceaux again. He died less than three years later in the Piedmont village of Vigelli, in the rear guard of the retreating French troops. In the museum of Capodimonte in Naples, there is a series of tapestries commissioned by the Hapsburgs to commemorate their victory at Pavia, which occurred the following year and which ended disastrously for the French, temporarily halting the mad "Italian Wars," the scourge of three generations of Frenchmen. Here we can see a realistic image of the disasters of war among which Thomas Bohier closed his eyes for the last time: peasants indifferent to the armies' fortunes but fearful for their cattle; knights helping themselves to booty or pillaging the inhabitants; camp followers and whores deserting to the enemy; noble lords staggering through the mud, trailing their plumed bonnets, their extravagant codpieces, and their embroidered crossbelts. Catherine settled down to her widowhood in the finally completed château; she survived her husband by a little over two years.

"One must be thirty years old in order to think of making one's fortune," writes La Bruyère; "nor is it settled at fifty; one builds in one's old age, and one dies when one has come to the painters and glaziers." This is virtually the story of the Bohiers. For this wealthy woman who for two years dragged out her widowed existence among these new walls, the rather ill-gotten estate was doubtless no more than an aborted dream. Yet it was to this financier's wife that the château, in which six queens lived or sojourned, owes the aspect it has retained to our own day. The bridge she planned to throw across the Cher was built only by Catherine de Médicis; the interior decoration was in large part renewed under Henri II, then more or less redone and spoiled by nineteenth-century restorers, but on the whole Chenonceaux remains what Catherine Bohier had made it.

Diane de Poitiers was forty-eight when, in 1547, the very year of his accession, King Henri II gave her Chenonceaux. In so doing he gave away what belonged not to him but to the crown, the château having meanwhile become state property. As it happened, the son of Thomas and Catherine Bohier, Antoine, and his wife, Anne Poncher, were soon forced to give up this residence in which they lived, if at all, only in fear and confusion. In 1527, Anne's father, the treasurer Poncher, had accompanied Semblançay to the scaffold at Montfaucon, and Antoine Bohier, implicated in what was one of the greatest financial scandals of the Renaissance, agreed to surrender his estate in payment of an enormous fine. But the prudent Diane insisted on the appearance of having bought Chenonceaux from a private person, lest her château someday be taken from her because illegally acquired, if by mischance the king's support should be withdrawn. She therefore schemed to annul the cession of Chenonceaux to the crown, which had already been ratified twelve years before, on the excuse of a falsification in the inventory of the estate. Her next move would then be to buy back at low cost the château which had been returned to Antoine Bohier only to be the more readily seized again and sold off. Threatened once again with having to pay his old debt to the state, from which he had presumed he was already released by surrendering Chenonceaux, Antoine Bohier fled to Venice, taking with him the deeds of the too-alluring property the favorite had just appropriated so cheaply. The king supported Diane de Poitiers in the course of this iniquitous judiciary comedy, which lasted seven years; Diane finally triumphed and remained the legal mistress of a Chenonceaux which had cost her nothing, since Henri had provided her with the cash necessary to buy it back at such an absurdly low price. It is worth recalling this sordid episode when we contemplate in museums those admirable portraits Clouet or Jean Goujon left us of this goddess of the Renaissance. The cold Diane had the cunning of a dishonest businessman and the temperament of a miser.

Diane de Poitiers is one of the rare women to have become, and to have remained, famous for their beauty alone, a beauty so absolute, so inalterable, that it casts into shadow the very personality of the woman endowed with it. Popular imagination has vainly tried to animate this splendid marble: to Diane has been attributed a melodramatic affair with François I, to whom she supposedly gave herself as a very young woman in order to save her father, who had been sentenced to death. The anecdote is in Brantôme, where Diane remains anonymous, but where the storyteller reports or rather invents the crude remarks of a father extremely pleased to have got off so cheaply; remarks which Hugo transformed into a long tirade of outraged virtue at the beginning of *Le Roi s'amuse*.

But this is merely legend, and there is a kind of generosity in this act of filial devotion of which it seems Diane was hardly capable. What we know about her is less dramatic and more peculiar. Of a very grand family, married young to an

old lord, a correct wife and the mother of two children, she
was a widow of thirty-seven when she met the future Henri
II, then seventeen, at a ball. This strange passion for a
woman twenty years his senior was the sole folly of this
prudent and gloomy prince, who was, all in all, a well-behaved
monarch. Immediately upon his accession he gave the widow
the crown jewels, made her a duchess, and lavished upon her
the funds of his privy purse. We have already seen to what
abrogation of justice his love for Diane had led him in the
affair of the Château of Chenonceaux.

Henri was married to an Italian girl of seventeen with
olive skin and fine eyes—that Catherine de Médicis who was
to become the dowager queen possessed of a genius for intrigue, unscrupulous when it came to defending her children's patrimony. But at the moment of Diane's entrance
on the stage, Catherine was still no more than an isolated
foreigner at the court of France, and wildly in love with her
young husband. She was discreet and did not importune with
complaints this Henri who continued to fulfill his conjugal
obligations faithfully enough (or rather, who ended by doing
so, for it appears that Diane's astute advice counted for
something in the king's attentions to the queen), so that after
nine long years of barrenness, Catherine gave him ten children. The queen arranged matters so as to have the most
brilliant court, the loveliest maids-of-honor; the refinements
of her taste and her realistic sense of affairs did honor to the
Florence of her origin. But beside the fair Diane, Catherine
was merely a woman too dark for the fashion of the time and
one whose pregnancies and passion for fine cooking had
brought her to an ungainly girth. The queen and the duchess
presided over every festivity together; Diane tended Catherine and her children when they fell ill; their relations were

characterized by these attentions and that superficial but not necessarily insincere good grace which is allied more often than is supposed with hostility and resentment in two women forced to share the same man. We know that Henri's monogram, everywhere repeated at Fontainebleau, at the Louvre, at Chenonceaux and elsewhere, was formed of an H overlapped by Catherine's two C's. But these two C's were in the form of crescents, the symbol of Diana the Huntress, and by intersecting with the shafts of the H they formed two D's, the first letter of Diane's name. A subtle arrangement which was likely to please the king and his mistress, and secretly to dishearten the queen as well.

Prudish historians have speculated whether this singular love, which lasted till the king's death in his forties, when the duchess was well over sixty, was merely a platonic cult of beauty; if so, it would be our sole example of a platonic passion that cost the state so dear. Chroniclers of the period supposed nothing of the kind, and it was certainly not the queen's opinion of the affair. Nor do the splendid images of her nudity, which Diane commissioned or allowed contemporary painters and sculptors to produce, give any suggestion of a prude. It seems, rather, that we are concerned here with a woman of a very familiar kind, vain rather than ardent, without scruples but intensely attached to the conventions of her milieu and her moment, and in love as in other matters of a miserly disposition. However passionately Henri loved her, Diane loved herself even more; such ardor excluded all others. She underwent the severest disciplines in order to keep this perfect beauty of hers intact; she made herself take daily cold baths; she skillfully distilled lotions and unguents—she would be the ideal patroness of our modern cosmeticians. And she realized her double ambition:

a body and face forever young, and a solid fortune which permitted her to sustain and embellish this masterpiece. The loveliest of her presumed portraits,* attributed to Clouet and now in the Worcester Museum in the United States, shows her naked in the diaphanous *déshabillé* of the period, her bust upright, her hair carefully braided and interlaced with pearls, her bright cold eyes contemplating a collection of jewels spread on the table before her. A richly framed mirror, placed beside her, reflects the profile of this female Narcissus. In the background, a servant is taking a gown out of a chest. Her contemporaries noted that Diane wore widow's weeds all her life—certainly not in deference to the old husband whose death had preceded her glory as the king's mistress, but perhaps out of a characteristic conformism to the proprieties, especially since the colors of mourning were so becoming to her. In any case, this black and this white add to the cold luster of her lunar beauty.

Chenonceaux was never her favorite château, she preferred her family estate of Anet, which Henri had helped transform into a princely domain. But she frequently visited the fine Touraine estate; here she received the queen and the court; the king came often. Henri and his sexagenarian mistress shared a passion for hunting and a hatred of heresy; the perfect countenance of Madame de Valentinois would not have frowned at the account of the execution in the place de Grève of that other handsome widow, Dame Philippe de Luns, whose tongue was cut out and who was burned

---

* Let us note, however, that another portrait of a woman at her mirror, an almost identical composition preserved at Dijon, is supposed to represent Gabrielle d'Estrées. Of course, it is possible that the same pictorial arrangement served twice over for two famous beauties of successive generations. It is also possible that these two portraits, as well as the one presumably of Diane in the Cook Collection at Richmond, actually represent only some anonymous beauty.

in 1557 along with other persons of the Protestant religion: by such measures the state protected true faith and order. But political necessities interested Diane less than the proper management of her fortune. At Chenonceaux this incomparable chatelaine was able to unite the agreeable with the useful; she rounded out her lands and managed to triple the estate's yield; she planted mulberry trees, silk being the fashion and consequently the great new industry of the sixteenth century. She developed a passion for the beauty of its gardens. She devised terraces and embankments and designed flower beds; she placed in her lawns a tennis court and a tilting ring, the latter an exercise at which she excelled; she set out one of those labyrinths whose secret and complicated paths recall in terms of boxwood and quincunxes the complex forms of Renaissance poetry; she invented a fountain. Her gardeners transplanted nine thousand feet of wild strawberries and violets, dug up in the still-virgin forests of the period, under whose great trees had passed the men of the Middle Ages. The catalogue of the rose trees and the lily bulbs her gardeners planted equals in floral grace a sonnet by Ronsard or by Rémy Belleau.

In 1559, Henri II signed the sad treaty of Cateau-Cambrésis, which confirmed the European supremacy of the Hapsburgs. Philip II thereby gained Piedmont, the Milanese, Montoferrato, Corsica, La Bresse, and several strongholds in northeast France. A recent widower of Mary Tudor, he thereby gained a wife as well: the young Elisabeth of France, who would die in Spain only a few years later, a victim, it was said, of this grim husband's jealousy. Among the festivities given to celebrate this brilliant marriage, Henri organized in the faubourg St.-Antoine one of those tournaments which were already a Renaissance way of reviving a legendary

Middle Ages: artificial duels embellished by the splendor of gowns, caparisons, and arms, and further decorated by the presence of a grandstand filled with ladies. An excellent horseman and a skillful duelist, the king announced as usual his intention of entering the lists. At the end of the second day, June 30, 1559, he insisted on breaking one more lance with the captain of his Scots guard, a certain Count Montgomery. A lance splinter passed through the gold grille of his helmet and entered the king's eye. He was carried to the Louvre in a dead faint. The despairing Catherine then recalled that the astrologers had predicted the king's death in a duel, an apparently absurd notion, since crowned heads were not in the habit of yielding their persons to deadly combat, nor of measuring themselves against their subjects. She also remembered that three years earlier a physician from Provence, a Jew baptized Michel de Notre-Dame, had described in mysterious prophetic quatrains the cruel death of a lion, his eyes put out in a cage of gold.

The king's death being no more than a matter of hours, Catherine immediately ordered Diane to surrender the crown jewels and the domain of Chenonceaux. The duchess refused: the king being still alive, she would renounce nothing she possessed without an express order from him.

But eleven days later, Henri died and Diane was obliged to restore the jewels. She held out with regard to Chenonceaux, which she was legally empowered to keep, having bought it back from the former owner by the means we have described, but Catherine was no less persistent in her attacks than Diane had been in hers against Antoine Bohier. The queen did not forget the indignities she had suffered in paying what was perhaps an obligatory visit to the favorite at her estate of Chenonceaux; she also remembered the beauty of the house and its gardens. While various courtiers were in all seriousness proposing that "the lovely duchess's nose be cut off," Catherine was shrewdly content to make the parliament decree that Diane must return the monies she had received from the king. Touched to the quick in what was dearest to her, her fortune, Diane realized she would have to come to terms with the queen. But she remained a woman who could keep her head. Gambling on Catherine's covetous desire for Chenonceaux, she offered in exchange for it the domain of Chaumont, which from a purely financial point of view was worth more. Catherine accepted. To the last, Chenonceaux was a "good thing" for Diane de Poitiers.

The duchess finally retired to her palace at Anet, over whose threshold Jean Goujon had represented her as a goddess reclining in the svelte, long-legged nudity so oddly related to the plastic canons of twentieth-century high-fashion models, one arm around the neck of a great stag almost as divine as herself, in a strange alliance of classical ideal and the medieval poetry of woods and wilds. One muses nowadays in a hall of the Louvre upon this group which transposes reality into a poem: for Madame de Valentinois the stag in the wild never meant anything but the still-panting beast whose bloody foot was presented as an honor at the *curée,* and then the smoking roast indispensable to the proper furnishing of her banquets. Only in the world of art is the stag a splendid companion for the beauty; only in the world of art is this nudity, hidden from all eyes beneath velvet and brocade, innocently revealed to the light of day; only in the world of art is a king's fifty-year-old mistress an immortal.

The real Diane continued to cut a great figure in her quasi-royal retreat. Her former friends, it is true, abandoned the superannuated favorite, but she remained rich, she was still beautiful, her religious sentiments made her respectable, and her hatred of Protestants endeared her to the ruling party to the last. She died in her seventies, following a fall from a horse. "I saw Madame the Duchess of Valentinois at the age of seventy," Brantôme writes, "as lovely of face, as fresh and as agreeable as at the age of thirty . . . Her beauty, her grace, her majesty, her fine appearance were all just as they had always been, and especially she had a great whiteness of the skin. I believe that had this lady lived to be a hundred, she would never have aged at all . . . Pity it is that the earth should cover up such lovely bodies!"

Catherine had immediately taken possession of Chenonceaux. Her arrangements, like Diane's, were both ornamental and practical: she enlarged the profitable mulberry plantations and established a silkworm hatchery and a spinning mill; she constructed cages for rare birds in the gardens and acclimated olive trees from her native Tuscany, which flourished; she assembled a library consisting, it was said, of the handsome books she had bought from her compatriot Marshal Strozzi (the Pierre Strozzi of Musset's *Lorenzaccio*). Above all, she brought here the turbulent horde of her children, whom she was determined both to control and to entertain: her oldest son, the young king François II, destined to die at seventeen of an acute otitis; her second son, Charles, carried off at twenty-three by galloping consumption, who in history chokes on the blood of St. Bartholomew; her third son, Henri, Duke of Anjou, the only one who inherited something of his mother's finesse and intelligence; her youngest son, the Duke of Alençon, a sly and quarrelsome child who would become an insufferable prince; her two daughters-in-law, adolescent girls stuffed into their brocaded gowns and pleated ruffs: Mary Stuart, child-bride of the child-king François II, fated to misfortune, to crime, to nineteen years of captivity ending on the block at Fotheringay, and Elizabeth of Austria, wife of Charles IX, shortly to be confronted by a widow's crepe and death in a Viennese convent after years of pious routine; and lastly her daughter Margot, soon married to the Protestant Henry of Navarre, whose nuptials were to end in a massacre, but who was stylish, giddy, untouched by the tragic resonance of her family, figuring in legend as in history as a lovely girl of easy virtue.

Chenonceaux might have housed this numerous family, but the court as well had to be accommodated. The queen undertook to add to the château the covered bridge already planned by Catherine Bohier's architect and by Diane's as well, and meant to serve as a banquet hall, but especially to join the present dwelling to a future annex symmetrically set on the far bank of the river; only lack of funds kept it from being built. Meanwhile, the bridge's upper story was divided into little rooms assigned to the servants and courtiers who quarreled with them for such accommodations, *faute de mieux.*

The banquets Catherine gave at Chenonceaux certainly had an avowed or secret political goal, but it was chiefly by temperament that this woman of intrigue created around herself so much noise and gaiety, so many splendid and frivolous entertainments. All these festivities, except the last, which deserves separate mention, partook of that allegorical and mythological genre then fashionable—there were ballets and serenades on the lawns and on the water, settings designed by Primaticcio, boar hunts managed as theater interludes, conveniently ending in the very gardens of the château, so that the young king coming down from his room could comfortably finish off a sow already torn by his dogs and stabbed by his courtiers. One saw lovely women disguised as classical divinities endlessly haranguing the royal family and—a new diversion imported from Italy—fireworks setting the waters and the woods aglow. The first of these entertainments occurred shortly after the summary executions following the Protestant attack known as the *tumulte d'Amboise*. These executions had initially entertained the court as a kind of bloody mummery, but one grows tired of everything: turning her back on the rebel corpses hanging like thrushes from the delicate balconies of Amboise, Catherine chose to rusticate her retinue and her children at Chenonceaux.

In May 1577, in the gardens of Chenonceaux, Catherine de Médicis, or rather her son Henri III, gave one of those parties which legend seizes upon after the fact in order to transform it into the fantastic, semi-scandalous symbol of an age, of a world, of a certain way of taking pleasure, of dreaming...

On May 15, at Plessis-lez-Tours, Henri had magnificently entertained his younger brother, the disagreeable Duc d'Alençon, and the noblemen who with him had won over the Huguenots the victory of La Charité and were, a few days later, to win that of Issoire, followed by the usual massacres. In the old royal residence of Plessis-lez-Tours, this banquet held against a backdrop of civil war seems to have been a typical May occasion in the tradition of medieval springtime festivities, revised and embellished by a disciple of Primaticcio: it had taken some sixty thousand francs' worth of green silk cloth to transform the ladies and the courtiers into dryads and sylvan swains. Immediately afterward, Catherine received all this company at Chenonceaux.

In these more characteristically Renaissance surroundings, the diversion offered by the old Italian queen was, it seems, even more unbridled and more sumptuous, perhaps better suited to a decor of Roman vines or Florentine villas than to that of a French park. The twenty-six-year-old king attended in his usual fashion, costumed and painted, though there is no evidence he wore on this night, as has been claimed, a somewhat feminine garment—with *décolleté* and three strands of pearls—which he had sported during the carnival masquerades of the same year. The ladies and maids-of-honor whose task was to serve at table wore the close-fitting and motley costumes of pages, or else, disguised as nymphs of the school of Fontainebleau, wore their hair loose and showed their bare legs and breasts. But if pleasure reigned at the party, it was certain that ease did not: the king loathed his brother. In truth, we have few details about this affair, which has so heated the imagination of modern historians; we do know that it cost so much that the queen mother, already in financial straits, once again resorted to her Italian moneymen, who immediately recouped their expenditures by taxing the people. But it is easy to imagine, beneath the still-pale branches, the usual apparatus of sixteenth-century pleasures: the gold tableware, the silk napery, the exquisite sound of rebecs and violas d'amore, and it is easy, too, to picture the couples straying away under the trees or meeting in the upper rooms of the new covered bridge, whose illuminated gallery was reflected in the water.

This orgy, if it was one, Catherine herself attended, enormous in her widow's weeds, at the side of Louise of Lorraine, Henri III's young and pious bride. Modern historians have speculated that the queen mother was relying on these lovely nymphs and these charming pseudo-pages to incline a relatively misogynist young king toward more conventional tastes; yet this would have been a very odd way of going about the matter, for such means were more likely to flatter his present passions than to dispose him to a quarter of an hour's intimacy with the queen. Rather than of Catherine, this night's folly bears the mark of Henri himself, revealing all his predilections, all his chimeras. The king was one of those men for whom a costume, a dance step, the unique discoveries of an occasion without precedent and without consequences are a living poem and merit as much effort and exhaustion as more lasting achievements. In the course of this imprudent, highly unpolitical party, the young king did not try out any new form of revelry; on the contrary, he was realizing the secret aspirations of the waning Renaissance, its love of the equivocal, its voluptuous sense of metamorphosis and disguise. He regaled himself that evening on the equivalent *avant la lettre* of Shakespeare's comedies or the mythological spectacles which Marlow's Gaveston offered to his Edward II.

Louise of Lorraine was destined to stroll beneath these same trees, a disconsolate shade clad in the white mourning of queens, during the last twelve years of her life. This pathetic Louise belonged to the same illustrious House of Lorraine from which descended, on the maternal side, Mary Stuart, and, on the paternal, Marie-Antoinette. But Louise belonged to a poor and relatively obscure branch of this great family; her father was Count de Vaudémont. Through her mother, Marguerite of Egmont, she was connected to the aristocracy of the Low Countries, being a niece of the great

Egmont, who had been beheaded at Brussels on the Duke of Alba's orders. But this memory, which so moves us today, no doubt left the sixteenth-century courts and chancelleries cold. Mademoiselle de Vaudémont was twenty in 1573 when Henri passed through Nancy on his way to Poland, that tempestuous kingdom whose diet had just elected him king. But this monarch of twenty-two barely noticed Louise, being distracted by a romantic passion for the lovely Marie of Cleves, charming wife of a Protestant prince who jealously kept her away from the court. This complex Henri, whose infrequent impulses toward women had hitherto seemed mere sensuous curiosity or else concessions to custom, conceived of having Marie's marriage annulled by Rome—he was, it appears, quite chastely loved by her. Perhaps his glimpse of Louise pleased him by some resemblance she bore to this Marie from whom he had tearfully separated just now, after many passionate sonnets and promises of eternal love.

A year later, in his palace at Cracow, Henri learned of the death of his brother Charles IX, survived by only a very young daughter. Accompanied by no more than eight or nine young Frenchmen of his intimate circle, Henri deceived the sentries' vigilance and galloped to the frontier, pursued by his Polish nobles, with their drooping mustaches and their long Oriental robes, who shouted to him in Latin to turn back. Henri stopped for breath only at Vienna, where his horse collapsed beneath him, victim of a cavalcade more romantic than royal. At Venice, where splendid entertainments of every nature had been prepared for him, he lingered with pleasure—tradition has it that here a courtesan infected him with syphilis, the disease of the epoch which, added to the family phthisis, partly accounts for the nervous imbalance of a prince so tragic, so futile, and so lucid.

At Lyon, the king was met by his mother and the court, and with them the two equally determined antagonists, Catholics on the one hand and Protestants on the other, who were tearing France apart. He was immediately faced with the question of marriage, ever the most pressing in a family whose sons died young. Henri had just learned with immense grief that he would never see Marie of Cleves again—she had died in childbirth at twenty, reluctantly faithful to that husband she herself had described as the most generous but also the most jealous of princes; her own death seemed to leave the field clear to a great dynastic union, one useful to the realm.

Catherine had recently proposed this favorite son to the aging Elizabeth of England, but her Virginal Majesty had rejected such a project, which, moreover, was anything but alluring to the young man in question; we may almost regret it: how curious it would have been to see united in one and the same bed the two most singular and overdressed creatures of their age. So Catherine now meditated a Swedish alliance, which would have been one way of bringing Catholic and Protestant Europe together; to this end she advocated a Northern beauty, the daughter of Gustavus Vasa. But the king was no longer the queen mother's docile son; nor was he the young generalissimo lately acclaimed for wreaking such cruel havoc in the Protestant ranks at the Battle of Moncontour. In politics, Henri claimed to take a moderate line, which he actually inherited from Catherine but which he intended to follow in his own manner. Moreover, we must regard such moderation as a means of astutely neutralizing each faction by the other, rather than as a concern to make either tolerance or justice prevail in his kingdom —to them no one gave a thought.

Physically too, Henri had changed. Clouet's first portraits of him evoke a proud and delicate boy of voluptuous, almost Italian beauty, and this aspect may explain certain elements of his history. Very quickly, however, this adolescent bloom faded, and the artist seems to have found himself facing a man with blurred features, a scanty beard, and a high, bony forehead, whose smile and glance alone suggested a certain grace. As for his private life, this Henri had acquired a taste in Poland for almost Oriental ceremony, which mixed poorly with the personal nonchalance of his manners, which he was to pay for with his life. He surrounded himself ever more exclusively with a group of arrogant and charming youths, almost all of mediocre birth and endowed with a great hunger for money and honors, troublesome favorites of whom many, however, served their prince with great intrepidity. Finally, the new king firmly opposed all his mother's matrimonial wishes; forced to marry, the only woman Henri would consent to accept was an obscure Mademoiselle de Vaudémont, glimpsed at Nancy a year or so before.

This union, which had nothing dynastic about it, scandalized Catherine. Moreover, she could well fear that such an alliance would only increase the importance in France of the House of Lorraine, whose princes, heading what we might call the Catholic right, were already only too dangerously powerful. Henri stood fast against all arguments. He lost no time sending one of his favorites to wed Louise for him, according to court custom. The girl had hitherto lived an obscure existence under the eye of two stepmothers her father had given her, one after the other; she assumed it was a bad joke when she saw one of them, Catherine d'Aumale, enter her bedroom early one morning and make a deep curtsey before informing her that she was to be Queen of France.

Henri and Louise were crowned together at Reims; the ceremony had to be postponed several hours until the king had finished dressing and adorning with his own hands this little queen described by all the texts of the period as enchanting. Was she really so? Less flattering, a portrait in the Louvre shows us a rather ovine young woman with large dreamy eyes and a sweet, rather stubborn expression.

This couple, whose marriage may well have been an unconsummated one, nonetheless presented for fifteen years the spectacle of a united *ménage*. Louise continued to engage in works of mercy, as she had done at Nancy: she tended the sick, washed and buried the dead with her own hands. Such pious occupations did not keep her from accompanying the king on most of his incessant moves from Blois to Chenonceaux to Plessis-lez-Tours to Amboise to Olinville, along with the queen mother and the gold-decked favorites, handsome warrior-boys who decimated each other in duels and whose death Henri mourned as he had mourned Marie of Cleves. One of them received Louise's own sister in marriage; on their wedding night, a splendid one, the little queen emboldened herself to offer the king a ballet of her own invention—in it she appeared disguised as a nymph graced, according to a chronicler of the time, with an almost celestial sweetness and gravity, beneath her pearls and cloth of silver.

The *Journal* of Pierre de l'Estoile tells us that she also participated in more sinister ceremonies: with the king and the queen mother, Louise attended the drawing and quartering of the traitor Salcève, watching from a box at the Hôtel de Ville, especially constructed and embellished for their majesties and where one may suppose no elegance and no comfort were lacking. After the horses had twice over supplied the effort required of them, the wretch was strangled by special mercy. Custom so utterly governs our sentiments that it is likely that the charitable little queen found such a scene of horror quite a natural one: the strength of the innocent stallions employed to rend a living body, the powerful creatures whipped or spurred forward with many oaths, the victim's screams, and even the crowd's fierce delectation . . . One wonders what she thought of those less bloody entertainments, the king's nocturnal cavalcades with his comrades, who insulted and molested passersby, or again those fits of religious lyricism whose equivalent we would find today only during Holy Week in Seville—episodes when Henri and his friends, in the traditional costume of Flagellants, breasts bared, heads covered with ashes, suddenly exhibited the cries and tears of penitence in the public squares.

One constant obsession united them: the zeal to produce that son it was believed, rightly or wrongly, would consolidate the dynasty. Here one hesitates—and the king and his little queen have preserved their pathetic bedroom secrets. The same year as the extravagant party under the trees, the king returns to Chenonceaux, then to Amboise, in search of Louise, who had hidden herself in Touraine, sick with disappointment, chagrined to the point of illness, and mistakenly fearing to be repudiated for barrenness. As for public opinion, it attributed this lack of progeniture to what it supposed it knew of the king's diseases and diversions. Whatever the case, Henri and Louise hoped for a miracle to the last; they multiplied their gifts to churches; they made exhausting pilgrimages, sometimes on foot; they piously brought back nightshirts from Chartres which had been blessed with a special intention

. . . One fine day, a lady-in-waiting advised the queen to procure an heir to the throne by the less recondite means of adultery. Louise sent this giver of evil counsel away in disgrace.

Despite his fits of dramatic devotion, this king, though a good Catholic, had nothing of the sectarian about him: he had managed to resist all pressure put upon him to establish the Inquisition in France. As a young man, he had even had his crisis of evangelism and carried a psalter about with him, less out of conviction, no doubt, than because it was the fashion. But by now the two warring religions were, as is almost always the case with rival ideologies, nothing but the pretext or the disguise of the violent and the ambitious, a means of rousing mass hysteria, a way of sanctifying the aims of the cunning in the eyes of the foolish and the dull. The Protestant princes were dreaming of their prerogatives and their slice of power; the leaders of the League had worse goals still. Tacking his whole life long between two factions almost equally fatal to the monarchy, it is not surprising that Henri sometimes made desperate lunges in one direction or the other, sometimes to the left, sometimes to the right.

Everyone knows, or supposes he knows, the sequel to these events, though the account of them is often distorted by partisan spirit or melodramatized by popular history. In May 1588, the king was forced to flee Paris, a victim of the League's demonstrations, more or less as he had once fled Cracow, but this prematurely exhausted man was no longer the carefree cavalier of old days. In August the hard-pressed king, impelled to concessions by his mother, gave promises by his Edict of Alençon to that same Catholic right and its disturbing leaders, the Duc de Guise and his brother the Cardinal, who were playing both dictators and demagogues.

In December, sequestered by the Guises in his château at Blois, unsupported by his disintegrating States-General, Henri refused to sign a decree which would have barred from the throne his Protestant cousin Henry of Navarre and have permitted the Duc de Guise to lay hands on the crown of France.

Lovers of great historic scenes, attracted by the melodrama at Blois, too readily forget that the Invincible Armada had finally set sail during the summer of 1588; French as it was, and Parisian specifically, the commotion of the League was actually part of that great movement to encircle Western Europe being prepared by Philip II. It appears that the harsh blow delivered to Spain by the wreck of her fleet encouraged Henri to resist the leaders of a party bribed by Spanish gold. In a sense, the winds and rain which lashed Touraine that season were the rear guard of the storms which a few weeks earlier had swallowed up the last vestiges of the redoubtable Armada. Henri had recovered his assurance: with all the cunning and the prudence of a prisoner, this prince, whom his enemies had judged ready to abdicate without resistance, now prepared to strike down the agitator by murder, the only means left to him.

The night before the murder, Henri, determined but a prey to anxiety, sought some rest beside the queen, from whom he doubtless concealed the cause of his insomnia. He had learned early in life to suspect everyone, even his mother, by now nothing but a sick old woman dozing between two potions, vaguely roused, however, in her room a floor below, by the slightest unaccustomed noise on this night of vigils. He had some reason to suspect his wife as well, related as she was to these very princes of Lorraine he had decided to put to death. The sequel was to prove Louise's utter loyalty, but it is likely she did not know, that morning, why Henri had left orders to be wakened and dressed before dawn. All went according to plan: the assassination of the Duc de Guise scarcely troubled the public opinion of Europe: "The King of Spain has lost another of his captains," murmured Pope Sixtus V. A note found in the duke's pocket, indicating that the civil war in France was costing 200,000 écus a month, proved to the king he had not been deceived as to the source of the evil.

But Paris was seething like a witches' cauldron. A few days later, when the old queen's death made Louise the only female figure in the king's entourage, a little Parisian peddler brought news from the great city. With the imprudent familiarity he showed to everyone, Henri had the man shown into the chamber where he and Louise lay in bed early that morning and asked him if it was true that his good people in rebellion no longer called him anything but Henri of Valois. The man said this was so. "Well then," the king replied merrily, "you can tell them you have seen Henri of Valois in bed with his queen." One imagines Louise's blush, and her smile, and her pleasure, in the midst of danger, in hearing a joke which seemed to crown her for the second time.

It was at Chinon that the king left Louise in relative safety when he set out to reconquer Paris with the help of Henry of Navarre. And on that July morning of 1589, shortly after the moment anticipated for retaking the capital, when Henri was stabbed in his wardrobe at St.-Cloud by a Parisian monk to whom he had rashly granted an audience, one of his first thoughts as a dying man was for the queen. Still unaware that his wound was a mortal one, or perhaps hoping in any case to spare the young woman a dangerous and exhausting journey, he wrote to advise her against joining him: "My

beloved, pray for me, and do not move from where you are."
Then, having once again recognized Henry of Navarre as
heir to his throne and having commended to him those favorites he still trusted, Henri III expired at the age of thirty-
seven. If we are to believe Brantôme, a young gentleman of
his suite named L'Isle-Marivaut immediately managed to be
killed in a duel in order not to outlive his master.

Henri III has been so disparaged by traditional history,
which has taken literally the insults showered upon him by
either party of his contemporaries, then so fiercely defended
by certain twentieth-century historians, that it is difficult to
judge this complex prince fairly. Tempered by an innate
good sense which resisted all his excesses, but also by the
effect of his intrinsic weakness, seeking peace of necessity at
a period when every man was gambling on war, a politician
rather than a statesman, ill served by his nerves and his
whims but sustained by the deep if narrow sentiment of his
royal function, this unstable monarch had withstood fourteen
years of crisis as best he could and on his deathbed bequeathed his crown to the man designated by his kingdom's
laws of succession. This was little enough, and yet a great
deal. There are figures of princes in history who are more
mediocre, and more ignoble ones as well.

Louise was about to leave Chinon, where an outbreak of
the plague had just occurred, when the same messenger
brought her the king's last letter and the news of his death.
Her intimates concealed the one from her as well as the
other. They managed to tell her nothing before bringing her
to Chenonceaux, which was of course less able to withstand
attack than the enormous fortress on the banks of the Loire
but more comfortable, more agreeable, and no doubt cooler
in the summer months, perhaps less exposed to epidemic.

Lucky for them that they did so. "My beloved, pray for me, and do not move from where you are . . ." Interpreting literally what was merely the advice of a wounded man and not the will of a dead one, Louise decided never to leave this residence where by chance she had unsealed this last message from Henri. That is the storybook explanation. Another more prosaic one is that Chenonceaux, bequeathed directly to Louise by the queen mother, was henceforth the only estate the young widow possessed. Whatever the case, for twelve years, this pleasure ground was to become a memorial chapel.

The Renaissance is the age of the great mourning widows: Joanna the Mad on the roads of Spain, Marguerite of Austria at Brou, Vittoria Colonna in her Roman cloister, and, perhaps less sincerely, Catherine de Médicis at the Louvre. But none of these bereavements is so touching as that of this little queen attached to the last to a prince insulted by those who had not forgotten him. Louise had the ground floor of Chenonceaux hung with black. The chapel itself, decorated with an image of Christ in agony, was perpetually in readiness for a funeral mass. She had the ceilings painted with the macabre funerary devices in fashion at the time: skulls, bones, gravediggers' spades, and, above all, by the thousands, tears. One vault decorated in this fashion is still to be seen on the great gallery ceiling, a faded testimony to this extraordinary grief. Looking at it, one realizes again that this age, which loved life so desperately, could also derive from death all its poetry, its splendor, and its intimations of eternity. The period when the delicate Louise ended her life in seclusion and mourning was also the period when Shakespeare was writing Hamlet's soliloquies and exchanges with the gravediggers.

Mihi, sed in sepulchro. Mine, but in the grave. This motto adopted by Louise translates precisely the reality of her widow's existence. In a sense, the modest spouse she had been asserted herself as a lover at Chenonceaux; here she took full possession of this husband so many voluptuary or tragic diversions had constantly taken from her. Never, surely, had Henri been closer to her; never had she supposed herself so necessary to him. At last she could repay him for having chosen her, for having made room for her in his heart to the very end. To describe these years of absorption in the memory of a dead man as a sterile and romantic nightmare is to risk forgetting the queen's pious confidence in the efficacy of prayer, her constant effort to sustain Henri in the other world, and to console him. On her knees in her private chapel, joints stiffened by the dampness rising off the river, Louise at Chenonceaux gave proof of the same simple devotion to this dead man as a woman tending a beloved invalid to the last. It was not to a poetic ghost that Louise dedicated her life but to a soul.

One imagines her in that white mourning which custom reserved for queens who were not, as Catherine had been, queen mothers, in her little circle of gentlemen and ladies-in-waiting. The household style was modest enough: Louise was poor. In the more than six years since Henri had died, civil war was still breaking out; prices were rising; the neglected estate brought in very little. But Louise had always been economical; more than once Henri had pared away his wife's pension in order to pay the expenses of a banquet or to shower gifts on a favorite. She used to be derided for the modest little presents she offered in return for the splendid gifts of her sisters-in-law. Only a few logs burned in the great fireplace. Shielded by a firescreen embroidered with tears, Louise perhaps kept on her lap one of those little spaniels for which she and Henri had shared a passion. Or perhaps, old-fashioned vestige of the fancies of the past, a monkey or a parrot was chained beside her. The garments worn by her retinue were cut, like her own, on the outmoded pattern of the old court fashions. What did they talk about? Country matters—the weather, which is never so good as might be hoped for the harvest; the latest sermon preached in the chapel and the way the anniversary Mass for the late king had been sung; the menu of the next meal—was it suitable to subtract from a meager budget the price of several pitchers of wine for a convalescent, or of a layette for a woman in labor? Monsieur Adam, the château steward, was critical of Henry of Navarre, who had allowed one of his colonels to billet his regiment on Chenonceaux land, cutting down trees and molesting the farmers. The château remained burdened with all the queen mother's debts; the scant yield of its farms was not sufficient to satisfy Catherine's creditors. Yet the parquet in the queen's bedroom had to be replaced—the other floors could wait. Among these persons sequestered in the château on the Cher as within a ship, there develop those petty rivalries, those little resentments habitual to people forced to live side by side for long periods; sarcastic observations were exchanged among the ladies-in-waiting. The Italian Countess of Fiesco may have selected a volume of Petrarch that had strayed among the various works of devotion on the shelves and read out a poem on fidelity beyond the grave. Or with a trembling hand Louise leafed through a collection of poems by Desportes, who had been Henri's court poet, and reread the strange sonnet about desperate ghosts prowling around the tomb in which a violent death has laid them. The queen took her leave, stood up to go to her private chapel or her room, and her retinue went to bed, musing that after all one was not too badly off at Chenonceaux in these difficult times.

The queen's chamber, placed in a suite overhanging the river and subsequently removed during a restoration of the château, is no longer in existence; the place where Louise's nocturnal reveries occurred is now impalpable air. But we possess the inventory of her furnishings at Chenonceaux; we can imagine her opening the complicated locks of one of her fine chests, perhaps rereading once more the king's message: "My beloved . . . do not move from where you are . . ." He had never written to her in his own blood, as he had to Marie of Cleves, but the last letter had been for her.

One wonders if the obscene lampoons which once had offered the public a magnifying glass for Henri's vices and weaknesses had ever fallen under the eyes of this touching little widow; had she scorned them, trusting the king in this realm as in all others? Had she lived in a kind of vague ignorance amid this court rustling with scandal; or on the contrary, knowing all of Henri's transgressions, had she regarded them as one more reason to spend her nights in prayer?

Standing at the window, she gazed absently at the dark mass of the trees, under which the man the poets used to compare to Achilles among women had given a costume party one May evening. Almost all the young lords covered with pearls and gems were dead now: Quélus, Livarot, Maugiron in duels; St.-Mégrin, Du Guast, who had fetched her from Nancy for Henri, murdered; her brother-in-law Anne de Joyeuse killed in one of those engagements of the civil war—and just in time, perhaps, at the very moment he was about to go over to the League . . . Henri himself was sleeping—badly, no doubt—in his temporary tomb. Long ago a Venetian ambassador had noted that during receptions at the Louvre, the queen's eyes continually rested on the king, doubtless out of affection, perhaps too because of her perpetual fear of an attack which finally occurred, but in her absence. Those faithful eyes must have recorded countless images of Henri. Again she would see the young king on the day of their first meeting, in Lorraine, the glass of fashion, the very model of a Renaissance prince; then the strange, painted creature, sparkling apparition in the uproar and confusion of the banquets, or again the haggard man plagued by incurable anxieties, as on that morning when, frightened by a dream in which he had seen himself torn apart by wild beasts, he had savagely had the lions in the moat of the Louvre killed by his archers, a crime assuredly more dreadful than the necessary liquidation of the Guises. And finally that prematurely aged Henri whose diseases she had tended, the cough, the earaches, the lachrymal fistula, the abscess on the left arm, the erysipelas . . . Six years, eight years, already eleven years . . . The house on the Cher seemed to navigate through time. Louise fell asleep to the murmur of water.

Apart from her concern for the eternal salvation of Henri's soul, two other preoccupations obsessed the White Queen: to punish the king's assassins, and to give his body a final sepulcher among his ancestors at St.-Denis. Of course, Jacques Clément, the murderous monk whom the king himself had seized by the throat, had fallen under the guard's pikes, but such a man was merely an instrument in more cunning hands, which had directed the blow; it came from that same House of Lorraine from which Louise was descended and from which, too, had come Henri's worst enemies. The dowager queen implored the new king, Henry of Navarre, who had finally mounted the throne, to punish those really responsible, whatever their rank or title. But Henri IV, busy pacifying his kingdom as best he could, preferred not to call new attention to these old crimes. Nor was Louise to see her second vow realized: there was not enough money to complete the sumptuous funeral arrangements for this king in whom a dynasty had perished.

But new plots were forming around Louise's seclusion. The mistress of Henri IV coveted Chenonceaux as Diane de Poitiers had done, and the newly crowned Bourbon was no less indulgent of his paramour than Henri II had been of his. Gabrielle d'Estrées parleyed with Catherine's creditors, who continued to harass the unfortunate little queen: their spokesman, one Du Tillet, promised, for the sum of 22,000 écus, to have Chenonceaux awarded to her. A process server from Paris ordered Louise to pay off the old queen's enormous debts at once; notice boards announcing the sale were posted on the gates of the château from which Louise was unceremoniously requested to decamp; the parliament of Paris confirmed this procedure of distraint and rejected an appeal from the widow of Henri III.

This series of judiciary nightmares seems to have been for Gabrielle and her royal lover the equivalent of the artillery pounding which precedes an offensive, for in February 1598, the astute Béarnais and his mistress appeared in person at Chenonceaux, where they came amicably enough to pay a visit to the dowager queen. It was decided to satisfy Catherine's creditors, provided the king's bastard, César de Vendôme, then four years old, inherited the estate after he was married off to one of Louise's nieces. It is easy enough to imagine what that visit must have been like, one misty or icy morning, finally putting a little life into the gloomy routine of the château, obliging, too, its poor occupant to prodigies of ingenuity in order to receive her guests fittingly. Louise would have recognized, around Madame d'Estrées's neck, the crown jewels she had worn in her own queenly days, and we can suppose that the charming Gabrielle, strong in her youth, her beauty, and a new pregnancy bestowed by the king, put a certain more or less deliberate condescension in her curtseys to this superannuated ghost, the widowed queen. The Vert Galant, always expert in matters of this kind, abounding in earthy remarks and compliments for the ladies, easily overcame the hard-pressed woman's last hesitations; in May, shortly before the birth of a second bastard, whose first name was that of the great Greek conqueror, Alexandre de Vendôme, the couple returned to Chenonceaux to put the finishing touches to the details of this project; it is likely that the triumphant fecundity of Madame d'Estrées inspired Louise with bitter thoughts about the barrenness which had been her misery as a woman and her worst misfortune as a queen.

In principle, this rather dishonorable agreement left Louise the usufruct of the estate, but Du Tillet had been able to ward off only some of the creditors, a fact perhaps concealed by the organizers of this transaction. Despite arrangements so laboriously concluded, therefore, the remainder of Catherine's moneymen were allowed to torment the wretched queen, who was obliged to sell her pearls in order to settle the most urgent claims. We may assume, moreover, that whatever was left to Louise did not represent, in the mind of Madame d'Estrées, anything more than a temporary compromise: perhaps the widow of the Valois would soon decide to seek refuge in one of her favorite convents, so that Gabrielle, meanwhile exchanging, perhaps, her title of duchess for that of queen, would not have too long to wait before enjoying herself at Chenonceaux with her young son. As it turned out, the dazzling duchess died in childbirth only a few months after the double visit to Touraine, and the royal quasi-widower returned alone the following year to sign the deed which assigned this desirable property to the young Vendôme.

On the occasion of this new royal visit, Louise once again begged that justice be meted out to the murderers of Henri III, and that the defunct king at last take possession of his tomb. But in vain. It was only ten years later, when Henri IV had perished in his turn under an assassin's knife, that the remains of the last Valois were hastily and unceremoniously carried into the royal basilica, etiquette decreeing that the reigning king's coffin be received at the vault's entrance by that of the king who had preceded him on the throne. But by then Louise was no longer of this world.

In 1601, in the dead of winter, the little queen left Chenonceaux to collect the revenues of her duchy of Bourbonnais, which Henri IV had finally constituted as her dower rights. Was this a final departure to which she had been compelled, or did she intend to return to Chenonceaux once some of her money worries were alleviated? We do not know. The fact of the matter is that the queen bore this journey badly in such weather: she fell ill at Moulins, where she died on January 29. They buried her there in a church of the town; later her body was transported to the chapel of a Parisian convent she had helped found. Certainly it had never occurred to her to claim a royal sepulcher for herself. She obtained it nonetheless. Two centuries later, after the French Revolution, when it was decided to restore the royal vaults at St.-Denis, which had been pillaged and emptied of their dead, a widespread search was made for royal bones to fill the disaffected crypt as well as possible. Someone remembered Louise, who now rests, paradoxically, amid the empty tombs and broken statues, beside the sad coffins of the last Bourbons. But too late: Henri III was no longer there. *Mihi, sed in sepulchro.* Henri and Louise were not destined to be entirely each other's, even in the grave.

For over half a century, Chenonceaux was nothing more than a splendid, rather neglected property whose rooms were aired and whose mirrors resilvered on the rare occasions when it happened to lie along the route of some royal progress. For twelve years, however, the Duchess of Mercoeur, mother-in-law and guardian of the plotting muddler César de Vendôme, had withdrawn there in a half-voluntary exile, caring as best she could for this estate which had barely escaped litigation, at the cost of having some of its parkland sold off in order to augment the farm revenues. She lodged a Capuchin convent under the eaves of the château. In 1677, the bailiffs reappeared, brought this time by the creditors of César's grandson, the ignoble and illustrious Phillippe de Vendôme; they obtained a sequestration which lasted twenty years. The debts of the great Vendôme almost equaled those of Catherine de Médicis; virtually every tree had to be chopped down to pay for the colossal feasting, the hunting dogs, and the onerous attentions of the valets of this most crapulous of princes. In 1696, his funds restored by the hazards of war, the fat Vendôme resumed possession of his estate, and installed a former companion of debauchery there; for this Monsieur d'Aulnay Chenonceaux was nothing more than a garçonnière. After the great and slovenly warrior's death, the château passed to the Condé family, an absurd marriage having belatedly united the scandalous Vendôme and a Mademoiselle de Condé, an ill-favored, heavy-drinking old maid. Chenonceaux was too onerous for Monsieur le Duc, into whose hands it had fallen; after a few years the Condé family sold the property to Monsieur Claude Dupin, who had started out in life as a tax receiver.

In the eighteenth century, Chenonceaux therefore became again what it had been at the beginning of its history, the property of a financier. Monsieur Dupin was a farmer-general; his wife, Louise de Fontaine, passed for the natural daughter of the Rothschild of the period, one Samuel Bernard, who in any case favored the young couple. Husband and wife belonged to that rich, restless bourgeoisie avid for fashionable literature and art which made the great days of the eighteenth century. The dark frescoes of Louise of Lorraine's apartments were whitewashed; the château once again became a residence of Fun and Games, as well as of the arts and even of the sciences, for in the era of Newton, people of fashion concerned themselves with physics.

The Dupins had as their protégé and almost as their parasite one Jean-Jacques Rousseau, not to be confused with his famous homonym Jean-Baptiste, a man widely admired for religious poetry and licentious epigrams. Our virtually unknown Jean-Jacques had fine eyes, mediocre manners, an atrabilious character softened by the desire to succeed and to please attractive women, and knew enough about music to compose certain charming trifles. Moreover, his literary or musical accomplishments were of the conventional sort: a comedy unperformed and probably unperformable; an opera whose libretto he had also written and which had *almost* been performed, as a matter of fact, thanks to the good offices of a member of the Dupin family; another opera in which he had merely collaborated and which had enjoyed some success, though without his name having appeared on the notice boards. Finally—a common enough phenomenon in a period when the systems and projects for reform abounded —he was the inventor of a new method of musical notation, scorned by professionals, but which he was advised to submit to ladies of fashion. At first glance, then, nothing distinguishes this man of talents from some dozens of scribblers or note spinners who came to Paris to make their fortune. Moreover, this Swiss seeking to make his way in the big city was thirty-five, which is both the end of adolescence and the beginning of senility for such enterprises. If, as no one dreamed of doing, someone had scrutinized his past more closely, what was visible would have seemed pitiable, ignominious, or even sinister: poverty, vagabondage, lackeydom, a penchant for sloth and even petty thievery, sickness or persistent hypochondria, timidities and sexual manias, the maternal generosities of a woman crazy but charming. Looking closer still, one might have discerned a tendency to passionate reverie which would have drawn a smile from this subtle and dry society. And finally, cohabiting with all these weaknesses, all these pettinesses, and even more hidden than these, the reformer's dangerous gift, an incapacity to revere or to accept the world as it is.

Rousseau's relations with Madame Dupin began with a misunderstanding. She had received him at her dressing table, her hair down, her arms bare, her peignoir loose about her: unaccustomed to this Parisian nonchalance, the timid favor seeker imagined he was being seduced. Madame Dupin possessed, at least if Nattier is telling us the truth, the delicate beauty of a Sèvres figurine; no longer exactly young, she was perhaps the age of the tender Maman des Charmettes, who had given Rousseau his first lessons in pleasure, and of Madame de Larnage, the enjoyment of whose favors he had owed to the accident of some evenings passed at the same inn; like these two mistresses, she belonged to that world of well-born or quasi-well-born ladies of which this craftsman's son had dreamed all his life. Witty, a friend to the arts, adorned with every elegance, Madame Dupin was for Rousseau, at least momentarily, that delicious fantasy he subsequently incarnated at greater length in Madame d'Houdetot, and to which he was ultimately to give life and reality in *Julie.* He wrote an impassioned declaration, which was contemptuously returned to him. Madame Dupin was virtuous, a fact worthy of notice in this daughter and sister of accessible ladies. Yet we may doubt whether she would have shown the door so coldly to an amorous duke.

But if he was too inconsiderable to be rejected with grace, Rousseau was also too inconsiderable for his effrontery to be held against him. Madame Dupin entrusted her son's care to him for eight days, the boy being temporarily without a tutor. Young Dupin de Chenonceaux was destined to dissipate at cards a good share of the money that his father earned by collecting the king's taxes or that Samuel Bernard gained by speculation. He ended his days on the Île Bourbon, where his family sent him after a scandal. This unstudious pupil exasperated Rousseau, who asserts he would never have consented to bother with him a second week, even if Madame Dupin had offered herself as the salary. Jean-Jacques's task was an easier one with his protectress's stepson, Dupin de Francueil, with whom he reviewed chemistry, a subject of which he was at least as ignorant as his pupil. He was also hired to correct certain trifles written by Madame Dupin herself, among which figures a *Treatise on Happiness*, a title and a subject very much in the air those days, as much in fashion for the eighteenth century as a *Treatise on Anxiety* would be today. Hence it was as an underling that Rousseau assiduously frequented the Hôtel Lambert, where these financiers lived in Paris, a setting no less splendid than that of Chenonceaux and one from which our Jean-Jacques was excluded on days when the family received the Academy.

These menial functions, interrupted by a sojourn in Venice as a secretary of the French ambassador, with whom Rousseau quarreled violently, lasted all in all nearly five years. A rather low annual salary of 900 livres was supplemented by discreet bonuses Madame Dupin granted to the false *ménage* of "her" man of letters, and Rousseau, always moved by presents from women, did not despise these little gifts, as later on, having become a philosopher, he would so furiously reject an admirer's crocks of butter. In 1747, the Dupins took him with them to spend the autumn at Chenonceaux.

The invitation must have pleased a man cooped up for two years in various Parisian lodgings, and perhaps one not sorry to leave behind the inept Thérèse, whom he had sworn never to abandon and never to marry, as well as a whole disastrous illegitimate family. But in every age, down to the Verdurins' Raspelière, the country houses of Parisian society have served chiefly as pastoral settings for entertainments exported from town, and what the Dupins' guest, who was still merely the composer of *Les Muses galantes*, would find— and moreover enjoy in this decor just picturesque enough to suggest an opera backcloth—was the luxury of the Hôtel Lambert transported to the water's edge under the trees, the violins, the harpsichords, the chance of showing off those minor society talents without which he would not have been of his time.

> In 1747, we went to spend the autumn in Touraine, at the château of Chenonceaux, a royal dwelling on the Cher, and now owned by Monsieur Dupin, *fermier général.* Life in this splendid setting was very agreeable; the dinners in particular were very fine: at that table I became as plump as any monk. Much music was made, and there I composed several trios for voice, filled with quite daring harmonies . . . Plays were also performed. In fifteen days I composed one in three acts entitled *The Rash Promise.* I also composed some other trifles, including a play in verse entitled *Sylvia's Allée,* after the name of an *allée* in the park bordering the Cher; and all this without leaving off my work on chemistry as well as the labors I was performing for Madame Dupin.

This brief text, the only document remaining to us of these vacations in Touraine, suffices to prove that for pre-Romanticism, the poetry of history still remained undiscovered. Jean-Jacques at Chenonceaux wasted no time sentimentalizing over the past.

Nothing essential, then, occurred for Rousseau during these four or five weeks of laborious enjoyment: an interlude à la Watteau, a blank measure in the life of this trifler who still had no idea where his true genius was to lead him. And yet, each man is so evidently contained entire in each fragment of his life that it is not difficult to recognize the whole of Jean-Jacques at Chenonceaux. The chatelaine was to count among those minor romantic experiences, more dreamed than lived, which ultimately led this clumsy suitor to that ardent mixture of wisdom and folly in the second part of *La Nouvelle Héloïse,* one of the most beautiful and one of the least known of all love stories. His two pupils, Dupin de

Chenonceaux and Dupin de Francueil, the lover of cards and the lover of chemistry, were for Rousseau one of his rare attempts at practical pedagogy; they may have inspired certain precepts or recommendations in *Émile*, which he dedicated in 1761 to the young and touching Madame de Chenonceaux, melancholy wife of the gambler expatriated to the Île Bourbon. The trios composed during the autumn at Chenonceaux served as a prelude to those of *Le Devin du village*; in the *allées* of the park he carried with him his reveries of a solitary wanderer; the measured courtesy of the lady of the house or of a distinguished guest, or perhaps the insolence of a valet divining the former lackey in this Monsieur Rousseau, may have obliged him to reflect upon inequality among men; what he knew of how Dupin's fortune was made is perhaps at the source of certain remarks in the *Social Contract* apropos of taxation in monarchies. These worldly people, so comfortable in their age that they accepted even its audacities, judging them to be without danger, did not suspect (nor did Rousseau any more than they) that what their overfed secretary was preparing at Chenonceaux was Romanticism on the one hand and on the other revolution.

"The scribe of Monsieur Dupin" returned to the rue St.-Jacques: "While I was growing fat at Chenonceaux, my poor Thérèse was doing the same in Paris, though in another manner." A difficult situation, which inspired him with the idea of utilizing the institution of the Foundling Hospital. He endowed his mental progeniture more generously, since his influence, direct or indirect, is perpetuated today in almost every subject that concerns us, whether in literature or education, in the individual's relations with nature or with the state, and since his craving for sincerity, even in the inadmissible, has helped transform our conception of man, and since his impassioned concern to prune life of everything conventional or superfluous in order to apprehend its essential values has been transmitted, through a long series of intermediaries, to Ibsen, to Shaw, to D. H. Lawrence, and, by means of Tolstoy, to Gandhi. In the *Confessions*, the visit to Chenonceaux brings to a close Jean-Jacques's period of social apprenticeship; his relations with the Dupins then became more distant, in part because he soon grew attached to the young Madame de Chenonceaux, and also because Madame Dupin seems to have enjoyed tyrannizing this daughter-in-law *née* Rochechouart, but especially because Rousseau became increasingly absorbed in his work. He remains today the only *man* whose traces we seek in the brilliant Chenonceaux of the eighteenth century, among the fluttering and spangled throng of a late summer's evening.

Madame Dupin withdrew permanently to her country house after the *fermier général's* death; again the property had fallen into the hands of a widow, one also named Louise. But this widowhood had nothing tragic about it. For thirty years, in this splendid residence, Madame Dupin lived the increasingly slackened life of the old. Even the Revolution scarcely disturbed this torpor of old age; the village curé, who inclined toward the new ideas, was a friend of the house; he permitted hotheads to hammer off the escutcheons and burn the documents covered with royal signatures, but when the tavern patriots proposed to destroy this residence that had once belonged to the tyrants, he managed, as we know, to trot out the old argument anticipated by the lawyers of Diane de Poitiers: Chenonceaux had passed from private person to private person, and had never been a property of the crown. Furthermore, this château was a bridge, and good republicans did not burn bridges. Madame Dupin subscribed to various Revolutionary charities; she lent to a theater founded "to instruct the people" certain decors which may have been those of *The Rash Promise*. Once the tempest had subsided and she had pardonably recovered from her taste for reforms, she smilingly showed her infrequent visitors the room of the man she called the Bear of Geneva, who had meanwhile shifted to the category of dangerous Jacobin and Great Man. It is possible that the memory of the amorous ardor Jean-Jacques had manifested forty years ago now flattered the nonagenarian lady. It is also possible that she had forgotten all about it.

The estate on the banks of the Cher belonged for almost two-thirds of the nineteenth century to the grandson of Dupin de Francueil, Comte de Villeneuve. In 1845, George Sand, *née* Aurore Dupin, paid a visit to her Chenonceaux cousins, accompanied by her son Maurice, then an adolescent; one of her letters tells us she marveled at the beauty of the place, especially appreciated the interior "arranged in the old style," and noted with maternal indulgence that Maurice was greatly amused by emptying his chamber pot from the windows of the château into the river. Later, the château came into the hands of one Madame Pelouze, sister of the peculator Wilson, the deplorable son-in-law of President Grévy. Brother and sister gave electoral parties at Chenonceaux in which we may discern the echo and the scent of the Third Republic's scandals. Madame Pelouze and her brother were of Scottish origin: perhaps the dubious businessmen from Paris, smoking their cigars on the terrace, turned a compliment or two for their hostess on the subject of Marie Stuart. It is more likely that their knowledge of the château's history was limited to the second act of Meyerbeer's *Les*

Huguenots, set, as we know, in the gardens of Chenonceaux and opening with Queen Margot's grand aria celebrating *la belle Touraine*. In any case, it is in the style of Meyerbeer and Scribe that the blond Pelouze and her shrewd brother took care to embellish their property.

In truth, this was not the first time that money from fraudulent dealings was spent on Chenonceaux, but taste at the very least had degenerated between the Bohier-Semblançays and the Pelouze-Wilsons: one of the worst misadventures the château suffered was to be redecorated by the latter, and under the direction of the architect of Ste.-Clotilde. Madame Pelouze incurred debts which her illegal sale of Crosses of the Legion of Honor did not suffice to cover, nor were the ensuing bankruptcy and confiscation new catastrophes to Chenonceaux.

Before this farcical episode, the old property received one more royal visit. In 1847, the twenty-six-year-old Gustave Flaubert made one of his first stops here on a long excursion to Brittany with Maxime Du Camp. The two travelers admired the château's "singular suavity" and its "aristocratic serenity." They were shown those apartments which could be visited at the time, and Flaubert's brief notes in *Par les champs et par les grèves* give us an idea of the severe and anything but luxurious interior, with its old hangings and its authentic Renaissance chimneypieces, before Madame Pelouze cluttered it up with Second Empire notions of *le style Henri II*. Nor was the kitchen overlooked, and Flaubert, perhaps hungry after the long day on foot and ever sensitive to the poetry of food, was delighted by the abundance and fragrance of the kettles, whose contents he had no opportunity to sample —in this he was less fortunate than Rousseau. But historical imagination had developed since the days of Jean-Jacques. In

L'Education sentimentale, it is at Fontainebleau that Frédéric Moreau, dismissing from his thoughts his charming and banal mistress, sinks into an ardent reverie over the images and emblems of Diane de Poitiers, but apparently it was at Chenonceaux that Flaubert himself first encountered this figure and this fantasy. In the chamber said to be Diane's, he was shown a bed canopied in rose and white damask and identified as the favorite's; he dreamed of the special delight of spending a night in the bed of someone who had been mistress of a Valois—voluptuousness worth more, he thought, than that afforded by the reality of a woman's presence. He was shown old portraits, which led him to imagine ancient balls and ancient duels. He was also shown a fencing room, a huge hunting horn, a stirrup said to have belonged to François I, and the china of Catherine de Médicis. The age of tourism had begun.

Suppose we shift perspective: let us put aside these all-too-familiar figures, these magic-lantern silhouettes of the history of France, or of the literary history of France. Let us give a moment's thought to other successive occupants of the château, anonymous inhabitants who outnumbered those we know or suppose we know: the servants with their tasks, their plots, their own concerns; the cooks who inside the pilings of the old mill plucked, gutted, sliced, roasted, and blanched, preparing thousands of meals over four centuries; the valets who season after season dragged in and out the traveling furniture which Renaissance princes carried with them from château to château; the ones who polished the sideboards of Catherine de Médicis and dusted the gilded woodwork of the Dupins; the Scapins and Mascarilles of the Chevalier d'Aulnay, and the white-aproned housemaids of the Comte de Villeneuve. Now let us walk outside the château—think of the gardeners who dug, grassed over, and redug these flower beds and these terraces, the obscure dynasties of farmers and gamekeepers who no doubt included their misers and their spendthrifts, their domineering wives and their sad widows. Let us think of the masons standing on their scaffolding, the architect consulting his plan and who was, without doubt, the most apt to take pleasure in the beauty of the materials and the boldness of the structures. Let us walk a little distance: think of the countless generations of birds which have circled these walls, of the cunning architecture of their nests; of the royal genealogies of the forest beasts and of their secret dens and lairs, their hidden life, their almost always tragic deaths, so often due to the aggressions of men. Another step along the paths: think of the great race of trees whose various species have succeeded or supplanted each other in this place, and compared to whose antiquity four or five hundred years is little enough. One step more, farther from all human preoccupation, and here is the water of the river, the water older and newer than all forms, and which for centuries has washed the dirty linen of history. A visit to old houses can lead to points of view we did not anticipate.

MOUNT DESERT ISLAND
1956 and 1961

The Dark Brain
of Piranesi

"THE DARK BRAIN OF PIRANESI . . ." said Victor Hugo in one
of his poems. The man to whom this brain belonged was born
in 1720 into one of those Venetian families in which the
crafts, the professions, and the Church harmoniously co-
habited. His stonecutter father; his uncle Matteo Lucchesi,
an engineer and architect from whom young Giovanni Battista acquired the rudiments of technical knowledge which
sustained his later work; his brother Angelo, a Carthusian
who taught him Roman history—all helped shape various
aspects of his future as an artist. Uncle Matteo in particular
was, one might say, a sort of early and rather mediocre version of Piranesi himself: from him the nephew inherited not
only an erroneous theory as to the Etruscan origins of Greek
architecture, which he stubbornly defended all his life, but
also his respect for the art of architecture considered as a
form of divine creation. To the end of his days, the great
engraver, who was the interpreter and virtually the inventor
of Rome's tragic beauty, proudly and perhaps somewhat
arbitrarily assumed the title of Venetian architect: *archi-
tectus venetianus*. It was also in Venice that he practiced
painting in the studios of the Valeriani brothers, and even

more significantly of the Bibbienas, those poets and virtuosi of theater architecture. Finally, having returned to Venice for several months in 1744, at a time when he was already beginning to establish himself in Rome, he seems to have frequented Tiepolo's atelier; in any case, he certainly came under the influence of this last master of the Venetian grand manner.

It was in 1740, at the age of twenty, that Piranesi, as a draftsman attached to the household of the Venetian ambassador Foscarini, first passed through the Porta del Popolo. No man, if we would than have foretold his future, better deserved a triumphal entrance into the Eternal City. As a matter of fact, the young artist began by studying engraving with a certain Giuseppe Vasi, a conscientious manufacturer of views of Rome, who found his pupil far too good a painter to be a good engraver. With reason, since engraving, in the hands of Vasi and of so many other manufacturers of prints, was hardly more than a rapid and economic process of mechanical reproduction for which excessive talent was more dangerous than useful. Nonetheless, and for reasons partly external, such as the difficulty of making a career as an architect and designer in the rather somnolent Rome of the eighteenth century, partly due to the artist's temperament itself, engraving becomes Piranesi's sole means of expression: the velleities of the painter of stage sets, the impassioned vocation of the architect apparently gave way; in reality, they imposed on his burin a certain style and certain themes. At the same time, the artist has found his subject, which is Rome, and with which for nearly thirty-eight years he will fill the thousand or so plates of his descriptive *oeuvre*. In the more limited group of early works, governed, on the contrary, by a free architectural fantasy, and in particular in the inspired *Imaginary Prisons*, he will audaciously combine elements which are Roman; he will transpose the substance of Rome into the realm of the irrational.

Apart from the brief absence of 1744, when he returned to Venice for the reason which invariably compels artists and poets to return home, lack of money, Piranesi never left Rome again except to explore its immediate environs and for two peregrinations that were more considerable, especially in those days of bad roads—one to Umbria in 1764, to investigate the Etruscan antiquities of Corneto and Chiusi; the other in 1774, to the Kingdom of Naples, where Pompeii and Herculaneum, recently discovered, and Paestum, rediscovered even more recently, were then brand-new attractions. Piranesi has left several haunting sketches of the dead streets of Pompeii; he brought back some splendid drawings from Paestum, which prove once again that the artist's eye and hand are wiser than his "mind," for he continued to the last to regard Greek architecture as a simple succedaneum of Etruscan, highly inferior to the art of the Roman mason. This theory, less indefensible at the time than today because of the learned world's almost complete ignorance of Greece itself, involved him in a long dispute with certain antiquarians of the day, among others the fervent Winckelmann, a lover and theoretician of Greek statuary. The incomparable abbé assigned Greece first place, as is fitting, but in an almost complete absence of Hellenic originals of the best periods, he happened to exalt certain mediocre Hellenistic or Greco-Roman copies as characteristic of Greek art, and to fall into systematization and error in his turn. This futile dispute doubtless served Piranesi as a stimulant or else as a kind of safety valve; it deserves to be forgotten, if it were not interesting to see it as the confrontation over an ill-framed issue of the two men who revivified our conception of the antique.

We know some of Piranesi's successive Roman domiciles: first of all the Palazzo di Venezia, the Serenissima's embassy to the Holy See at the time; then the shop on the Corso where, having returned from his visit to his native city and quarreled with his family, who had cut off his funds, he set himself up as the agent of the Venetian print dealer Giuseppe Wagner; finally, the studio in the via Felice (today the via Sistina), where the second states of the *Prisons* were on sale at their creator's for the price of 20 écus, and where Piranesi breathed his last, a thriving artist covered with honors, a member of the Academy of St. Luke since 1757, ennobled by Clement XIII in 1767. Like so many men of taste then settled in Rome, the Cavaliere Piranesi did not disdain to practice the profitable trade of dealing in antiquities; certain engravings of his *Vasi, Candelabri, Cippi, Sarcophagi, Tripodi, Lucerne ed Ornamenti antichi* served to circulate the image of one or another splendid item among enlightened amateurs. He appears to have been chiefly surrounded by a group of foreign artists and connoisseurs: the goodnatured Hubert Robert, who sometimes seems to have undertaken to retranslate Piranesi's Baroque Rome into rococo terms, the publisher Bouchard, who printed the first states of the *Prisons* and the *Antiquities of Rome*—"Buzzard," as Piranesi spelled it, and no doubt lisped it as well, in the Venetian fashion. Of the English colony, Piranesi's circle included the architect and decorator Robert Adam, who adapted Italian classicism to British tastes and habits, and that other London architect George Dance, who was inspired, it is said, by the *Imaginary Prisons* to design the very real dungeons of Newgate. The thread which continued to attach Piranesi to

Venice during these years was the friendship of the papal and banking family, the Rezzonicos: Pope Clement XIII employed him as a decorator and appointed him architect for certain projects at St. John Lateran, which, however, were never carried out or even begun. In 1764, one of the Pope's nephews, Cardinal Rezzonico, entrusted Piranesi with the task of partly rebuilding and entirely redecorating the Church of Santa Maria Aventina, the property of the Order of the Knights of Malta, of which he was the Grand Prior. This modest commission required less majesty than grace: Piranesi transformed the little façade of the church and the great walls of the Piazza dei Cavalieri di Malta into a harmonious ensemble embellished with escutcheons and trophies in which, as in his *Grotesques*, certain ancient architectural elements combined with a Venetian whimsicality. This was the sole occasion this dedicated architect would have to express himself in actual marble and stone.

What we know of Piranesi's private life is limited to his marriage to a gardener's daughter, a handsome young woman with fine black eyes whom the artist regarded as incarnating the pure Roman type. Legend has it that he met this Angelica Pasquini in the then nobly deserted ruins of the Forum, where he was sketching on that particular evening, and took her for his wife after having possessed her then and there on ground sacred to the memory of Antiquity. If the anecdote is authentic, this violent dreamer must have imagined he was enjoying the favors of Magna Tellus herself, Dea Roma incarnate in the solid flesh of this young *popolana*. A different but not necessarily contradictory version informs us that the artist urged marriage when he learned that the beauty would bring a dowry of 150 piastres. Whatever the case, this Angelica gave him three children, who continued his own labors without

genius but assiduously: Francesco, the most gifted, followed
his father in uniting the engraver's profession with that of
archaeologist and dealer in antiquities; it was he who obtained
for Gustave III of Sweden the mediocre (and in some cases
dubious) marbles which today form a touching little eighteenth-century collection "of an enlightened amateur" in a
room of the Royal Palace in Stockholm.

It is a Frenchman, one Jacques-Guillaume Legrand, whom
we may thank for gathering from Francesco Piranesi's lips
most of our details as to his father's life, views, and character;
what remains of the artist's writings confirms his observations.
We see a man of passionate feelings, intoxicated by work,
careless of his health and his comfort, disdaining the *malaria*
of the Roman Campagna, sustaining himself on nothing but
cold rice during his long sojourns in such solitary and un-
healthy sites as, at the time, Hadrian's Villa or the ruins of
Albano and Cora, and lighting his scanty campfire only once
a week in order to waste none of the time reserved for his ex-
plorations and his works. "The verisimilitude and the vigor
of his effects," notes Jacques-Guillaume Legrand, with that
sober pertinence which is the mark of eighteenth-century
intellectuals, "the accurate projection of his shadows and their
transparency, or the fortunate liberties taken in this regard,
the very indication of shadings of color are due to the exact
observation which he was to make from nature, either under
the burning sun or by moonlight." It is easy to imagine, beneath the unendurable noonday sun or at an almost luminous
midnight, this observer on the prowl for the ineffable, seeking
in this apparent immobility whatever moves and changes,
scrutinizing ruins to discover the secret of a highlight, the
place for a crosshatching, as others were to do in order to dig
up treasures or to raise ghosts. This great overworked artisan

died in Rome in 1778, of a neglected kidney ailment; he was buried at the expense of Cardinal Rezzonico in the Church of Santa Maria Aventina, where his tomb may be visited today. A portrait inserted as a frontispiece to the *Prisons* shows him in around his thirtieth year, hair close-cropped, eyes intense, features somewhat soft, very Italian, and very much a man of the eighteenth century, despite the naked shoulders and pectorals of a Roman bust. From the viewpoint of chronology alone, we may note that he was a contemporary of Rousseau, of Diderot, and of Casanova, and the elder by a generation of the Goya of the *Caprichos*, of the Goethe of the *Roman Elegies*, of Sade the obsessed, and of that great prison reformer Beccaria. All the eighteenth-century angles of incidence and reflection intersect in the strange linear universe of Giovanni Battista Piranesi.

At first glance it seems possible to make a selection from Piranesi's almost overabundant production—to relegate, for instance, as certain timorous critics of the past have done, the sixteen plates of the *Prisons* to the wing reserved for madness and delirium, and to extol, on the contrary, in the *Views* and the *Antiquities of Rome*,* a logical discourse, a reality scrupulously observed and nobly transcribed. Or else, fashion having as always intervened and paradoxically reversed the terms, to regard the *Prisons* as the sole series in which the great engraver freely expressed and exercised his

---

* It is for the sake of convenience and simplification that we here designate as *Views of Rome* or *Antiquities of Rome* the countless representations of ancient monuments Piranesi has left us. Aside from the *Antichità Romane* and the *Vedute* and the *Varie Vedute di Roma*, a complete list of Piranesi's descriptive work would also include the *Antichità Romane de' Tempi della Repubblica*, the *Antichità d'Albano*, the *Antichità di Cora*, the engravings which embellish his great polemical study *Della Magnificenza ed Architettura de' Romani*, and several other series as well.

genius, and to degrade the *Antiquities* and *Views* to the level
of admirably fluent commonplaces fabricated to please a
clientele in love with historical clichés and famous sites, and
thereby certain of a ready market. And of course it can never
be said too often that the voluminous series of *Views* and
Antiquities represented, for the eighteenth-century dealer
and connoisseur, the equivalent of the coffee-table albums of
artistic photographs offered nowadays to the tourist eager to
confirm or complement his memories, or to the sedentary
reader who dreams of faraway places. We might almost say
that in relation to the engravers who preceded him, the
Piranesi of the *Views* occupies the position enjoyed, among
his mediocre and literal confrères, by the virtuoso photogra-
pher who exploits backlighting, effects of mist or twilight,
unexpected and revealing angles . . . And yet we should be
completely denaturing Piranesi's productions by establishing
for them a scale of values ranging from the quasi-artisanal
level of his album *On Various Fashions of Embellishing
Chimneypieces*, or from his diagrams of clocks or gondolas,
to the still semicommercial stage of the *Views* and *Antiquities of Rome*, and finally attaining, in the *Prisons*, a kind of
pure subjective vision. In reality, the slender album of the
Prisons, with its dark images resulting, it is said, from a bout
of fever, also corresponds to an established genre and almost
to a vogue: a painter like Pannini, engravers like the Bibbienas, compiled at the time or even earlier their audacious
decors for operas or imaginary tragedies, constructions consisting of real architectural elements skillfully juxtaposed with
dream-like perspectives. Furthermore, Piranesi's artisan drawings attest not only to the same temperament but to the same
obsessions as his boldest or most powerful masterpieces. The
chimneypiece covered with symbols and fabulous animals in

the *Arte d'adornare i cammini*, worthy of imprisoning fire in the cabinet of a Rosicrucian, is indeed from the same hand which drew the gigantic lions of Plate V of the *Prisons*; the study of a project for a carriage attests to the same exquisite sensibility as the complicated schema of the *Grand Thermae of Hadrian's Villa*. Without the help of his more artisanal work, we should perhaps fail to place his major productions in their period and in the fashion of the time; we should overlook in him the part of the clever decorator. Without the *Antiquities* and *Views*, the phantasmagorical universe of the *Prisons* would seem too studied, too factitious; we should not discern in it the authentic materials reappearing obsessionally amid his own nightmares. Without the almost demonic boldness of the *Prisons*, we should hesitate to recognize, in the apparent classicism of the *Views* and the *Antiquities*, the *deep song* of a meditation on the life and death of forms at once visual and metaphysical.

The subjects of Piranesi's descriptive engravings fall into two categories, which of course intersect. On one hand, the Baroque edifice, still new or virtually so: the rectilinear façade with its unbroken walls; the obelisk dividing perspectives; the street where rows of palaces produce a slightly curving line, which is one of the miracles of Rome; the ellipse or the irregular polygon of the bare, flat piazzas; the parallelepiped of the interior views of basilicas; the cylinder and the sliced-off sphere of cupola-churches' interiors; the rotunda revolving open to the sky; the monumental fountain whose rounded basin imitates the curve of a wave; the smooth and polished facings of floors and walls. On the other hand, the ruins already fifteen centuries old: broken stone and crumbling brick; the collapsing vault that welcomes light's intrusion; the tunnel of dark rooms opening in the distance on daylight streaming through a broken wall; the overhanging plinth, suspended on the brink of its collapse, the great broken rhythm of aqueducts and colonnades; temples and basilicas lying open and as though turned inside out by the depredations of time and of man, so that the interior has now become a kind of exterior, everywhere invaded by space like a ship by water. Piranesi establishes an equilibrium of communicating vessels between what is for him still modern and what is already, for him as for us, the antique, between the new monument solidly established in a time which is still his own, and the monument already touching the last extremity of its trajectory through the centuries. If it tumbled down, this *St.-Paul's-outside-the-Walls* would be no different from the ancient temple to which its columns once belonged; in ruins, this *Colonnade of St. Peter's* would closely resemble the porticoes of Nero's Circus, which it has replaced. Intact, this *Temple of Venus* or these *Baths of Cara-calla*, by the luxury of their marbles, by the abundance of stuccos and the proliferation of gigantic statues, would correspond to the same preoccupations with pomp and prestige as an edifice by Bernini. The genius of the Baroque has given Piranesi the intuition of that pre-Baroque architecture created by Imperial Rome; it has preserved him from the cold academ-icism of his successors, with whom he is sometimes confused, and for whom the monuments of Antiquity are no more than scholarly texts. It is to the Baroque that Piranesi, in his *Views*, owes these sudden breakdowns of equilibrium, this very de-liberate readjustment of perspective, this analysis of mass which is for its period a conquest as considerable as the Im-pressionists' analysis of light later on. To the Baroque as well he owes these great unexpected interplays of shadow and shafts of light, these shifting illuminations, so different from the skies of eternity which the Renaissance painters set behind their imitation-antique palaces and temples, and which a nineteenth-century Corot was to rediscover in his Italian period. Finally, it is to the Baroque that Piranesi owes a sense of the superhuman which he carries to dizzy heights in the *Prisons*.

Of course, the creator of the *Views* and the *Antiquities of Rome* invented neither the craze for ruins nor the love of Rome. A century before him, Poussin and Claude Gelée had also discovered Rome with a foreigner's fresh eyes; their work was nourished on these inexhaustible sites. But while for a Claude, for a Poussin, Rome had been chiefly an admirable background for personal reverie or else for discourse of a general order—in short, a sacred site purified of any contemporary contingency, situated halfway to the divine country of Fable, it is the City itself, the City in all its aspects and in all its implications, from the most banal to the most unwonted, that Piranesi has fixed at a certain moment of the eighteenth century, in a thousand plates at once anecdotal and visionary. He has not merely explored the ancient monuments as a draftsman looking for a point of view; he has explored the remains in person, in part to unearth the antiquities he makes a business of, but above all to penetrate the secret of their foundations, to learn and to demonstrate how they were built. He is an archaeologist in a period when the word itself is not in common usage. To the last, he docilely follows custom, which consists in numbering on the plates each part of the structure, each fragment of ornament still in place, and making certain explanatory notes in the lower margin correspond to them, without its ever occurring to him, as it certainly would to an artist nowadays, that these schoolbook specifications or engineering diagrams might diminish the aesthetic or picturesque value of his work.

"When I realized that in Rome the majority of the ancient monuments were lying forsaken in fields or gardens, or even now serving as a quarry for new structures, I resolved to preserve their memory with the help of my engravings. I have therefore attempted to exercise the greatest possible exactitude." There is already something Goethean about this sentence in its assertion of a modest desire to be useful. To grasp the importance of this rescue work, we must recall that at least a third of the monuments drawn by Piranesi have since vanished, and that what remains has most often been despoiled of the surfacings and stuccos then still in place, or again modified, and restored, sometimes clumsily, between the end of the eighteenth century and our own time. Nowadays when artists believe they are liberating themselves by breaking the links which connect them to the outside world, it is worth noting what a precise solicitude for the object contemplated is at the source of Piranesi's almost hallucinatory masterpieces.

Many painters of genius have been architects as well; very few have thought solely in terms of architecture in their painted, drawn, or engraved work. Further, certain painters who have also tried to be archaeologists—the Ingres of *Stronice*, for example—have generally produced no more than a cheap and disappointing imitation. On the contrary, Piranesi's studies as an architect taught him to reflect thoroughly and continuously in terms of balance and weight, of blocks and of mortar. His antiquarian research, furthermore, accustomed him to recognize in each fragment of antiquity the singularities or specifications of kind; they were for him what the dissection of cadavers is for a painter of the nude. It seems in particular that the passion for building, repressed in this man limited throughout his career to the two dimensions

of a sheet of copper, rendered him particularly apt at redis-
covering in a ruined monument the energy which originally
raised it from the ground. We might almost say that the raw
materials, in the *Antiquities*, are expressed for their own sake:
Piranesi's image of the ruin does not release a discourse on
the grandeur and decadence of empires and the instability of
human affairs, but rather a meditation on the duration or the
slow erosion of things, on the opaque identity of the block
continuing, within the monument, its long existence of stone
as stone. Conversely, for Piranesi Rome's majesty survives in
a broken vault, rather than in an association of ideas with
some buried Caesar. The edifice is sufficient unto itself; it is at
once the drama and the drama's decor, the site of a dialogue
between the human will still inscribed in these enormous
masonries, inert mineral energy, and irrevocable Time.

This secret metaphysical poetry sometimes seems, in the
hands of this compatriot of Arcimboldo, to end by producing
double images, due not so much to caprice as to the intensity
of his visionary gaze. The collapsed cupola of *Canopus* and
that of the *Temple of Diana at Baiae* are the fractured skull,
the bony casement from which dangle filaments of grass and
weeds; the *Antonine Column* and *Trajan's Column* irresistibly
suggest, in this *oeuvre* so apparently lacking in eroticism,
certain frenzied verses by Théophile Gautier on the Vendôme
Column; the obelisk lying in sections at the foot of the
Palazzo Barbarini is a corpse hacked to pieces by nameless
bravi. Even more often, instead of simply identifying the man-
made shape with the human body, visual metaphor tends to
reinstate the edifice within the ensemble of natural forces, of
which our most complicated architectures are never anything
but a partial and unconscious microcosm. The ruin leans

against the new palace like a dead log against living trees; the half-collapsed dome seems to be a mound scaled by a troop of bushes; buildings assume the aspect of lava, of sponge, having reached that degree of undifferentiated matter where we no longer know if this pebble picked up on the beach has once been carved by the hand of man or was fashioned thus by the tides. The extraordinary *Foundation Wall of Hadrian's Tomb* is a cliff against which the centuries have washed and broken; the empty *Coliseum* is an extinct crater. This sense of great natural metamorphoses is perhaps never more evident in Piranesi than in the drawings which he brought back from Paestum, and which his son Francesco honorably completed after his death, peopling them with shepherds and Theocritan cattle. But here violence gives way to peace; metaphor is dissolved into a simple affirmation of the object contemplated. Greece, which the draftsman approached without knowing it, suffuses these images with a robust beauty at once individual and abstract, so different from Rome's simultaneously utilitarian and romantic grandeur. The ruined temple is not merely a wreck on the sea of forms; it itself is nature: its shafts are the equivalent of a sacred wood; its rhythms of projection and recession are a melody in the Dorian mode; its wreckage remains a precept, an admonition, an order of things. The work of this tragic poet of architecture comes to its close upon this ecstasy of serenity.

Before leaving the *Views*, let us consider for a moment, magnifying glass in hand, the minuscule humanity which gesticulates on the ruins or in the streets of Rome. *Fantoccini, burattini, puppi*: these ladies in paniered gowns, these gentlemen wearing swords and capes *à la française*, these hooded monks and these *monsignori* belonging to the repertoire of eighteenth-century Italy—they give off an atmo-

sphere of Goldoni or of Casanova, a fragrance more Venetian than Roman. With these characters from genre painting
reduced to infinitesimal proportions by the enormity of the
edifices, Piranesi has mingled the picaresque personnel of the
Roman Campagna, muleteers, Trastevere girls lugging their
broods, beggars, cripples, and almost everywhere the hairy
and agile goatherds, scarcely more human than their flocks.
Nowhere has the artist attempted, as have so many Baroque
or Romantic painters of Rome before or since, to harmonize
human nobility and gravity with architectural dignity. It is a
rare thing if, here and there, a small figure of a handsome
youth standing or prone, solitary wanderer, dreamer, or simply local guide, suggests among these human will-o'-the-wisps
the equivalent of an ancient statue. "Instead of studying from
the nude or from the only good models, which are those of
Greek statuary," writes Piranesi's first biographer, Bianconi,
toward the end of the eighteenth century, "he preferred to
draw the most wretched cripples and the most hideous hunch-
backs to be found in Rome. When he had occasion to find
one of these monsters begging upon some church doorstep,"
he rejoiced as if he had discovered a new Apollo Belvedere."
The presence of these vagabonds sometimes endows Piranesi's deserted sites with a suggestion of danger. In one of the
plates of the *Antiquities*, two dancer-like graverobbers are
quarreling over a skeleton almost as graceful as themselves;
another thief has snatched up the skull, while two steps away,
under the split lid of the sarcophagus, a carved bucranium
adds an image of the animal death's-head to the human one.
The ruin literally seethes: each new glance reveals a new
group of human insects rummaging through the rubble or the
brush. Rags, cowls, and flounces consort in the shining
church interiors, not to mention the dogs snapping at each
other and scratching their fleas at the very foot of the holy

altars. Piranesi's strollers and prowlers betray that easy, devil-may-care, occasionally alarming behavior, Mephistophelean before Goethe invented his Mephistopheles, which, if we are to believe painters from Watteau to Magnasco and from Hogarth to Goya, was typical of the century from beginning to end.

The grotesque contrast between papal pomp and antique grandeur on the one hand, and on the other the miseries and absurdities of contemporary Roman life, had already been felt some two hundred years earlier by the Du Bellay of *Les Regrets*, who was also one of the first poets to celebrate *in situ* the majesty of Rome's ruins. It erupts again in the strident opening of Voltaire's *Voyages de Scarmentado* ("I left Rome, highly pleased with the architecture of St. Peter's"); we will encounter it all over again a century later in Belli. It would seem only natural to attribute to the creator of the *Views* the same intention of mocking counterpoint, but these little characters from the comedy of manners or picaresque romance are too stereotyped in aspect and format for us to assume in Piranesi any depth of irony or well-concealed disdain: this trivial *hoi polloi* and this preening world of fashion simply served him, as so many engravers of his period, to accentuate the elevation of the vaults and the depth of the perspectives. At most they constituted for him a *scherzo* contrasting with the architecture's solemn *largo*. And yet these homunculi whom we discover absurdly perched on the dizzying stories of the *Prisons* correspond too closely to a certain sense of mockery and of the futility of human life not to acquire, at least implicitly, a value as very minor symbols; not to remind us of a half-mathematical, half-satirical badinage which obsessed certain of the best minds of the eighteenth century: *Micromégas, Gulliver's Voyage to Lilliput.*

. . .

The first album of the *Prisons*, or, to translate their title more precisely, of the *Imaginary Prisons* (*Invenzioni Caprice di Carceri*), bears no date, but it is thought to have been published in 1745. Piranesi himself assigns them an earlier date in the catalogue of his works: "Plates produced in 1742"; the artist have been twenty-two at the time. Thus these fourteen plates of the first *Imaginary Prisons* are just about contemporary with two youthful works, *Prima parte di Architettura* and *Opere varie di Architettura*, in which Piranesi draws certain fictive edifices with cunningly complicated perspectives, virtuoso pieces almost obligatory for artists trained in the Baroque tradition, and among which already figures the isolated image of a *Dark Prison*. They closely follow the publication of Giuseppi Bibbiena's architectural fantasies, *Architettura e Prospettiva*, which appeared in Augsburg in 1740. Their completion, or their first revision, is set around the period of the 1744 stay in Venice, when Piranesi is supposed to have worked under Tiepolo, another magician of theatrical architecture. But these images, which in many aspects refer to a fashionable genre, deliberately depart from it by their intensity, their strangeness, their violence—as if struck by the rays of a black sun. If, as is asserted, the delirious *Prisons* were created in a fit of fever, the Campagna's paludism favored Piranesi's genius by momentarily releasing certain elements which might have been repressed to the last, merely hinted at in his work.

We must define the word "delirium." Supposing his legendary malaria of 1742 to be authentic, fever did not open for Piranesi the doors to a world of mental confusion, but to realms dangerously vaster and more complex than the one the young engraver had hitherto lived in, though composed after all of virtually identical materials. It increased the art-

ist's perception to the point of erethism, and almost to torment, thereby making possible on one hand the dizzying
energy, the mathematical intoxication, and on the other the
crisis of agoraphobia and claustrophobia combined, the anguish of captive space from which the *Prisons* certainly re-
sulted. From this point of view, nothing could be more useful
than to compare these *Imaginary Prisons* with one of the
technically perfect but coldly linear plates of the *Prima parte
de Architettura*, for instance, the academic *Project for a
Temple*, dated 1743, which is contemporary with or even
very slightly posterior to the first states of the *Prisons*. Extend
these perspectives; raise this drum vault already dispropor-
tionately high; bathe these still-conventional edifices and
these tiny inhabitants in an atmosphere of dreams; make the
smoke from these classical urns rise up in a more disturbing
coil; intensify and simplify each line; and what you achieve
will differ little from these hallucinated *Prisons*. Which sig-
nifies, in short, that in the *Prisons* Piranesi's genius shows
itself at work for the first time.

This unexpected series of fourteen plates and the gayer
series of four decorative compositions, the *Grotesques* of
1744, are the only works in which Piranesi abandons himself
to what he called his caprice, or to put it better, to his obsessions and to his hallucinations. Diverse as they may be,
Prisons and *Grotesques* both record the first shock of the
antique and the Roman on Piranesi the Venetian. The *Grotesques* combine in a charming rococo *potpourri* certain
fragments of columns, broken bas-reliefs and skulls which
remind us a little of the gracefully macabre ornaments on
some seventeenth-century tombstones, and a little of the delicate skulls and skeletons of Alexandrian carving. The
enormously lofty *Prisons*, for their part, offer an inverted

image of Roman and Baroque grandeur reflected in the dark-room of his visionary mind. The somber fantasy which, later on, reabsorbed within the actual and the concrete, still steeps the *Roman Antiquities*, is in these youthful works in a free state and, so to speak, chemically pure. For the *Prisons* especially, we must remember that the creator of this extraordinary series was only twenty-two years old. If we could compare an artist of the Baroque era to a poet of the post-Romantic period, we might risk calling these *Prisons* of the young Piranesi the equivalent of the *Illuminations* of a Rimbaud who did not subsequently give up writing. Perhaps they were his *Season in Hell* as well.

These *Prisons*, which modern criticism hails as a crowning achievement, were in their own day, as we might expect, very mildly appreciated and not at all understood, and consequently seldom purchased. In 1761, *i.e.*, seventeen years after the series' publication in its first form, Piranesi, now forty, offered the public a second, greatly reworked edition (*Carceri d'invenzione di G. B. Piranesi*), one which now contained sixteen plates. At the same time, the word "*Caprice*," which figured prominently in the frontispiece of the first state, disappeared from this definitive edition, by an omission perhaps significant, or perhaps due merely to the formal rehandling of the title page.

If we look closely, we see that Piranesi's other changes in the *Prisons* are almost all of two kinds: he has multiplied the crosshatchings, permitting more generous inking, has diminished the great bright spaces, has darkened and augmented the areas of shadow; almost everywhere, too, he has added wheels, pulleys, cranes, winches, and capstans to the mysterious machines sketched in the foreground or in the corners of the halls; details which certainly transform them into instruments of torture rather than seeming the mere engines of construction they might have been; the wheels and platforms now ominously bristle with nails; from a brazier paradoxically flaming at the edge of a gallery opening out into the void rise blackened stakes, vaguely suggesting tortures; in Plate IV of the second state, a huge dark St. Catherine's wheel has replaced the noble column which constituted the axis of the perspective; clusters of chains hanging along the walls have proliferated like those of some hateful vine. Further, Piranesi has added two new plates (II and V) to the series, more vehement and more crowded with architectural reminiscences than the others. Finally, he has suppressed the fourteenth and last sheet of the first album, where we saw, against an almost bright background, two characters descending the steps of a central staircase, while a tiny veiled figure, a kind of mysterious counterweight, appeared at the right in a secret stairwell. This masterpiece of strange grace, which seemed to prophesy a kind of finale, *avant la lettre*, to an ideal *Fidelio*, has been replaced by the image of a black cellar decorated with grimacing Roman busts and lugubrious inscriptions, emphasizing almost to excess that the place we are in is indeed a prison.

Among the many reasons an artist of genius may have for modifying his work, the most common one does not apply here. There can be no question of a labor still blemished by inexperience now rehandled by the creator who has since achieved mastery: nothing, on the contrary, equals or exceeds the virtuosity manifested in these second states, if it is not perhaps that of the first ones. The most we can say is that meanwhile Piranesi has studied Rembrandt further, for we know that he admired the Dutchman's engraved work and that it certainly influenced his own productions, typically Italian though they are. It is possible, of course, that Piranesi, like his entire century, was swept by the current which drew Baroque art toward what we call pre-Romanticism, and that he deliberately modified his work in the direction of the gothic novel. It is also possible that, for some other reason, the notion of crime and the idea of legal prosecution increasingly preoccupied the creator of the *Prisons*. But above all, let us not forget that the eighteenth-century artist was supposed to offer his public an organized discourse whose signification would be patent to all, and not the more or less indecipherable product of a subjective reverie. Everything in these *Prisons* suggests that Piranesi had attempted in a lucid state to rationalize images which had perhaps lost the manifest meaning they possessed in his delirium, to justify their title by adding to these transcendental dungeons and dizzying torture chambers some unimpeachable detail of real dungeons and actual tortures—in short, to replace on the level of concepts and comprehensible emotions of the waking state, darker but also less unexpected, what had initially been the prodigious hallucination of an architect, the dream of a builder drunk on pure volumes, pure space.

Taken together, in either the edition of 1761 or in an earlier state, what first strikes us is that the *Prisons* bear very little resemblance to traditional images of a prison. In every age, the nightmare of incarceration chiefly consists in *confinement*, in being shut up in a dungeon which already has the dimensions of a grave. *Tu in questa tomba* . . . It also involves physical misery, ordure, vermin, rats swarming in the darkness—all the hideous decor of the *in-pace* and the *oubliette* which so obsessed the Romantic imagination. To these lugubriously permanent characteristics, our age will add the cold functionalism of its model prisons, the sinister banality of concentration-camp barracks which conceal the modern forms of torture and death, the mocking hygiene of the shower rooms of Belsen, the image of human crowds penned in the abattoirs of the first half of the twentieth century and in those the future holds in store. We are far from that loathsome horror and that sordid hypocrisy with Piranesi's megalomaniac and sublime *Prisons*. The sight of ancient Rome's places of incarceration could not have inspired him: the dreadful Mamertine Prison, where victims of the Republic and of Caesar suffered their last agony, consists of no more than two superimposed black holes, the lower barely the height of a man; Jugurtha and Vercingetorix suffocated in this pit with no outlet but the sewer of the Cloaca Maxima. Nor was Piranesi reminded of the medieval jails of the Castel Sant'Angelo, though he might have retained certain elements of its internal structure from this ancient mausoleum of Hadrian, like its helical corridor or underground room with the tombs, in order to serve them up again, much modified, in some plates of the *Prisons*; and the "leads" or "wells" above and under the Ducal Palace in his native city, which could have haunted this Venetian when he was drawing imaginary jails, also belonged to that type of prison in which the captive stifles or freezes in a narrow space. The pictorial art of the past, and in particular old Italian religious paintings, to which this eighteenth-century man doubtless paid very little attention, offer the one variant of the iron cage or heavily barred cell, scarcely spacious enough for the saint to receive the angel who comes to prepare him for martyrdom or else to save him; it was in this constricted form that Raphael had represented St. Peter's prison in the Vatican *stanze*.

Most of Piranesi's commentators, seeking a point of departure for the delirious *Prisons*, refer, for want of better models, to a certain Daniel Marot, a French draftsman and engraver who worked in England and who in 1708 published a little series of prints, one of which, the *Prison of Amadis*, already heralds the extravagant style of Piranesian dungeons. But this thread is very slender; actually it appears that the two engravers set out to depict quite independently an imaginary or a real setting: a tragedy king enslaved by his usurper, an opera knight imprisoned by a magician might fill with the *bel canto* of his distress these dizzying palaces related to no real prison. For example, Act III, Scene 1 of Metastasio's *Artaxerxes*, written in 1730, supplies the following brief indications, which, given contemporary taste for *trompe l'oeil* and perspective in the grand manner, might have inspired a designer less concerned with verisimilitude than with splendid effects of shadow and mass: *Parte interna della Fortezza nella quale e ritenuto Arbace. Cancelli in prospetto. Picciola porta a destra, per la quale si ascende alla Reggia.* It is probably from a description of this kind that Piranesi embarked to attain a region in which reigns a more mysterious anguish than that of the theater, and which sometimes seems to translate that of the entire human condition.

Let us consider these *Prisons*, then, which with Goya's *Black Paintings* are one of the most secret works bequeathed us by a man of the eighteenth century. First of all, what we are shown here is a dream. No connoisseur of oneiric matters will hesitate a moment in the presence of these drawings evincing all the chief characteristics of the dream state: negation of time, incoherence of space, suggested levitation, intoxication of the impossible reconciled or transcended, terror closer to ecstasy than is assumed by those who analyze the visionary's creations from outside, absence of visible contact between the dream's parts or characters, and finally a fatal and necessary beauty. Next, and to give the Baudelairean formula its most concrete meaning, it is *a dream of stone*: powerfully hewn stone, set in place by human hands, constitutes virtually the sole substance of the *Prisons*, with an occasional wooden rafter, iron jack, or chain; contrary to the program of the *Views* and *Antiquities*, here stone, iron, and wood have ceased being elemental substances—they now become no more than a constituent part of the edifice with no relation to the life of things. Animal and plant are eliminated from these interiors where only human logic or human madness rules; no trace of moss touches these bare walls. The natural elements are absent or narrowly subjugated: earth appears nowhere, covered over by tiles or indestructible pavings; air does not circulate—no puff of wind, in Plate VIII, animates the frayed silk of the flags; a perfect immobility reigns in these great closed spaces. At the very bottom of Plate IX, a fountain rim on which a woman is leaning (and both figure and object seem to have come out of the *Views of Rome*) is the only sign of water's presence in this petrified world. In several plates, though, fire is present: smoke rises from a cauldron strangely set on the brink of the void at a cornice's jutting edge, suggesting an executioner's brazier or a magician's crucible. In reality, it seems that Piranesi chiefly delights in setting smoke's pale and shapeless ascent against the verticality of the stones. Nor does time move any more than air; the perpetual *chiaroscuro* excludes the very notion of the hour, and the dreadful solidity of the structure defies the erosion of the centuries. When Piranesi could not help introducing into these buildings a rotted beam or a noble patch of ancient wall, he sets it, like a precious jewel, in the midst of timeless masonry. Finally, this void is sonorous: each *Prison* is conceived as an enormous Ear of Dionysus. Just as in the *Antiquities* one heard the faint echo of an aeolian harp in the ruins, the rustling of the wind in the weeds and rushes, here the roused sense of hearing perceives a formidable silence in which the lightest footstep, the faintest sigh of the strange and diminutive strollers lost in these aerial galleries would echo from one end of the enormous structures to the other. Nowhere sheltered from sound, one is nowhere sheltered from sight either, in these hollow, apparently vacated chambers linked by stairs and gratings to other invisible chambers, and this sense of total exposure, total insecurity, perhaps contributes more than all else to making these fantastic palaces into prisons.

The major protagonist of the *Antiquities* is Time; the hero of the *Prisons* is Space. Discrepancies, deliberately warped perspectives also abound in Piranesi's Roman albums; he remained faithful to the method of the engraver able to reproduce the totality of a building or a site—its various aspects, which in reality the eye does not simultaneously perceive but which our memory unconsciously collects after the fact. Almost everywhere in his interior views of Roman basilicas, Piranesi seems to place himself, and to place us, at the entrance of the edifice he is drawing, as if we had just crossed its threshold with him. As a matter of fact, he has stepped back some hundred paces, mentally suppressing the façade rising behind us, a trick allowing him to include in his sketch the whole interior but dwarfing the figures in the foreground as if they were glimpsed in a middle distance, while those at the very back become simple dots in this universe of lines. The result of this trick of perspective is to increase further the already existing disproportion between human size and the man-made monument. The stretching or warping of the perspectives of streets and squares produces the same effect, distancing or removing structures which would hamper the view, majestically raising the *Fountain of Trevi* or the colossal statues of *Monte-Cavallo* into a space greater than that actually around them; this procedure has influenced all subsequent architects and urbanists. In the *Prisons*, these games played with space become the equivalent of what in an inspired novelist's work are the liberties taken with time.

The irrational world of the *Prisons* dizzies us not from its lack of measurements (for never was Piranesi more of a geometrician) but from the very multiplicity of calculations which we know to be exact and which bear on proportions which we know to be false. For these figures high on a gallery at the back of the hall to have such infinitesimal dimensions, this balcony, which is extended by other still more inaccessible cornices, would have to be separated from us by hours of walking, and this discrepancy, which suffices to prove that this somber palace is only a dream, fills us with an anguish analogous to that of an inchworm trying to measure the walls of a cathedral. Often the arch of a vault in the upper part of the image conceals the top steps of a staircase or the end of a ladder, suggesting heights still loftier than those of the steps and rungs visible; the hint of another staircase plunging lower than the level on which we are standing warns that this abyss is also to be extended beyond the plate's lower margin; the suggestion grows even more specific when a lantern hung almost on a level with the same margin confirms the hypothesis of invisible black depths below. Moreover, the artist succeeds in convincing us that this disproportionate hall is hermetically sealed, even on the face of the cube we never see because it is behind us. In the rare cases (Plates II, IV, and IX) where an inaccessible opening gives onto an exterior itself imprisoned by walls, this sort of *trompe l'oeil* merely aggravates the nightmare of closed space in the center of the image. The impossibility of discerning any overall plan adds another element to the discomfort inspired by the *Prisons*: we almost never have the impression of being in the main axis of the structure, but only on a vectorial branch; the preference of the Baroque for diagonal perspectives inevitably gives us the feeling we exist in an asymmetrical universe. But this world without a center is at the same time infinitely expansible. Behind these halls with their barred bull's-eyes, we suspect there are other halls just like them, deduced or deducible in every direction. The frail catwalks, the drawbridges in midair which almost everywhere double the galleries and the stone staircases, seem to correspond to the same desire to hurl into space all possible curves and parallels. This world closed over itself is mathematically infinite.

Contrary to all expectation, this disturbing architecture is discovered, upon study, to be formed of very concrete elements which Piranesi elsewhere reintroduces into his work under apparently more real but actually no less visionary aspects. These subterranean chambers resemble the ancient reservoirs of the *Emissarium of Lake Albano* or the *Cistern of Castel Gandolfo*; these trophies at the foot of the splendid staircases of Plate VIII suggest those of Marius on the ramp of the Capitol; these posts linked by chains derive from the façades and the courtyards of Roman palaces where they quite banally serve to keep out carriages; these staircases whose balusters, flight after flight, encage the abyss are, but on a nightmare scale, those which princes and prelates of Baroque Rome mounted and descended every day; this hemicycle glimpsed in Plate IV through an arch decorated with ancient bas-reliefs resembles—but in the way things "resemble" in dreams—the colonnade at St. Peter's; this complicated system of volutes and semicircular arches is but an exaggeration of the Baths of Caracalla or Diocletian; these bronze rings between the teeth of granite masks are there not so much to tether weak captives as to moor Caesar's galleys. The preoccupation with specifically Roman archaeological details ultimately imposes itself on us with grim insistence in the three plates added in 1761: these piled-up blocks at the brink of a yawning excavation, these reliefs populated by monstrous wild beasts, these busts glimpsed in a sepulchral half-light increasingly suggest that the architect's delirium has been supplemented by the residue of the antiquary's nightmares.

Similarly, the fantastic machines which so redoubtably embellish the *Prisons* are nothing other than old construction devices whose use has persisted to our own day, and which an engineer familiar with archaic equipment recognizes and identifies at first glance. The gibbet added to the second state of Plate IX is the corner brace supporting a pulley which has served from time immemorial to raise loads; the ladders evocative of hangings are actually mason's ladders which here and there, in the *Antiquities*, lean against the walls of Rome; the cylinder armed with long points is a winch; this trestle which Piranesi has cunningly bristled with nails is the kind carpenters use for sawing; this ominous pyramid of beams is a jack the artist himself has diagrammed in his *Method of raising large blocks of travertine and other marbles used in the construction of the tomb of Cecilia Metella*; those scaffolds are scaffoldings. The very real resemblance between a historical period's instruments of torture and its technical machinery has permitted Piranesi to suggest in the *Prisons* the executioner's omnipresence, and at the same time to maintain, at the foot of these already titanic walls, the sense of the incomplete and the temporary, exhausting symbols of the architect's forced labors. Piranesi determined early on to explain the presence of these dreadful machines by their use as implements of torture, since even in the *Dark Prison*, published in 1743 in the *Prima parte de Architettura*, and which the artist did not subsequently add to the *Prisons*, we find the following mention: *Carcere oscura con antenna pel suplizio de' malfattori*. As a matter of fact, nowhere in his works do we see a corpse hanging from these immense gibbets, like Félicien Rops's *Bell Ringer* dangling from his clapper. Even in the blackest second states of the *Prisons*, the rope of a pulley and the plumb line of a pendulum serve only to score with a curve and a magisterial stripe the abyss these walls enclose. The same is true of the gigantic wheels set up almost everywhere in the depths of the dungeons, and which we occasionally find in the *Antiquities of Rome*, reduced to the modest role of hydraulic wheels or capstans: no human being is crushed on their enormous rims.

In reality, and though commentators have deliberately emphasized the "extraordinary torments" to which so many prisoners would be subjected in the *Prisons*, we are on the contrary surprised by the relative infrequency and above all by the insignificance of these images of torture. At the margin of the enormous bull's-eye which paradoxically fills the upper part of Plate IX, tiny figures are whipping a minuscule prisoner lashed to a stake; an imp, detached from a St. Andrew's Cross, falls like an acrobat from a prodigious height; and these wavering silhouettes here play the same part as the little windswept bushes atop the walls in the *Antiquities*. In Plate XIII, two figures descending the steps are indubitably captives with bound hands; in one of the plates added in 1761 (II), deep in a gigantic trench like some gutted ruin of an

ancient monument, two pygmies drag by the feet a huge prisoner, himself exactly like a toppled statue; idlers scattered
around the brink of this latomia urge on the executioners,
unless of course their gesticulations are addressed to a stonecutter who is chiseling a block a little lower down. Here and
there, by dint of plumbing the remotest corners of the *Prisons*, the eye discerns other captives, other jailors. But these
tiny images take up scarcely more room than the battles or
death throes of insects. Only once (Plate X) has Piranesi
represented very distinctly a group of men being tortured; a
sculpturesque group of four or five titans attached to stakes,
limp or prostrate at the top of an immense voussoir. They
look something like a Christ or a Prometheus facing each
other in identical figures, as in some dream images. Colossal,
with no relation to the tiny humanity strolling along the canti-
levers or climbing the stairs, they move us no more than the
prisoner in the frontispiece—brother of Michelangelo's
Ignudi and also of the boys in Carracci's ceiling painting—
wearing his chain around his neck like a ribbon tied in a bow.

Like their kind in the *Antiquities*, the tiny inhabitants of
the *Prisons* surprise us by their alacrity, which is indeed
typical of the eighteenth century. Strollers, captives, or jailors, some of these pirouetting marionettes hold a wand which
may be a pike but which looks more like the bow of some
shrill stringed instrument or a tumbler's balancing pole, and
which here replaces the cattle prod the creator of the *Antiquities* likes to put in his rustics' hands. A suggestion of
torment floats in the air of the *Prisons*, but is almost as vague
as the suggestion of a sinister meeting with highwaymen in
the *Views* of deserted stretches of the Campagna. The true
horror of the *Prisons* is less in their few mysterious scenes of
torture than in the indifference of these human ants roaming

through enormous spaces, whose various groups seem almost never to communicate among themselves or even to take note of their respective presences, and still less to realize that in some dim corner a prisoner is being tortured. And perhaps the most singular feature of all this disturbing little multitude is everyone's immunity to vertigo. Sure-footed, at ease in these altitudes of delirium, such gnats do not seem to notice they are buzzing on the brink of the abyss.

But why has Piranesi given the *Imaginary Prisons* such characteristics, at once factitious and sublime, or, what comes down to the same question, why has he chosen to name these sumptuous architectural hallucinations *Prisons*? The influence of an illustration from a knightly romance produced nearly forty years earlier by a virtually unknown engraver, the hypothesis of a project for an opera decor of which not even the name has come down to us, are very inadequate explanations for the choice of this theme and this series of eighteen masterpieces.*

Certainly the *Prisons* may well be one of the first and most mysterious symptoms of that obsession with torture and incarceration which increasingly possesses men's minds during the last decades of the eighteenth century. One thinks of Sade and of the dungeons of the Florentine villa in which his Mirsky imprisons his victims—not, as we have seen, that Piranesi heralds the cruel manias of the author of *Justine* as much as we might think, but because Sade and the Piranesi of the *Prisons* both express that abuse which is somehow the inevitable conclusion of the Baroque will to power. One thinks of Beccaria's argument against the atrocities of the

* Eighteen, if we count, as well as the sixteen plates of the 1761 edition, the admirable Plate XIV of the first state, subsequently replaced by Plate XVI of the definitive edition, and the *Dark Prison* of the *Prima parte de Architettura*, which obviously belongs with the *Prisons* series.

prisons of the time, a plea soon to touch men's conscience and lay siege to the *Ancien Régime*'s bastilles. One thinks, above all, realizing the almost grotesque contrast between the poets' inner vision and history's anecdotal reality, that scarcely thirty years separate the fantastic *Prisons* from the very prosaic prisons of the Terror, and that the kindly Hubert Robert, Piranesi's friend and follower, would soon have occasion to paint, in the sordid bourgeois comfort of the Conciergerie, Camille Desmoulins waiting for his execution between a straw pallet and a chamber pot, an inkstand and a miniature of his Lucile. But despite the Promethean group of captives of Plate X, despite a gesture of pity or terror which the tiny characters sometimes seem to be making in the darkness, it is by no means certain that Piranesi himself was touched by the onset of horror and pre-Revolutionary revolt which his *Prisons*, in spite of everything, portend. In the last plate of the second state, the somber incomplete inscriptions: *Infamos . . . Ad terrorem increscen . . . Audacias . . . Impietati et malis artibus . . .* suggest that the author sides with public punishment, with Roman law and order, and make out the prisoners of the *Prisons* to be malefactors rather than martyrs.

If we cannot account for them as an anticipation of Sade or the excesses of the Revolution, perhaps we should seek the secret of the *Prisons* in a concept which especially preoccupied Italian imaginations and which has always been fruitful in masterpieces—that of the Last Judgment, of Hell, of the *Dies Irae*. Despite the total absence of any religious atmosphere in the *Prisons'* formulation, these black abysses and these lugubrious graffiti are nonetheless the sole and grandiose equivalent which Italian Baroque art has produced of Dante's terrible funnel and his *Lasciate ogni speranza . . .* In his *History of Art*, Elie Faure noted in passing that the creator of the *Prisons* remained in the great tradition of Michelangelo's *Last Judgment*, and this is true even of the single point of view of the steep perspectives and the disposition of space, and truer still of the viewpoint of interior perspectives. Michelangelo's work, impregnated by Dantesque concepts, seems to have served as an intermediary between Piranesi's entirely secular *Prisons* and the old sacred conceptions of an Immanent Justice. No God, it is true, assigns the Damned their places down the stages of the abyss in the *Prisons*, but His very omission makes the image of man's excessive ambitions and his perpetual failure only all the more tragic. These sites of hard labor from which Time and the forms of living nature are eliminated, these sealed chambers which so readily become torture chambers, but in which most of the inhabitants seem perilously and obtusely at their ease, these abysses which are bottomless and yet without means of escape, are no ordinary prison: they are our Inferno, our Hell.

"Denmark's a prison," Hamlet says. "Then is the world one," retorts dull Rosencrantz, for once foiling the black-clad prince. Are we to suppose Piranesi had a conception of the same sort, the distinct vision of a universe of prisoners? For ourselves, darkened by two more centuries of human strife, we recognize only too well this limited yet infinite world in which tiny and obsessive phantoms writhe; we recognize the minds of man. We cannot help thinking of our theories, our systems, our magnificent and futile mental constructions in whose corners some victim can always be found crouching. If these *Prisons*, for so long relatively neglected, now attract the attention of a modern public as they do, it is perhaps not only, as Aldous Huxley has said, because this masterpiece of architectural counterpoint prefigures certain conceptions of abstract art but above all because this world, factitious and yet grimly real, claustrophobic and yet megalomaniacal, cannot fail to remind us of the one in which modern humanity imprisons itself deeper every day, and whose mortal dangers we are beginning to recognize. Whatever the quasi-metaphysical implications of the *Prisons* (or, on the contrary, their total absence) might have meant for their author, there exists among the observations from Piranesi's own lips one sentence, uttered perhaps in jest, which indicates that he was not entirely ignorant of the demonic aspects of his own genius: "I have need of great ideas, and I believe that if I were commanded to design a new universe, I should have the folly to undertake such a thing." Once in his life, consciously or not, the artist kept that almost Archimedean pledge, which consists in drawing a series of diagrams of a world uniquely constructed by the power or the will of man: here is the result: the *Prisons*.

Like that of most artistic geniuses, Piranesi's glory has been intermittent and fragmentary, in that it has successively touched the various phases of his work. The *Views* and the *Antiquities of Rome* were immediately famous, especially outside Italy, where they initially met with less enthusiasm. One might say that they established forever a certain aspect of Rome at a certain moment of its history. They have done even more; since we possess, with regard to the periods preceding Piranesi's, no documentation equal in abundance and especially in beauty to his, and since furthermore we shall never know ancient Rome's physical aspect except through the cold and hypothetical reconstruction of archaeologists, the image Piranesi has left us of the Roman ruins of his day has gradually and retroactively extended in the human imagination; and it is almost mechanically of the ruins of Rome as Piranesi depicts them, and not of the monuments in their initial or older state, that we catch ourselves first thinking when we happen to name this or that Roman edifice.

Since the final years of the eighteenth century, there has probably nowhere been a student of architecture who has not been influenced by Piranesi's albums, and one can assert that from Copenhagen to Lisbon, from Petersburg to London, or even to the young state of Massachusetts, the buildings and urban perspectives drawn at this period and for the next fifty years would not have been what they are had their authors not leafed through the *Views of Rome*. Piranesi certainly counted for something in the obsession which ultimately swept Goethe to Italy, there to find a second youth, and Keats as well, who was to die there. Byron's Rome is Piranesian, Piranesian too Chateaubriand's and the more forgotten city of Madame de Staël, and the same is true of Stendhal's "city of tombs." At least until 1870 and the wave of building speculation which followed on the choice of Rome as the new kingdom's capital, the city's appearance remained Piranesian, and it is still in large measure the memory of this half-antique, half-Baroque Rome that irresistibly lures us today toward this increasingly transformed city.

While infecting the great public with a taste for ruins hitherto limited to a few artists and poets, Piranesi's influence has had the paradoxical result of modifying the ruins themselves. The longing to preserve and to restore, sometimes abusively, the ancient works of art greatly antedated the desire to preserve and restore the rubble from which they emerged. Until the development of this later poetry of archaeology, of which Piranesi's albums are one of the first signs, classical ruins, with few exceptions, had been regarded as mines from which to extract masterpieces subsequently added to papal or princely collections, or again, as Piranesi himself complained, as marble quarries exploited with a view to the erection of new monuments by popes eager to turn to Christianity's (and their own) glory what had been the pagan grandeur of Antiquity. These tragic and gutted ruins which Piranesi engraved, and the very circulation of his works, counts among the elements which have gradually changed the public's attitude, and finally that of the authorities themselves, and which have led us to the labeled, scrubbed, and replastered ruins of today, object of state solicitude and a national treasure of organized tourism.

The vogue of the *Views* and the *Antiquities* was substantially based not on an aesthetic or a technical merit few are competent to judge but on their subjects, which corresponded to the tastes of amateurs, acquainted since schooldays with the names and sites of Roman history which constituted a part of the baggage of learning. With subsequent generations, such learning tended to shrink to little or nothing. Further, archaeological interest, strictly speaking, shifted for the most part to the monuments of hitherto inaccessible Greece, now restored to her European patrimony, then to a newly explored Egypt and the Middle East. Rome ceased to be that sole queen of the ancient world she had hitherto been, down to the end of the eighteenth century. Finally, these plates, admirable from so many points of view, suffered from the inflation sustained by the art of engraving in the nineteenth century and vanished into the inglorious host of images of famous sites or monuments, whose wide-margined, rosewood- or mahogany-framed examples embellish the dining rooms of so many provincial homes. Gradually Piranesi's *Antiquities* and *Views* passed with all the rest into an obscure corner of the hall or even of the attic. We come upon them there today with that entirely new and freshly motivated admiration we often experience in the presence of works which have outlived fashion and then that oblivion which follows fashion.

Piranesi's decorative albums, those drawings which, past Louis XV, Louis XVI, and the Directoire, anticipated Empire style, immediately found a certain echo in England, where the author had in 1757 become a member of the London Society of Antiquaries; they certainly contributed almost everywhere in Europe to the shift from Baroque to Neo-Classical. But in a more general sense, for this almost frenzied obsession with the antique to be imposed on the imagination of decorators and cabinetmakers, we had to wait until events had once again made fashionable Consular Rome and that of the Caesars, as well as forty centuries of pharaonic Egypt. It is curious to note, in particular, that the first germ of this so-called Egyptianizing style, with its profusion of sphinxes, Osirises, and mummies, is to be found not, as one might think, in the drawings of statues from the Nile Valley of Jomard's *Description of Egypt*, begun under Napoleon and completed under Louis XVIII, but in the Piranesian album of the *Arte d'adornare i cammini* of 1769, itself inspired by the modest pseudo-Egyptian statues found in the Villa Adriana between 1740 and 1748, and today in the Vatican.

The fate of the *Imaginary Prisons* was different from that of the rest of Piranesi's legacy. They were, as we have seen, somewhat overlooked in their own time, except by a few connoisseurs. In 1763, however, the *Prisons* figured in the library of Louis XV, and the accession memorandum praises their fine effects of light. Almost unknown to the great public during the nineteenth century, these structures created by the wand of a somber sorcerer were nonetheless to enchant several poets: Théophile Gautier said he would have liked to see *Hamlet* performed in a setting based on the *Prisons*, whereby he was at once very far behind and very much in advance of his century's notions of theatrical decoration. But it was above all Victor Hugo who seems to have undergone Piranesi's influence most profoundly, and allusions to the great Italian engraver are quite frequent in his works. It is obviously through the *Antiquities* and the *Views* that this man, who saw Rome only once in the course of his life, and then with the eyes of a very young child, imagined the city of the Caesars; it is likely that the "Ode to the Arc de Triomphe," with its evocation of the ruins of cities of the past and of the rubble of Paris to come, would not be what it is had not the author frequently leafed through those great images of Roman decrepitude. Hugo the poet (and perhaps, too, Hugo the draftsman) was haunted by the *Imaginary Prisons*. These "horrifying Babels Piranesi dreamed of" probably served as a backdrop to some of Hugo's poems; in them he recognized his own penchant for the superhuman and the mysterious. Here one visionary encountered another.

However, it is in England most of all that the *Prisons'* influence seems to have worked most powerfully on the imaginations of certain poets and artists. Horace Walpole saw them as "chaotic and incoherent scenes where death sneers in the darkness," an appreciation in itself more melodramatic than exact, but these dark images seem to reappear in his novel *The Castle of Otranto*, published in 1764, *i.e.*, three years after the definitive edition of the *Prisons*, and set in an imaginary Italian dungeon. The fantastic William Beckford numbered among Piranesi's admirers, and the vast subterranean halls of his *Vathek*, published in 1786, perhaps show the trace of these smoky *Prisons*. Curiously, Walpole and Beckford, both masters of the gothic novel, were also both passionate builders, and their whimsical structures, rococo-

Gothic in one case, Gothico-Moresque in the other, though without in any way imitating Piranesi's Baroque grand manner, nonetheless betray the same obsession with a subjective architecture. But the finest British text concerning Piranesi comes from neither of these *rich amateurs*—it occurs, rather, in De Quincey's *Confessions of an English Opium-Eater*, or rather, in De Quincey's recollections of Coleridge. Let us reread the passage.

> Many years ago, when I was looking over Piranesi's *Antiquities of Rome*, Coleridge, then standing by, described to me a set of plates from that artist, called his 'Dreams', and which record the scenery of his own visions during the delirium of a fever. Some of these (I describe only from memory of Coleridge's account) represent vast Gothic halls; on the floor of which stood mighty engines and machinery, wheels, cables, catapults, etc., expressive of enormous power put forth, or resistance overcome. Creeping along the sides of the walls, you perceived a staircase; and upon this, gasping his way upwards, was Piranesi himself. Follow the stairs a little farther, and you perceive them reaching an abrupt termination, without any balustrade, and allowing no step onwards to him who should reach the extremity, except into the depths below. Whatever is to become of poor Piranesi, at least you suppose that his labors must now in some way terminate. But raise your eyes, and behold a second flight of stairs still higher, on which again Piranesi is perceived, by this time standing on the very brink of the abyss. Once again elevate your eye, and a still more aerial flight of stairs is described, and there, again, is the delirious Piranesi, busy on his aspiring labors: and so on, until the unfinished stairs and the hopeless Piranesi both are lost in the upper gloom of the hall. With the same power of endless growth and self-reproduction did my architecture proceed in dreams.

What immediately strikes us in this admirable passage is first of all De Quincey's entire fidelity to the spirit of Piranesi's work and then his extraordinary infidelity to the letter. First of all, the title is erroneous, for the *Prisons* have never been called "Dreams"; and it is interesting to see the two poets dropping, so to speak, from the title pages—the pediments of these prodigious palaces—their appellation of *Prisons*. Then appears the image of Gothic vestibules, unconsciously introduced by the two great romantics into this specifically Roman architectural world. But above all, one would seek in the eighteen plates constituting the total series of the *Prisons* in vain for that delirious staircase continuing its ascent, occasionally interrupted by missing steps, and where one and the same figure, evidently Piranesi himself, reappears a little higher up each time on new steps separated from the preceding ones by the abyss. This representation, so characteristic of a certain type of obsessional dream, was either transmitted by Coleridge to De Quincey, or else De Quincey himself, who had never seen the *Prisons* album with his own eyes, inserted it after the fact into the description Coleridge gave him. One or the other poet was pardonably misled by the very nature of this strange series. As a matter of fact, the *Prisons* seem to belong to that type of semihypnotic work in which one might say that the figures have moved, vanished, or reappeared between two winks of an eye, and that the sites themselves have mysteriously changed. The *Carceri d'Invenzioni di G. B. Piranesi* thereby provoked, in the author of *Christabel* or else in the author of *Suspiria de Profundis*, the image of a symbolic staircase and a symbolic Piranesi, truer than true, emblems of their own ascent or of their own vertigo. Thus the dreams of men engender one another.

The history of Piranesi's plates deserves separate mention. Brought to Paris by Francesco Piranesi during the Revolutionary period, they passed into the hands of the publisher Firmin Didot, who later resold them to the Academy of St. Luke in Rome, where they remain to this day. Piranesi calculated he could pull a total of three thousand examples from each copper plate, a figure much higher than that of most of the engravers of the time, whose plates sometimes deteriorated after one hundred proofs. This astonishing resistance of the plates, which permitted the abundant circulation of Piranesi's work, was due to the admirable simplicity of his engraving methods. He worked as much as possible by parallel lines, and appeared parsimonious of crosshatchings, which tend to form a little eroded islet on the plate where ink gathers unduly in the course of many inkings. Despite this technical perfection, Piranesi's originals ultimately eroded from use, and are no longer utilizable today. In his own lifetime, he often reengraved the crosshatchings, which tended to blur. This is what causes his latest impressions to be the blackest ones as well. It is important that we not forget this detail when we seek out psychological reasons for the darkening of the second states of the *Prisons*, although the necessity of such retouching must have been less evident in their case than for other more frequently reproduced works by the same artist. However this may be, it seems appropriate to conclude our study by these few technical details, which prove once again how much a modest concern for artisanal perfection contributed to the great virtuoso's disturbing masterpieces.

MOUNT DESERT ISLAND
1959–1961

Selma Lagerlöf,
Epic Storyteller

NOVELISTS OF GENIUS are rare; novelists of genius who are
women are, of course, even rarer. Great women poets, though
scarcely numerous, are still sufficiently so for us to assort them
into an entire bouquet, but a great novel presupposes a free
look at life which social custom has not hitherto permitted
women to take; it also supposes, in the best cases, an opulence
of creative power which women rarely seem to have had, or at
least to have been able to manifest, and which till now has
followed its free course only in physiological maternity. One
admirable exception: Murasaki Shikibu, surely one of the
world's greatest novelists, flourished in eleventh-century Japan.
Despite two or three intermediary names which might be cited
but which, on reflection, give way of their own accord,* the
other great women novelists are all to be found in the nineteenth or the twentieth century. The list, which each of us
will draw up according to individual preference, includes at
most a dozen names, and even some of these—say George
Sand's—figure on it more as a function of the woman's per-

---

* Marie de France is an exquisite storyteller, and Madame de La Fayette
transposes something of Racine's discretion and intensity to the order of
the short story. But neither of these women is a novelist, strictly speaking.

sonality than of the writer's genius. We realize with some surprise that Anglo-Saxon figures, and after these the Scandinavians, form the majority. Among these women of great talent or of genius, none, in my opinion, is to be placed higher than Selma Lagerlöf. She is in any case the only one who consistently mounts to the level of epic and of myth.

A commonplace life, to all appearances: a happy childhood on the old estate of Mårbacka, where she is born on November 20, 1858, into a family of landed gentry, civil servants, and pastors. A disease, which turned out to be a blessing in disguise, a congenital coxalgia appearing in her third year, made her a little girl absorbed by her books, attentive to the stories told by the old people around her. A melancholy adolescence and young womanhood: a first ball during which no one asks this lame girl to dance; a father more chimerical than practical who toward the end of his life takes to brandy as a medicine for all his ills; the certitude of soon losing the beloved estate which was her home. After great struggles, Selma gains permission to study for the state normal-school examinations, hoping to enter the ill-paid, but safe, profession of teaching—a project regarded with suspicion by relatives in a period when the liberal careers were still a novelty for women. Some featureless years spent as a teacher at Landskrona, near Malmö; Mårbacka sold at auction, as the Ingmarssons' farm and that of Marianne Sinclair's father were to be in her novels; after long efforts to find a tone and a style of her own, the publication, at the age of thirty-three, of *The Story of Gösta Berling*. An almost immediate celebrity soon followed by real fame, bringing with it the possibility of exclusive devotion to literary work; in 1909 the Nobel Prize, allowing Selma to buy back Mårbacka.

For the rest, a few long trips, courageously undertaken by

this semi-invalid; a long, fervent friendship with a young widow belonging to the Jewish bourgeoisie of Göteborg, a beautiful, sickly woman injured by life who also, and with some talent, writes books. "Traveling companion" is the cryptic expression used by Selma, who, when Sophie Elkan dies, some twenty years before herself, sadly confesses: "I was sure of her affection; she often hurt me, and I often hurt her." Beyond this, a tender loyalty to her family, to her mother above all and to the Aunt Lovisa so sympathetically evoked in *Mårbacka*. A guarded participation in the feminist movement of the day, when this movement was still new in Sweden (young Selma is a contemporary of her country's first woman doctor and of the first woman to hold a doctorate of letters). A landowner's financial worries, caused by the restoration of Mårbacka; her early participation in the pacifist movement even before 1914; generous gifts to her peasant community and to indigent writers; a generosity lavished without counting the cost during both wars, in the financial realm as well as in personal efforts, writing articles, giving lectures and readings for the displaced and the hungry, later for the relief of German or Russian populations suffering from effects of the blockade or inflation, and finally for Finland during the "winter war." In fact, it appears that the impossibility of affording personal aid to this beloved country delivered a telling blow to the aging and exhausted Selma, who died of a stroke at Mårbacka, on March 16, 1940.

A life is what one makes of it: these details, which I take from Elin Wagner's very rich biography of Selma Lagerlöf, tell us both everything and nothing at all. A few more will shed some light: we learn that this woman whose genius seems to have emerged straight from the folk tradition read a great deal and in several languages, and that she took very

much to heart her functions as a member of the Swedish
Academy and of the Nobel jury. Carlyle had influenced her
youth: it seems that by the effect of a singular osmosis *Gösta
Berling*'s tone and style owe much to the austere Scots
prophet. Later on she read Swedenborg and in him found a
confirmation of her own second sight, which put her in com-
munication with other worlds.* Yoga exercises helped her
improve her physical condition and doubtless to confirm as
well her surprising serenity in spite of the world events which
were later on to overwhelm her generation. It does not seem
she explored very widely in this field, but this method, even if
only earnestly approached, must enrich and permanently
transform its practitioners to some extent. Yet the use of this
Asian technique initially surprises us on the part of the great
storyteller of Värmland peasant life: one thinks of those tiny
mysterious figures seated in the classic contemplative position, legs and arms folded, which embellish certain Viking
bronzes—imperceptible points of contact between the far
North and an Orient closer than one might have supposed. A
woman sculptor of contemporary Sweden, Tyra Lundgren, in
a bas-relief dedicated to famous Swedish women, has put
Selma Lagerlöf in the center, under a bo tree, surrounded by
a brilliant group including St. Bridget and Queen Christina,
Frederika Brenner and Ellen Key. Selma's wisdom, her
humanity, her tranquil ease in both visible and invisible
worlds deserve this place of honor.

---

* Of the more or less convincing parapsychological experiences Selma
Lagerlöf records, I shall note, for its beauty, only this instance of thought
transference: late one night the novelist was finishing a novel at the bed-
side of her ill mother, who was too confused and exhausted for Selma to
tell her about the book she was working on; the story ended with an impassioned improvisation by the old gentleman-rider of Ekeby, the violinist
Lilien-crona. In the morning the old lady said she had heard in her sleep a
marvelous tune played on the violin.

Various kinds of fiction have been described as a *roman-fleuve*; but Selma Lagerlöf's epic current wells up from the very sources of myth. Its source is among the streams and waterfalls which impetuously feed the forges of Ekeby, in *The Story of Gösta Berling*, with their eddies of melted snow, their foaming superstitions, their dead leaves and debris of the past century mingled with the wild joy of youth. This first work is perhaps the great writer's most spontaneous, a vast hymn to life and at the same time a song of innocent rebellion. The stream then passes through sterner straits: in the first part of *Jerusalem* it reflects the somber green mountains, the storm-raked forests, the fields immemorially hallowed by human labor which Ingmar Ingmarsson and old Matts refuse to leave, even for the Holy Land. Its floodwaters bear the tree trunk which strikes down huge old Ingmar, struggling to save a little band of children swept away by the waters. In the second part of *Jerusalem* the river runs underground, beneath the aridity of the desert. In *The Wonderful Adventures of Nils* it floods all of Sweden, from Lapland to the Sund, reflecting the triangular flights of wild geese accompanied by the rascal Nils, who, by dint of traveling all over the land, participating in man's struggles and sufferings, sharing in the hunted existence of wild creatures, acquires the heart and wisdom he needs to help his old parents on their poor farm. Broadening to an estuary, mingling with the ocean's waters, it surrounds that huge archipelago of sometimes smiling, sometimes somber islands and islets which constitute the tales and novels of Selma Lagerlöf—*Invisible Links, From a Swedish Homestead, The Girl from the Marsh Croft*, many others. In a tale evoking the harsh Sweden of the sixteenth century, *Herr Arne's Hoard*, its icy waves embrace the island where the old priest's murderers are hiding. In *The Outcast* and in *Charlotte Löwensköld*, heavy, tormented, debatable works written later in her career, it is contaminated by the detritus of wickedness and mad selfishness; it sweeps in its eddies the corpses of the Battle of Jutland. Finally, its subsiding wavelets lap the landscapes in which an old lady tenderly reconsiders her childhood.

The characters, too, are of epic scope. Drinker, gambler, debauchee, the renegade minister Gösta burns like a flame, spreading around himself the joy and passion of life. Yet he is also the vagabond who trades for brandy the sacks of grain entrusted to him by a pauper child; the superstitious ungrateful rider of Ekeby who allows his protectress to be driven from her home because she is accused of witchcraft, though he later reinstates her and keeps vigil at her deathbed; the romantic desperado who dreams of dying in the peace of the Finnish forests, seducer of every beauty and lover of none till the day he weds an abandoned woman who needs his aid, and thereby makes a Faustian end as a useful man. At his side, the Dowager of Ekeby, pipe and oath in her mouth, sometimes decked out in satins and pearls, receiving her Christmas guests, sometimes helping her ore barges navigate the treacherous lake, is one of the most robust female figures the nineteenth-century novel has produced. We hardly know which to prefer among so many unforgettable scenes: the one where she confesses to the young renegade who wants to die that her own life has been as fierce and hard as any vagabond's, and that she would have as many reasons to take her own life as he, if she allowed herself to heed them; the scene where she gives a dinner for her mother, who has come to reproach her for her sins, and the two women insult each other while placidly continuing to eat, the petrified guests not daring to speak or touch the food; or the scene, finally, where, fallen in her turn, she walks to the estate of this virtually centenarian mother and finds her in the dairy, busily ordering the servants about; without a word, the old mistress hands her prodigal daughter the creaming ladle she has hitherto entrusted to no one, thereby restoring her to her rank in her home.

In the two volumes of her novel *Jerusalem*, the current's rhythm matches the slow gait of the peasants. Here the characters move with caution so as to disturb nothing in established custom or in the mysterious harmony between the spirits of nature and of man, until a crisis of fanaticism hurls some of them on the roads to Palestine. The book begins with the famous pages where Ingmar Ingmarsson, walking behind his plow, imagines he is consulting his father and his forebears gathered on some celestial farm: should he or should he not resolve to seek out, when she has been released from prison, his fiancée condemned to three years' detention for infanticide? Ingmar realizes that Brita would have been ashamed to celebrate her child's baptism before her own wedding, yet the old people are not unaware that the custom of anticipating the nuptial ceremony inveterately prevails in the countryside. "It is hard for a man to understand a bad woman," the imagined father muses. "No, Father, Brita was not bad, she was proud." "That comes to the same thing." How could he marry, as a matter of fact, when the old man's burial in the spring occasioned such heavy expenditures, when there is not enough money to paint and plaster the farm and also give a wedding banquet? But Ingmar, seeing a housepainter passing by on the road with his pails of paint and his brushes, believes he has received the advice his ancestors had promised him: in a long, slow trajectory, each stage of which is a station of the Cross for his pride, he will fetch his fiancée from prison, though she hesitates, fearing the scorn which will be poured on her in her own village. It is Sunday: Ingmar musters the courage to enter the church with her, for she is seized with a sudden desire to attend the service; the other women leave the bench near the door where she sits down. But soon scorn turns to respect; the peasants will recognize in this man capable of enduring his own hard ordeal the worthy successor of the old folk of Ingmarsgard.*

When we seek out the source from which Selma Lagerlöf's men and women draw their strength, we think first of the powerful reserves of Protestant austerity in which the author herself was brought up. Accurate in part, this answer is nonetheless too simple. These characters so close to the natural world seem chiefly motivated by a strict adherence to the order of things; their good resolutions grow like trees or well up like springs. We must also take into account a long human heritage which includes not only the warmhearted pre-Reformation folk piety (Swedish Lutheranism never completely broke with the rites and legends of medieval Christianity) but also the legacy of rich and obscure "pagan times." Beneath the Protestant rigidity, her characters' virtue, in the ancient meaning of the word, derives less from the observance of this or that precept or from faith in this or that dogma than from man's deepest powers, those of the race itself. It is not only metaphorically and in the course of a waking dream that Ingmar Ingmarsson is counseled by his ancestors. On one hand, we are so accustomed to despise the conventional morality, considered factitious by so many of us, and on the other to regard greatness of soul as no more

* Selma Lagerlöf told her biographer Hanna Astrup Larsen that she sometimes put herself in her books, but generally as her male characters. "Especially Ingmar Ingmarsson, that heavy, stubborn laborer." Does one not divine a faint smile here?

than a theatrical convention, that it is difficult, at first, to find such virtues as intimately contained in a human existence as the grain of its wood is present in the oak.

The Danish critic Georg Brandes, who "launched" Selma Lagerlöf, immediately noted in *Gösta Berling* the "cold purity" of the love scenes. Perhaps he was mistaken: this coldness scorches. His point of view at least suggests that the naturalism of the 1880s could be as mistaken as the paneroticism of our own times about what constitutes a work's passional and sensual depths. The characters of *Gösta Berling*, it is true, do not copulate, or at least do not do so before our eyes, and the adulterous passions of the old mistress of Ekeby manor occurred long before the first chapter. But, as in all high art, it is symbolically and not by physiological details that carnal love is expressed. Even more than the kisses Gösta gives to the little Countess Donna, fierce songs and the speed of the sledge, the cold and the night's flaring torches evoke the lover's orgasm. In the tale from *Invisible Links* in which a peasant ravishes a Troll girl sleeping in the forest, the orgy of butterflies plundering flowers prefigures the young man's emotions in the presence of the lovely naked girl: one is reminded of Baudelaire's "young giantess," but here there is a primeval innocence as well. Selma Lagerlöf inherits her art from the great epic tradition in which sexual relations are either implied or chastely described, whatever the raw realities might have been in the society of the time. Beautiful Helen is presented by Homer as the worthy spouse of Paris; the enormous conjugal delights of Zeus and Hera are signified by the blossoming of flowers on the ground which serves as their couch. In Selma Lagerlöf, marriage, with its joys and its torments, is situated at the very center of life, its sensuous rites remain secret, but under the full skirts and peasant bodices of Brita, of Barbro, or of Anna Svärd, under the well-padded toilettes of that provincial lady Charlotte Löwensköld, we do not doubt the presence of warm flesh.

Symbol again intervenes in the representation of Gabriel and Gertrude's young love in the two parts of *Jerusalem*: it becomes the pure water of the underground spring which Gertrude craves in the delirium of her fever and which Gabriel risks his life to find. On other occasions, the deferred joys of betrothal are allegorized by the building of the house that the bridegroom works at so joyously, and by the sheets and tablecloths woven by the bride. Shameful though it is, as in all traditional societies, adultery is ennobled by a certain aristocratic unconcern in the old mistress of the manor of Ekeby, by a poignant courage in the farmer's wife Ebba, at first driven to despair by the fear of scandal but finally determined to erect, for all to see, a wooden cross engraved with her own name over the grave of her child, to whom her husband has denied the right to sleep in the family plot.* Finally, in this rustic society a wronged girl does not fall quite so low as she would have done in the bourgeois world of the period. Brita, as we have seen, recovers her status despite her infanticide; the girl from the Marsh Croft who forgoes charges against her seducer, rather than causing him to perjure himself before the judge, regains her status in public opinion by this very feat and marries a prosperous peasant.

For us the pagan-Christian opposition is seen at a quasi-primal level, the term "pagan" being supposed to signify the largely imaginary sexual freedom of Antiquity, and the term "Christian," often evoking a religiosity of pure routine, narrowly allied to proprieties and social forms, but from which the great and specifically Christian virtues of charity, humil-

* "The Epitaph," in *Invisible Links*.

ity, poverty, and love of God are absent. In this Scandinavia still so close to its pagan era, the contrast is very differently seen. Pagan elements are perceived as cosmic, *elementary*, in the literal sense of the word, benign or terrible presences irreducible to the human order and surrounding us on all sides; contacts with them remain possible as long as our mind is capable of seeing the invisible within the visible. Thus the enchanting Maja Lisa encounters "The Neck," the fine white magic horse, immemorial genius of the waters, which regards her with the eyes of a human lover.* The "tomte" watches over the proper upkeep of the house and eliminates its bad masters; it is, as much as the old servants themselves, the conscience of the house.† Forest spirits warn the charcoal-burner Stark when his rick catches fire, but disappear forever when fanatics cut down the rosebushes in which the "little people" take shelter on his threshold.‡ The fisherman helped in his work by mermaids drowns himself when his priest, in order to exorcise him, makes him drink out of the communion chalice a few drops of the lake water which a magical ban forbids him to touch.§ In the powerful tale "Banished," one of two criminals reduced to living in the woods is a rich Christian peasant outlawed for having killed a monk, while the other, a pagan and the son of a pirate shipwrecker on an isolated island, has never known the relatively settled customs of village life. The peasant whom the half-wild youth reveres as a god gradually teaches him the precepts of the faith he still believes in, though he has broken its commandments. This moral progress paradoxically leads to betrayal: the youth betrays and murders the friend whose soul he believes he is

* *Mårbacka.*
† "The Tomte of Toreby," in *The World of the Trolls.*
‡ *Jerusalem.*
§ "The Water of the Lake Bay," in *The World of the Trolls.*

saving by forcing him to undergo punishment.* Christian faith and the heroic modes of primitive life destroy each other.

It appears, from certain parts of her early work, that the Selma Lagerlöf of these years saw Christianity as a religion too narrow and too demanding to embrace the whole of reality, and the Cross as the symbol of a salvation which did not necessarily save all mankind. Late in her life, she still said she did not believe in the Redemption; on the other hand, we find an invocation to Jesus in the margin of a book she was reading at the time. These states of her personal belief signify less than the profoundly Christian accent of certain great tales imbued with what we might call the existential fervor of medieval piety. The child who was outraged that an intolerant priest should cast the brightly daubed village saints into the pond reacts to this obtuse puritanism as intensely as to the pietists cutting down the fairies' rosebushes: she, for one, is willing to drink at every spring. The story of King Olaf Trygvasson, killed by a fierce Viking queen whose advances he has rejected, contains one of the purest Marian visions in literature: Olaf, in a premonitory dream, sees himself defeated during a naval battle, his bloody body lying on the sea's floor; the merciful Mother of God advances into the murky depths which form a cathedral's pillars and vaults around her, raises him up, presses him to her bosom, and slowly bears him out of the sea's blue into the blue of the sky.† Even more poignant is the story of King Olaf Haraldson, flouted by a monarch who has sent him for his bride not his legitimate daughter but a slave's bastard. Strongly tempted to kill her, Olaf nonetheless spares the accomplice of this impos-

---

* In *Invisible Links*.
† "Sigurd the Proud," in *Invisible Links*.

ture, feeling strong enough to raise this woman to his own level rather than being degraded by her. "Your face shines, King Olaf!" But we must make no mistake here: Olaf is motivated less by Christian humility than by an inner certainty which wells up from deep within his being. On a very high level, this difference vanishes altogether: nonetheless, it is true that Olaf Haraldson, like Ingmar Ingmarsson or Anna Svärd, derives most of his strength from his own inner depths.*

In certain tales whose simplicity, even whose good humor, might mislead us, we hear a discordant note, not of irony, as at the same period in the work of Anatole France, but of clear-sighted bitterness, tempering what we took for naïve Christian folklore. Upon St. Peter's supplications, Jesus sends an angel to seek the apostle's mother in the depths of hell and to bring her to heaven. Some of the damned have clung to the angel's wings and the hem of his garments, but the implacable old woman manages to make them let go. When the last of these wretches has fallen back into the abyss, the angel, as though exhausted, lets the woman fall back in her turn and wings his way up out of the infinite abyss. We bear our hell with us: God Himself has not the power to change us sufficiently to enter into heaven.†

In many of the tales, pagan and Christian currents run together. Old Agneta, in her cabin on the edge of a glacier, too far from the road to be able to offer a drink to passing travelers, suffers from her useless life. A monk counsels her to aid the dead souls prowling on the mountain, and henceforth, each night, she burns her faggots and candles in order to bestow a feast of light and warmth upon the damned en-

* "Astrid," in *Invisible Links*.
† "Our Lord and St. Peter," in *Invisible Links*.

during the torments of cold of the ancient Scandinavian hell; she will never again be useless and alone. Old Beda of the Shadows* offers food to the neighborhood crones to celebrate the sun which, that day, recovers from an eclipse indicated on the kitchen calendar. In her cold hamlet overhung by the mountain wall, the sun is her best friend: she honors it as an ancestor in the Edda might have done. But a mention of the Lord to whom one owes the sun leads us back from the action of pagan grace to St. Francis's Canticle of the Sun.

The climax of this instinctive syncretism occurs in the "Legend of the Christmas Rose,"† an exquisite tale one might be tempted to overlook, so many stupid Christmas stories in illustrated magazines having disgusted us with that form of literature. It is the tale of the Goinge Forest, inundated by a flood of light and warmth which melt the snow just before midnight, when all the valley bells begin to ring in the Nativity. The quasi-polar night triumphs anew, but a second, stronger flood makes the grass green again and the leaves sprout; a third brings the migratory birds, which make their nests, lay their eggs, and teach their young to fly, while the creatures of the earth give birth, feed their young, and fearlessly mingle with the lives of men . . . One more pulsation of light and the songs of angels will mingle with that of the birds—but this prodigy, in which even the outlaws hiding in the forest are entitled to participate, ceases when a suspicious monk who regards this phantasmagoria as the work of the Devil strikes down a dove which had perched on his shoulder. The splendor of Christmas will never again return to Goinge. Beyond the profoundly satisfying notion of a biblical Eden, we here approach the sacred world of India: time explodes;

* Ibid.
† In *The Girl from the Marsh Croft.*

plants, animals, and seasons flourish and pass in an instant which we might say was measured by the breath of the Eternal.

Animals, as we have seen, have their share in this reappearance of Eden. It is in the order of things: the Beasts ever fierce or cunning precede the Fall; it retains that primal innocence we human beings have sacrificed. In Selma Lagerlöf's work, it is often a crime committed against an animal which is responsible for the series of human maledictions. During the Christmas season, old Ingmar, surprised by a storm, has boldly taken refuge in a bear's den; he then breaks God's truce by hunting down the powerful creature, who strikes him dead, and the peasant's family buries without honor this man who has violated the terms of a pact.*

In the first part of *Jerusalem*, Barbro's ancestor has whipped to death a blind horse sold him by a dishonest horse trader: his male descendants are born blind and idiot, until the day Ingmar Ingmarsson redeems this sin by a heroic good deed. In other tales, animal innocence consoles us in our despair over the way of the world. The hermit Hatto,† arms raised motionless like an Indian fakir's, implores God to annihilate this world in which Evil rules. But his knotty arms resemble the branches of a tree, and the wagtails build a nest in the hollow of one of his palms. As though in spite of himself, the holy man takes an interest in the birds' intelligent labor and in their frail masterpiece of twigs and moss. When the nestlings have grown, he protects them against a sparrow hawk, though he knows that all life necessarily proceeds to death. Finally, he stops praying for total annihilation, unable to endure the thought that these innocents should be de-

---

* "God's Truce," in *The Sinner's Ring*.
† In the tale of that name, in *Invisible Links*.

stroyed. A nest has won out over the iniquity of mankind: "Men, of course, were not worthy of the birds, but perhaps God regarded the universe as Hatto regarded that nest."

In that *Bildungsroman* of 1906, *The Wonderful Adventures of Nils*, birds teach a boy prudence, tenacity, courage. He learns pity by restoring its young to a caged squirrel, and comes to comprehend something about resignation from the old dog that expects nothing but a bullet from its master, and from the old milk cow good for nothing but the knacker since the death of the farmwoman who used to whisper so many secrets over her milking as she leaned against the creature's side. The animals in La Fontaine's fables are human beings deliciously disguised as barnyard or forest creatures; here, sympathy and the feeling of a shared insecurity surmounts the wall between species. When the old lead-goose Akka of Kebnaikaise asks the boy if he doesn't think wild geese deserve to have some patches of land where they will be safe from the hunters, there are some of us on whom the lesson has not been lost.

Two masterpieces immersing the human child in primitive life—Lagerlöf's *Adventures of Nils* and Kipling's *Jungle Books*—were created at about the same time, the turn of that century which has most fiercely sacked and desecrated nature, and thereby man. Selma Lagerlöf acknowledged having been influenced by Kipling, but these two books, produced by such different temperaments, resemble each other as little as the Hindu jungle and the Lapp steppe. The adolescent Mowgli is a kind of young god who possesses "master words," and is aided by the animals to destroy the village against which he seeks revenge, restored to the human world (and for how long?) only by the amorous summons of the spring festival. Nils merely returns to his little farm—we recognize the humble utilitarian ethic which allows the Dalecarlians to survive in the "Jerusalem that kills." *The Jungle Book* and *The Wonderful Adventures of Nils* have suffered the same fate: to be considered as children's books, whereas their wisdom and their poetry are addressed to us all. Selma Lagerlöf, it is true, had consciously written for Swedish schoolchildren, but it is to us that she speaks, over their heads.

In this work so dominated by the notion of a divine or cosmic good, evil seems to be perceived as an accident or a human crime. Lagerlöf's darkest fantastic tales rarely provoke in us the quasi-visceral horror sought by so many lovers of the supernatural. The Devil in *Gösta Berling* is merely a man in costume, and his diabolism is rudimentary. Selma Lagerlöf always refused to say whether the hurricane which precipitates the peasants' conversion in the first part of *Jerusalem* was actually a spiritual tempest, the passage of the Evil One signified by the ancient Wild Hunt of Northern mythologies, or merely a big storm. But it suffices to compare the two parts of *Jerusalem* to that other murkier masterpiece, Maurice Barrès's *La Colline Inspirée*, to realize that the visionary Dalecarlians retain a kind of heroic integrity to the last; Barrès's dreamers, on the other hand, are mired in a more or less demonic zone where ghosts seethe and riot. This happens, surely, because Barrès, a Catholic by inheritance and by determination, recoils in a terror not untouched by desire before whatever represents for him the temptations of carnal disorder; whereas the Dalecarlians, despised or persecuted as they are, remain in the great tradition of Protestant dissidence.*

* Several tales, and *The Miracles of Antichrist*, testify to Selma Lagerlöf's sympathy for the Italian Catholicism of her day; she betrays a shade of amused condescension and makes a number of small mistakes. Perhaps more interesting is her respectful treatment of Islam. It is a pious vagabond,

Evil nonetheless lurks in these books of goodness, in its habitual forms of violence, debauchery, or hypocrisy: these are not merely blackberry-syrup idylls. As early as *The Miracles of Antichrist*, we encounter the story of a feast given by an old Englishwoman to some Sicilian villagers in the ruins of their ancient theater: after singing a few politely applauded ballads of her own country, the foolhardy woman risks an aria from *Norma*; jeers and laughter result, and the delighted crowd compels the wretched woman to repeat her aria over and over again, a grotesque victim flung to wild beasts. The murder of an entire family, in *Herr Arne's Hoard*, is as violent as the reportage by Truman Capote. In *The Outcast*, the scene in which human riffraff, half-sailors, half-malefactors, compel a wretch even viler than themselves to devour a serpent's flesh is virtually unbearable. The Selma Lagerlöf of *Gösta Berling* sympathetically describes the punch flames illuminating the faces of the "riders of Ekeby"; the drunkard mistreated by life in "the Fallen King" from *Invisible Links* is still a kind of sublime wreck, a Rembrandt in a Salvation Army setting. But in "The Balloon"* the alcoholic is nothing but a sick man, odious as only the weak can be; the story would read as a temperance tract except for the subtle relations between the father and his sons, gentle dreamers who, if they were not lucky enough to die young, would probably end like him. The same refined art in simple forms is orchestrated, at the beginning of *The Ring of the Löwenskölds*, in

---

descendant of the Prophet, who comes to the aid of the persecuted Dalecarlians in *Jerusalem*. Gertrude, stricken with mental illness, imagines she sees Christ in the solemn gaze of a dervish in a mosque doorway; later she learns that this man is a shouting dervish and attends, horrified, the vocal rites of his sect; but having completely recovered her wits, she goes to kiss his hand before leaving Jerusalem: "It was not Jesus, but all the same he was a holy man."

* In *The Girl from the Marsh Croft*.

the conversation of a peasant couple egging each other on to commit a sacrilegious theft without ever uttering the slightest compromising word.

Hypocrisy, vice of self-righteous societies, is everywhere courageously assigned to the lowest circle of all. *Charlotte Löwensköld,* published in 1925, is dominated by the disagreeable personality of Pastor Karl Arthur Ekenstedt, a monster of self-deception who sows misery around him without once ceasing to claim that he is approved and guided by God. With the poisonous Thea, the organist's wife, a wheedling female who has managed to take him for her own, he forms the only repugnant couple in the Swedish novelist's writing; their loathsome figures wandering from fair to fair seem to have emerged from some canvas by Bosch. We are amazed that Selma Lagerlöf should have granted to the two daughters of her old age, the aristocratic Charlotte and the rustic Anna Svärd, such treasures of indulgence in behalf of this crapulous clergyman. Are we to suppose in one of the two women a vestige of tenderness for the man she once loved, and in the other a certain respect for this husband socially so far above herself? Or are we rather in those zones of sensuous penumbra where Selma Lagerlöf sheds no light? One thinks of the charming little Elsalill of *Herr Arne's Hoard,* first loving without recognizing, then loving quite knowingly the murderer who has exterminated her entire family and who, had he been able to, would not have spared her either. "I have loved a wolf," she tells herself. But she continues to love him.

Despite certain touches of almost inevitable moralism, given the time and the place, Selma Lagerlöf does not judge her characters; their actions suffice. The great novelist rarely judges; he is too sensitive to the diversity and specificity of human beings not to see in them the threads of a tapestry whose entirety we do not grasp. Like the French peasant, these Swedish ones obscurely believe it takes a little of everything to make a world. In the tale entitled "A Story of Halland,"* one of those where Selma Lagerlöf makes us most clearly aware of the inexplicable attraction of one person for another, the young farmer who has abandoned his wretched lands to follow the vagrant Jan, his mother's servant and husband, is not indignant at having been ruined by him or at having been involved in a shady deal which sends him to prison: "He was of another race and had to act according to the laws of his kind." It is not only between the two men but between two modes of life that the author does not choose: that of the sedentary peasant who has never known anything but his heavy habitual burdens, and that of the dissipating vagabond, sometimes faithless and treacherous, but sometimes sweeping others with him into a dance of ecstatic joy.

I have written enough to show that Selma Lagerlöf, where she excels, is the equal of the greatest writers. She does not always excel. Even in her best years, certain works give the impression of troughs between the crests. *The House of Liliencrona* or *From a Swedish Homestead*, among others, though they have the charm of old tales or ballads, would be pale narratives indeed if they were not illuminated by reflections cast upon them by their author's great works. The *Miracles of Antichrist*, published soon after *Gösta Berling*, was received with a mixture of praise and objections; the latter are mainly what prevail today. Lagerlöf's Italian folklore, too hastily absorbed, remains superficially picturesque, and the obviously prefabricated story of a baby Jesus replaced on the altar

* In *The World of the Trolls*.

by a counterfeit who is the Antichrist, *i.e.*, socialism (forty years later, one would have said Communism), is almost irritating in its simplicity. The author has the merit of having seen beneath the tourist's Sicily to an underlying peasant poverty, and it was something to have dared to say in 1894 that the exclusive cult of progress is an atheist form of idolatry, but perhaps it should not have been said in this fashion. A short novel, *Death's Carter*, written in 1912 at the request of a society for the prevention of tuberculosis, deals with problems of the after-life, but despite the experiences to which the author had been exposed, it teaches us little about these marginal regions which has not already been said better elsewhere.* The *Emperor of Portugallia*, which dates from 1914, was received admiringly, but it now seems all too easily framed, this tale of a gentle megalomaniac who imagines he is raising his daughter, actually a prostitute in Lund, to the rank of empress.

"My soul has become poor and dark; it has reverted to the wild state," Selma Lagerlöf noted in 1915. Two or three years later, in a poem which remained unpublished during her lifetime, she sits down at her desk, exhausted by her writer's task, which seems to consist in a "desperate gathering up of twigs, straws, and useless bits of bark," then suddenly feels her soul, "that deserter," return to her—and here soul seems to signify genius: "I soared alone above the battlefields," the soul sadly reports. "I advanced with the tormented men in the trenches, I accompanied the refugees on their roads into misery and exile; I was wrecked with the torpedoed ships and lurked in the murderous submarines, waiting for my prey . . .

* Moreover, Selma Lagerlöf kept her distance from spiritualism. After Sophie Elkan's death, a medium who claimed to be bearing a message from her was shown the door.

I have suffered the fate of starving peoples; I have kept vigil in cities on which unexpected bombs rained down . . . I have lived with dethroned princes and among the persecuted who have seized power." Such experiences of identification with the world's pain and suffering should have inspired Selma Lagerlöf to further great achievements as she grew to be an old woman. But exhaustion had come, and the doubt that literature could still serve any real purpose; there was not enough time to let these new experiences ripen as they must in order to be expressed. *The Outcast*, which ends in wartime landscapes, had not been, she knew, a successful work. The twenty years which remained to her were to see the slow gestation of *The Ring of the Löwenskölds*, in which several poignant scenes alternate with delicate portrayals of provincial life of the last century, but in which lengthy digressions and repetitions also abound, and occasionally the melodramatic sequences of a gothic novel. The author, evidently, no longer dominates her work. She struggles to invent an epilogue in which Karl Arthur Ekenstedt dies in the odor of sanctity: this she failed to achieve.* Every authentic novelist knows that one does not do as one likes with one's characters.

"I remain perplexed as to the meaning of life," Selma had imprudently confessed to a journalist in 1926. This sage admission provoked the indignation of her public; philosophic doubt was not what her readers expected of their idol. As invariably happens when a writer achieves great fame, her enthusiasts had created a summary notion of her, partly drawn from her great books admired on trust or read only in the hope of finding in them exciting stories, partly from the

---

* Yet it is regrettable that in the last pages of the published version, the character is described as regenerated after two or three years spent in Africa converting the natives. Selma Lagerlöf must have known that hypocrisy is not to be got rid of so cheaply.

inevitable publicity organized around her person and her writings. Two years earlier, *Mårbacka*, more accessible than the early masterpieces, had offered her readers a sentimental and playful image of the writer's family past, from which filial piety eliminated all pettiness and conflict. The child Selma was painted with charm but according to conventions adults use in speaking of childhood. There is no harm in an old lady's tenderly evoking her early years, and it would indeed be a hardhearted reader who could resist *Mårbacka*'s half-smiling, half-tearful grace. But the great epic storyteller was dead.

Everything is a danger for the writer who grows old (young writers run no fewer risks, but different ones). Obscurity and solitude are dangerous; so is popularity. It is dangerous to sink irretrievably into one's private world; just as dangerous to scatter oneself in works and tasks of another order. Covered with honors, Selma Lagerlöf was perhaps not so free as the obscure schoolteacher at Landskrona. Her celebrity took the form of official receptions, of speeches to make or to listen to, of squads of Boy Scouts camping on the grounds of Mårbacka, of cantatas performed on her birthday by visiting schoolgirls, of visits from journalists and curiosity seekers of all kinds, flies drawn to the honey of fame. A septuagenarian, she had expressed her intention of "entering into the silent country of old age." She never even reached its borders. Her readers kept her away from it, as did her need of money, less for itself than for the enterprises and causes to which she had dedicated herself, and also, no doubt, the humble desire of any good writer to go on writing. But she doubted herself. "I wanted to believe as long as I could that all this"—her recent works—"had some value. But it doesn't; I know that now," she confessed in 1937. Sometimes she was mistaken. *Written on the Earth,* composed in 1933 and for which she gave her royalties to persecuted German intellectuals, contains an almost visionary description of the court of lapidations in the Temple of Jerusalem quite worthy of the old Selma, that is, the young one. Despite the overemphatic morality of its conclusion, her Jesus converting the woman taken in adultery ranks alongside another Christ, one imbued with an unexpected sensuality, *The Man Who Died,* by D. H. Lawrence, over twenty years younger than Selma Lagerlöf and dead ten years before her. Poets of successive generations contradict each other—and say the same thing.

From time to time, however, Mårbacka opened its gates to other visitors besides schoolboys seeking autographs or delegations of postal employees. In 1938, a young woman stirred —as she herself avows—as if by a love, paid her homage to this old lady of seventy-eight: Greta Garbo. Forty-six years earlier, Sophie Elkan, *née* Sophie Salomon, had introduced herself in the same way, but she wore, according to the fashions of the time, a thick veil which Selma crossed the room to raise with her own hands in order to admire her visitor's beauty. Since then, all of life had passed.

But little did it matter. The great works, already a little blurred by distance, were still there, like landscapes in the background of a painting: the forests and falls of the riders at Ekeby, the severe mountains and green hills of the first part of *Jerusalem,* the moorlands Nils saw from the clouds, and above all the admirable tales, pure as the unpolluted lakes. In one of these, old Colonel Berenkreuz, retired to a farm, spends the time he has left weaving a gigantic tapestry with yarns that are sometimes bright, sometimes dark—a tapestry into whose design he has secretly put everything he knows of life. One bright midsummer eve, he hears someone he cannot see passing through the web though not disturbing it, then approaching his bed, clicking his heels and presenting arms: "Death reporting for duty, Colonel." Death could come now and interrupt at her task the weaver of Mårbacka.

MOUNT DESERT ISLAND

1975

A Critical Introduction
to Cavafy

CONSTANTINE CAVAFY is one of the most famous poets of modern Greece; he is also one of the greatest, certainly the subtlest, perhaps the most modern, though sustained more than any other by the inexhaustible substance of the past. The poet was born, of Greek parents from Constantinople, in 1863 in Alexandria, where he worked for thirty years in the Ministry of Irrigation and where he died in 1933. Cavafy soon discovered his vocation, but preserved only a small number of all the poems written before he was fifty.* Few of them figure among his masterpieces; even these early compositions, moreover, show signs of subsequent retouching. During his lifetime Cavafy permitted only a few poems to be published in periodicals; his fame, which was to be gradual, depended on printed sheets handed out parsimoniously to friends or disciples; thus a body of work which at first glance seems astonishingly detached, almost impersonal, remained

---

* It is unfortunate that a considerable quantity of these early poems, which are little more, for the most part, than student's exercises, have lately reappeared and been published against what had been their author's wishes. Half a dozen, at least, deserve to be known; the rest add nothing to Cavafy's glory, and very little to the psychological image of him we already have.

"secret" to the end, subject to constant revision, profiting from the poet's experience until his death. And only in his last years did Cavafy express more or less openly his most personal obsessions, emotions, and memories, which had inspired and sustained his work all his life, but more vaguely, in a more veiled fashion.

A few lines account for Cavafy's external biography; his poems tell us more about this existence apparently limited to the routine of office and café, library and low tavern, confined in space to a monotonous itinerary through one city, yet extraordinarily free in time. We might attempt more—to decipher what the poet's art consists precisely in encoding, to extract from this or that poem a plausible if not a verifiable personal memory. For example, "Apollonius of Tyana in Rhodes" echoes, we are told, Cavafy's distaste for the copious and often declamatory works of his contemporary Palamas; again, two or three profiles of noble Byzantine or Spartan mothers ("In Sparta," "Come, O King of the Lacedaemonians," "Anna Dalassané"), the only feminine figures in the corpus of poems decidedly alien to woman,* appear to be inspired by the memory of his own mother, widowed when Constantine was seven, and left to raise him and his six older brothers. Clearly autobiographical, "Dangers" records that brief moment when the young man wavered, like so many

---

* To complete the list: Demeter and Metaneira ("Interruption"), Thetis ("Infidelity"), an old servant woman ("Kleitos' Illness"), the sailor's mother ("Prayer"), and Aristoboulos ("Aristoboulos") are also personifications of maternity. We may note three or four allusions to the political role of Byzantine women: Irene Doukaina ("A Byzantine Nobleman in Exile"), "Anna Komnina," Irene Assan ("Of Colored Glass"), Anne of Savoy ("John Kantakuzinos Triumphs"); a few names of Jewish princesses ("Aristoboulos," "Alexander Jannaios"), a reference to Cleopatra as Caesarion's mother ("Alexandrian Kings"). Never has a female cast been more reduced. Erotic concerns aside, Cavafy's poems resemble those Near Eastern cafés frequented only by men.

others, between pleasure and asceticism. "Satrapy" translates the bitterness of a man who to succeed in the material world must renounce high literary ambitions: Cavafy the functionary must have suffered such misgivings. "Sculptor of Tyana" and "For the Shop" are suggestive, with their allusions to works of art apart from what is shown and offered to the public, objects created exclusively for the artist. With the help not only of the few erotic poems in which Cavafy speaks in his own name ("Gray," "Far Away," "Afternoon Sun," "On the Deck of the Ship," "The Next Table"), but also of the many more numerous ones in which the lover is designated by an impersonal "he," we might establish the habitual catalogue of pursuits and encounters, of pleasures and partings. Finally, his almost obsessive insistence on specifying ages ("Two Young Men 23 to 24 Years Old," "Portrait of a 23-Year-Old Youth," "For Ammonis, Dead at 29," "Cimon, Son of Learchos, a 22-year-old student"), along with a few descriptions of faces and bodies, would suffice to delimit what for Cavafy were the beloved's ideal age and type. But to use the poems in the hunt for biographical details contradicts the poetic goal itself: the most clear-sighted poet often hesitates to retrace the route which has led him from the more or less chaotic emotion, the more or less insignificant incident, to the serene precision and enduring beauty of the poem. A commentator is therefore all the more likely to go astray. Cavafy said many times that his work originated in his life; henceforth his life abides entirely in his work.

Accounts by the poet's disciples and admirers afford at most a characteristic or colorful touch; however, the most enthusiastic see little and describe badly, not from a failure of attention or of eloquence, but for reasons which relate, perhaps, to the very secret of life and of poetry. I have ques-

tioned Greek friends who saw something of the sick and
dying poet, already famous at the time of his last stay in
Athens, around 1930; he lived, they told me, in a seedy hotel
on Omonia Square, a new and noisy business neighborhood;
this supposedly solitary man seemed to be surrounded by devoted friends whose praise he welcomed politely, merely smiling when it seemed excessive; he corrected the manuscripts of
young admirers with gentle severity. His anglomania surprised them; they found he spoke Greek with a faint Oxford
accent.* As often happens, these young people were disap-
pointed that the great man's literary tastes were less advanced
than their own; the singularity, novelty, and boldness of this
poetry they so admired seemed to be nourished, by an incomprehensible osmosis, on works they regarded as superannuated. Cavafy enjoyed Anatole France and had no use
for Gide; he prized Browning above T. S. Eliot; he scandalized them by quoting Musset. I inquired as to his physical
appearance and was assured he looked quite ordinary—like a
Levantine broker. A photograph of him at about forty shows
a face with heavy-lidded eyes, a sensual judicious mouth; the
reserved, pensive, almost melancholy expression may have
more to do with milieu and race than with the man. But let us
turn to E. M. Forster, who knew Cavafy in Alexandria a few
years before this photograph was taken:

> Modern Alexandria is scarcely a city of the soul. Founded
> upon cotton with the concurrence of onions and eggs, ill
> built, ill planned, ill drained—many hard things can be said
> against it, and most are said by its inhabitants. Yet to some of

* This same anglomania dictated, I am told, the poet's use of the double
initial C.P. instead of his given name, Constantine, as is customary in
Greek. The surname itself, traditionally written Kavafis, can be transcribed
in various ways, but the poet's heirs have chosen Cavafy, eliminating the
final *s*, which is no longer pronounced in modern Greek.

them, as they traverse the streets, a delightful experience can occur. They hear their own name proclaimed in firm yet meditative accents—accents that seem not so much to expect an answer as to pay homage to the fact of individuality. They turn and see a Greek gentleman in a straw hat, standing absolutely motionless at a slight angle to the universe . . . He may be prevailed upon to begin a sentence—an immense complicated shapely sentence, full of parentheses that never get mixed and of reservations that really do reserve; a sentence that moves with logic to its foreseen end, yet to an end that is always more vivid and thrilling than one foresaw. Sometimes the sentence is finished in the street, sometimes the traffic murders it, sometimes it lasts into the flat. It deals with the tricky behavior of the Emperor Alexius Comnenus in 1096, or with olives, their possibilities and price, or with the fortunes of friends, or George Eliot, or with the dialects of the interior of Asia Minor. It is delivered with equal ease in Greek, English, or French. And despite its intellectual richness and human outlook, despite the matured charity of its judgments, one feels that it too stands at a slight angle to the universe: it is the sentence of a poet . . .

We might contrast Forster's irreverent sketch with a few sober lines by Ungaretti which evoke, in a milk-bar in the Ramleh district of Alexandria, at the table of the young editors of the review *Grammata* (one of the first to present his work to the public), a sententious, measured, but affable Cavafy, occasionally uttering a remark not to be forgotten. To which may also be added the account I once heard from a young woman who, as a child, had known the poet in Alexandria, at the end of his life. The little girl would hide in order to spy on this mild, courteous old gentleman who occasionally visited her parents and who inspired her with a passionate curiosity, along with a certain terror, because of his way "of looking like no one else," his pallor, his bandage-swathed neck (Cavafy was to die of throat cancer a few months later), his dark clothes, and his habit, when he thought he was alone, of pensively murmuring something. An indistinct murmur, the young woman told me, for the sick man was already almost voiceless, but one which suggested all the more the incantation of a sorcerer . . . We may allow such fragmentary testimonies to complete each other and turn instead to the poems themselves, a distinct murmur, insistent, unforgettable.

What strikes us first is the almost complete absence of any Oriental or even Levantine "picturesque." That this Alexandrian Greek should have given no room to the Arab or Moslem world can surprise no one even slightly familiar with the Near East, its juxtaposition of races and their separation rather than their mixtures.* Cavafy's Orientalism, that Orientalism perpetually in suspension in all Greek thought, is located elsewhere. The fact that nature, that landscape explicitly, is passed over in silence relates chiefly to his personal sensibility. The one poem which specifically considers natural objects yields the secret of this soul voluptuously immured in the human.

> *I'll stand here and look at nature a while.*
> *The brilliant blues of the morning sea, the cloudless sky,*
> *and the yellow shore: all lovely,*
> *all bathed in light.*
>
> *I'll stand here and make myself believe I really see it*
> *(I did, for a moment, when I first stopped)*

---

* The abstract yet ardent tone of certain erotic poems irresistibly recalls some Arabic, or rather Persian, poetry, but Cavafy would surely have rejected any such comparison.

and not just my illusions, my memories,
my fantasms of sensuality.

We may not call this indifference to landscape Greek or Oriental without having to limit, define, explain. Greek poetry abounds in natural images; even the later epigrammatists who lived for the most part in that "resolutely modern" world of ancient Antioch or Alexandria constantly invoke the shade of a plane tree, the waters of a spring. And the Oriental poets ecstatically apostrophize fountains and gardens. In this realm, Cavafy's dryness is a distinctive feature; quite his own are those perspectives deliberately limited to the streets and suburbs of the great city, and almost always to the decor, to the stage set of love.

> *The room was squalid and mean,*
> *hidden above the dubious tavern.*
> *From the window you could look down*
> *into the dirty narrow alley. From below*
> *came the voices of some workmen*
> *playing cards and having a good time.*
>
> *And there, on the filthy sheets of that bed,*
> *I possessed the body of love, possessed the lips,*
> *the swollen dark lips of intoxication—*
> *so swollen with such intoxication that even now*
> *as I write, after so many years,*
> *in my lonely house, I am drunk again.*

Workmen's cafés, avenues darkening at nightfall, dubious establishments frequented by young and suspect figures, are presented only in terms of the human adventure, of encounter and parting, and it is these terms which lend such an accurate beauty to the slightest sketches, street scenes, or interiors. The poet could be speaking of Piraeus, of Marseilles, of Algiers, of Barcelona—of any great Mediterranean city just as well as of Alexandria. Except for the color of the sky, we are not so far from Utrillo's Paris; certain bedrooms suggests those of Van Gogh, with their rattan chairs, their yellow pots, their bare, sun-drenched walls. But a wholly Greek light touches everything here: vitality of air, clarity of atmosphere, the sun on human skin, and that incorruptible salt which also saves from total dissolution the characters of the *Satyricon*, that Greek masterpiece in Latin. And indeed the Alexandrian underworld often suggests Petronius; the casual realism of a poem like "Two Young Men 23 to 24 Years Old" irresistibly evokes the fortunes of Ascyltus and Encolpius.

> *His friend brings unexpected news:*
> *he has won sixty pounds playing cards . . .*
>
> *And filled with excitement and longing*
> *they go off—not to their respectable families*
> *(where they are no longer wanted anyway)*
> *but to a very special house, one they know well,*
> *they ask for a room and they order*
> *expensive drinks, they drink again . . .*

Perhaps not everyone will appreciate these singular realistic sketches in Cavafy's final manner, almost banal in their exactitude. Yet nothing deserves our interest more than these dry, delicate poems ("The Tobacco-Shop Window," "He Asked about the Quality," "In the Dull Village," "Lovely White Flowers That Became Him": I deliberately select those most likely to try the reader's indulgence), where not only the erotic or sometimes picaresque element but even the stalest situations and settings, the occasions dearest to sentimental ballads, scoured here by a kind of pure prosaicism, regain their true resonance, their values, and, so to speak, their uprightness.

> *But now there is no need of suits of clothes*
> *or silk handkerchiefs or twenty pounds*
> *or twenty piasters, for that matter.*
>
> *On Sunday they buried him, at ten in the morning.*
> *On Sunday they buried him, almost a week ago.*
>
> *On the cheap coffin he put flowers,*
> *lovely white flowers that became him,*
> *that became his beauty and his 22 years.*
>
> *In the evening when a job came his way—*
> *he had to live on something—and he went to the café*
> *where they used to go together, it was a knife in his heart,*
> *that dreary café where they used to go together.*

But I was speaking of the setting, the decor of these poems: by a transition inevitable in Cavafy, any mention of the decor leads us back to the passions of the characters.

"Most poets are exclusively poets. Not Palamas, he writes stories too. I am a poet-historian. I cannot write novels or plays, but inner voices tell me that the historian's calling is within my reach. But there is no time left . . ."* Perhaps there was never time: Cavafy does not care for broad perspectives, the great movements of history; he makes no attempt to grasp a human being in his deepest experience, his changes, his duration. He does not paint Caesar; he does not

---

* Quoted by Theodore Griva in his preface to a translation of Cavafy's poems, Lausanne, 1944.

revive that mass of matter and passions which was Mark Antony; he shows a moment in Caesar's life, he meditates on a turning point in Mark Antony's fate. His historical method is related to Montaigne's: he extracts certain examples, certain counsels, sometimes very specific erotic stimulants from Herodotus, from Plutarch, from Polybius, from the obscure chronicles of the late Empire or of Byzantium.* He is an essayist, often a moralist, supremely a humanist. Intentionally or not, he confines himself to the swift glimpse, to the naked, sharply etched feature. Yet this narrowly limited field of vision is almost always of the strictest accuracy.† This realist never burdens himself with theories, ancient or modern, thereby discarding that stew of generalizations, clumsy contrasts, and clotted scholarly commonplaces which give so many minds indigestion at the feast of history. This precisionist breaks, for example, with a long romantic tradition when he shows us Julian the Apostate as a young fanatic marked despite himself by Christian influence, unwittingly distorting the Hellenism he claims to defend, a butt for the mockery of the pagans of Antioch.

> *"I find you very indifferent toward the gods,"*
> *he says solemnly. Indifferent! What did he expect?*

* A man of letters rather than a professional scholar, Cavafy did not necessarily read so widely in every instance. Most of the poems in his *Ptolemys–Seleucids–Greek Defeats* cycle were apparently inspired by E. R. Bevan's splendid book *The House of Seleucus* (London, 1902), where Cavafy could also have found the detail he borrows from Malalas ("Greek since Ancient Times") and the photograph of the young king's profile "that seems to smile" ("Orophernes"). The poems of the Byzantine cycle, on the other hand, appear to be documented from the chronicles rather than, as has been said, by a reading of Gibbon.

† Yet we must distinguish, in Cavafy, between the superb poems of an authentic Hellenism and those in which he yields to a period taste for a knickknack Greece. I wanted to indicate at once this mixture of the exquisite and the mediocre so that ultimately I could indicate only the exquisite.

He could reform the priesthood to his heart's content,
write every day to the high priest of Galatia
or to other pontiffs of the kind, exhorting . . .
His friends were not Christians, granted . . .
But they couldn't get involved, as he did
(brought up a Christian as he was) in that whole
system of religious reorganization,
as ridiculous in theory as in practice.
After all, they were Greeks . . . Nothing in excess,
   Augustus.

We may indicate further points of detail, such as noting that the Homeric period has inspired only some fine early poems, the somber "Infidelity" or the subtle "Ithaca."* Fifth-century Greece, the traditional Hellas of Attica and the Peloponnesus and the islands, is virtually absent from this Alexandrian poetry, or approached obliquely by an interpretation dating from six or eight centuries later ("Demaratos," "Young Men of Sidon"). It is the exile and death of King Cleomenes in Alexandria which appear to have drawn Cavafy's attention to the drama of Sparta's decline ("In Sparta," "Come, O King of the Lacedaemonians"); Athens is mentioned only once, apropos of one of the great sophists of the imperial epoch ("Herodes Atticus"); the Roman world is seen from Greek perspectives. The poet prefers to deal with a period of Antiquity known chiefly to specialists, the two or three centuries of cosmopolitan life which followed the death of Alexander in the Greek Orient. Cavafy's humanism is not ours: from Rome, from the Renaissance, from the academi-

* "Infidelity," inspired by a fragment, quoted in Plato, from Aeschylus' *Tragic Iliad*, and the three or four poems more or less directly inspired by Homer, represent Cavafy's only borrowings from the poets of Antiquity. Elsewhere he draws almost exclusively on the historians and the sophists, *i.e.*, on the Greek prose writers.

cism of the eighteenth century, we inherit a heroic and classical image of Greece, a white marble Hellenism: the center of our Greek history is the Acropolis of Athens. Cavafy's humanism passes through Alexandria, through Asia Minor, to a lesser degree through Byzantium, through complex phases of Greece more and more removed from what seems to us the golden age, but in which a living continuity persists. Moreover, we must not forget that by an age-old mistake we have regarded "Alexandrianism" as a synonym for decadence: it was during the rule of Alexander's successors, it was at Alexandria and at Antioch, that an extramural Greek civilization was elaborated, one which assimilated foreign contributions and in which patriotism of culture prevailed over patriotism of race. "We call Greeks," Isocrates said, "not only those who are of our blood, but also those who follow our ways." In every fiber of his being Cavafy belongs to this civilization of the *koine*, the common tongue—to that immense outer Greece resulting from diffusion rather than from conquest, a Greece patiently formed over and over again down through the centuries, a Greece whose influence lingers still in the modern Levant of merchants and shipowners.* The array of compromises, participations, exchanges, the image of the young Oriental more seduced than defeated, gives a touch of pathos to that admirable historical narrative "Orophernes."

> *The figure on this tetradrachma*
> *who seems to be smiling, the face*
> *with the pure outline, beautiful, delicate,*
> *is Orophernes, son of Ariarathis . . .*

---

* Neither here nor elsewhere, moreover, is Cavafy representative of the tendencies of his neo-Greek milieu. Modern Greek poets are usually more Romaic, more Italianizing, or more vehemently Westernized. Even their humanism (if it exists) has an Occidental stamp.

It is a destiny to be Greek, or to desire to be, and we find in this Cavafian poetry the whole range of the mind's reactions to this destiny, from pride ("Epitaph of Antiochus, King of Kommagine") to irony ("Philhellene"). These short poems, overinscribed like palimpsests but haunted by no more than two or three problems of sensuality, politics, or art, frequented by a type of beauty always the same, vague yet very specifically characterized, like those burning-eyed Fayum portraits that stare out at you with a kind of dizzying insistence, are unified by climate even more than they are diversified by time. For a French reader, despite obvious differences, this authentically Levantine climate of Cavafy's suggests that Greco-Syrian Orient so miraculously divined by Racine: Orestes, Hippolyte, Xipharès, Antiochus, Bajazet himself have already made us familiar with this atmosphere of refinement and passion, this complex world which dates back to the Diadochi if not to the Atridae, and which does not end with the Osmanli Turks. Whether Cavafy speaks of the young prince "adorned in Greek silks, with turquoise jewelry" from pre-Christian Ionia, or of the young vagabond in a cinnamon-colored suit ("Days of 1908"), we always catch the same accent, the same just-perceptible pathos, the same reserve, I was about to say the same mystery. Voluptuaries, too, have their sense of the eternal.

Suppose we group in cycles these historical poems Cavafy has distributed, like all the others, according to their order of composition; we shall then see the poet's preferences, his rejections, even his lacunae more clearly focused. First, the *Ptolemys–Seleucids* cycle, which we might also call the *Fall of the Hellenistic Monarchies–Triumph of Rome*, the largest, since it includes at least two dozen poems and the ones most charged with pathos and irony; the four *études de moeurs* in the *Hellenized Jews* cycle; seven poems in the fine Alexandrian *Caesar–Caesarion–Antony* cycle; ten poems in the *Sophists–Poets–Ancient Universities* cycle, which constitutes the equivalent of Cavafy's *ars poetica*; two poems on Nero, one still decked with the futile ornaments Cavafy was later to discard, the other among the subtlest and surest in the canon; some twenty poems in the *Pagans–Christians* cycle, as we may call it, making little of the banal contrast between Christian austerity and ancient license, showing life persisting beneath all formulas; two poems about Apollonius of Tyana; seven poems on, or rather against, Julian the Apostate; seven in the *Orthodoxy–Byzantine Chronicles* cycle, jumbling together an encomium of Orthodox ceremonies ("In Church"), an erotic notation ("Imenos"), glosses on the poet's reading such as the exquisite "Of Colored Glass," filled with a tender piety for the past of the race, but also including "Aimilianos Monai," one of the purest of all Cavafy's threnodies. It is again to Alexandrianism that we must attach most of the *Illnesses–Deaths–Funerals* cycle, which cuts across the others; this group, which contains some of the most famous of Cavafy's poems ("In the Month of Athyr," "Myris," and the modern, very picaresque "Lovely White Flowers," which, curiously, is in this same vein), also includes some overly literary poems of a rather flaccid charm, more or less related to the traditional genre of the erotic elegy or the fictive funerary epigram. Putting matters in the best possible light, "Cimon, Son of Learchos," "Kleitos' Illness," and "The Tomb of Lanes" afford Cavafy masculine equivalents of the young Clyties and the young Tarentines of that other poet—half Greek by parentage —André Chénier.

Instead of this purely external classification of the historical poems, let us now take deeper soundings: *poems of fate*, in which disaster befalls man from without, the consequence of unexplained forces which seem to take a conscious pleasure in leading us into error—more or less the ancient view of man's relation to fatality, to the huge mass of causes and effects inaccessible to our calculations, indifferent to our prayers and our efforts. Cavafy, haunted from the outset by this problem of fate, has inventoried these recipes of defiance, of acceptance, of prudent audacity: "Prayer," "Nero's Respite," "Interruption," "On the March to Sinope," "The Ides of March," and above all "Infidelity," that harsh acknowledgment of what seems to man the incomprehensible perfidy of his god or his gods.

> At the wedding feast of Peleus and Thetis,
> Apollo stood up to salute the bride and groom.
> They would be fortunate, he said, in the son
> who would be born of their union. Never
> could sickness harm him, and his existence
> would be long . . . And as Achilles grew up,
> the admiration of all Thessaly,
> Thetis remembered the god's promises . . .
> But one day, old men came bearing news,
> and they told how Achilles had been slain at Troy.
> And Thetis tore off her purple robes, tore off
> and cast upon the ground her bracelets and rings . . .
> Where was he, the poet-god who had spoken
> such fair words at the feast? Where was he,
> the prophet-god, when they had murdered Achilles
> in the flower of his youth? And the old men answered
> that Apollo himself had come down before Troy
> and that with the Trojans he had slain Achilles.

The tragicomic predominates in the *poems of character*, outlines sure as an Ingres drawing, exact tracings of weaknesses, follies, failings of a lively, frivolous, and yet lovable humanity, inventive in trifles, almost always baffled by the tremendous, swept by misfortune to extreme solutions, by misery or indolence to timid or base ones, though not without a certain quick wisdom: "From the School of the Renowned Philosopher," "Alexander Balas' Favorite," "The Gods Should Have Bothered." A perspective without illusions, but not desolate even so: we should hesitate to call it bitter, yet it is certainly bitterness and rigor that we discover under the imperceptible curve of a smile. Consider, for example, "The Gods Should Have Bothered":

> *I am virtually a pauper now, a vagrant:*
> *Antioch, this fatal city*
> *has swallowed all my money—*
> *this fatal city with its extravagant life.*
>
> *But I'm young and in good health.*
> *My Greek is extremely good . . .*
> *I have some notion of military matters . . .*
> *So I regard myself as quite qualified*
> *to serve this country, my own*
> *beloved Syria . . .*
>
> *I'll apply to Zabinas first*
> *and if that dolt doesn't appreciate me*
> *I'll go to his rival, Grypos,*
> *and if that fool doesn't hire me either*
> *I'll go straight to Hyrkanos . . .*
>
> *As for my conscience, it's clear:*
> *why should I worry which one I choose,*
> *all three are equally bad for Syria!*

> *But what can a poor devil like me do?*
> *I'm only trying to make ends meet.*
> *The almighty gods should have bothered*
> *to create a fourth, an honest man.*
> *I'd gladly have gone over to him.*

The *poem of character* almost always coincides with the *political poem*: Cavafy devotes to Ptolemaic or Byzantine intrigues that chess player's sagacity, that passionate interest in the fine art of public life, or what is called public life, which almost no Greek is without. Further, like many of his compatriots, Cavafy seems bitterly sensitive to the spectacle of perfidy, disorder, futile heroism, or base inertia which so often characterizes Greek history (though scarcely more than any other, ancient or modern): his absence of moralism, his disdain for the sensational and the grandiloquent, afford such themes, compromised by so much pompous oratory, a striking immediacy. It is hard to believe these poems of humiliation and defeat were not inspired by the events of our own day, rather than having been written over thirty years ago on themes dating back twenty centuries. Neither the cunning opportunist nor the myopic patriot who sacrifices his country to his grievances nor the adventurer who openly profits from the miseries of the moment is denounced with vehemence: each is accurately judged. They continue to belong—though at their own level, an extremely low one—to that civilization which they are helping to destroy and to which they owe the remains of that elegance in which they drape their selfishness or their cowardice. Similarly, the heroes are surrounded by no applause which might distract us from the spectacle of their serenity: the symbolic soldiers of Thermopylae or a noble mother like Cratesicleia move silently toward "that which is willed for them." A

slightly intensified conviction, an almost imperceptibly deep-
ened pathos in the monologue's movement is enough to turn
the cynicism of "The Gods Should Have Bothered" into the
heroic sadness of "Demetrius Soter," with its undertone of
indignation and scorn.

He used to dream he would achieve great things,
ending the humiliation that had oppressed his country
ever since the battle of Magnesia. He was convinced
Syria would be a powerful nation again, with her fleets,
her armies, her great fortresses, her wealth.

He suffered bitterly in Rome when he realized,
listening to his friends, young men of prominent families,
that for all the delicacy and politeness they showed him,
the son after all of King Seleucus Philopator—
when he realized that nonetheless there was always
a secret contempt for the fallen Hellenized dynasties:
their time was past, they weren't fit for serious things,
for governing people—quite unfit.
Left to himself he would grow angry, and swore
it would not turn out the way they thought . . .
He would struggle, would do what had to be done,
awaken his country . . .

If only he could get back to Syria!
He had been so young when he left, he hardly
remembered what it looked like. But in his mind
he had always seen it as something sacred,
to be approached reverently, a vision
of a lovely land, with Greek cities, Greek harbors.

And now?
 Now despair and desolation.
The young men in Rome were right.

*The dynasties created by the Macedonian Conquest
could not survive any longer.*

*Still, he had made the effort, struggled all he could.
And in his black disillusion, there is one thing
he is still proud of: even in disaster
he still shows the world the same indomitable courage.*

*The rest was dreams and wasted energy.
This Syria almost seems not to be his country anymore—
This Syria is the land of Valas and Heracleides.*

In a sense, the political poems are still poems of fate, but
in them fate is created by man. From the Theophrastian
technique of the *Character*, in which an individual's qualities
and defects are supremely important, there is a gradual shift
to those astonishing poems where the interplay of expedients,
fears, and political calculations acquires the dry clarity of a
blueprint. Here emotion is deliberately suppressed; if there
is irony, it is honed so exquisitely that its wounds are imperceptible. The allegorical (and almost too famous) "Waiting
for the Barbarians" is a demonstration *ad absurdum* of the
politics of defeat; "In Alexandria, 31 B.C.," "Alexander Jannaios," "In a Large Greek Colony," "In a Township of Asia
Minor" epitomize—in street scenes, in the gossip of bureau-
crats—the eternal comedy of state; poems like "Displeasure of
the Seleucid" or "Envoys from Alexandria" bring political
realism to the level of pure poetry, a very rare success shared
by Racine's historical plays. Their beauty consists in a complete absence of vagueness and inaccuracy.

*For centuries, no one had seen gifts at Delphi
so fine as those sent by the two brothers,*

the rival Ptolemys. But now that they have them
the priests are uneasy about the oracle expected of them:
they will need all their wits to determine which one
of two such brothers will have to be offended.
And so they meet secretly, at night,
to discuss the family affairs of the Lagides.

But now the envoys are back, to take their leave.
They are returning to Alexandria, they say, and want
no oracle whatever. The priests are delighted
(it is understood they are to keep the marvelous gifts)
but also totally bewildered, not understanding
what this sudden indifference means.
For they don't know that yesterday serious news
reached the envoys. The oracle was pronounced
in Rome; the dispute was settled there.

Setting aside the historical poems of erotic inspiration, which overlap the personal poems and should be studied with them, I come at last to those splendid half-gnomic, half-lyric poems I prefer to call *poems of passionate reflection.* Here the concepts of politics, of character, and of fate seem to melt into an ampler, looser concept of destiny, of a necessity at once external and internal, associated with a freedom implicitly divine. "Theodotos," which suggests a Mantegna drawing, is such a poem, as is the one entitled "The Gods Abandon Antony,"* accompanied by that "mysterious music" of the tutelary gods abandoning their former favorite on the eve of battle—a fanfare out of Plutarch which has also passed through Shakespeare.

---

* Literally, "A god abandons Antony." But the poem describes a procession, and I have tried to include in the title, as well as Bacchus, this whole cortege of accompanying divinities.

At midnight, when suddenly you hear
an invisible procession passing
with exquisite music, with voices calling,
don't mourn your Fortune that's deserting you,
your work that has failed, your plans
that have all turned out to be illusions—
don't mourn them uselessly:
as if long prepared for this, and bravely,
bid her farewell, the Alexandria that is leaving.
Above all, don't make this mistake, don't say
it was a dream, that your ears deceived you;
don't stoop to empty hopes like those.
As if long prepared, and bravely
as becomes you, who are worthy of such a city,
with emotion but not with regret
or a coward's whining, listen to the voices,
to the exquisite music of that mysterious procession
and bid her farewell, the Alexandria you are losing.

Alexandria . . . Alexandria . . . In the poem just quoted, Antony seems to see not his tutelary gods leaving him, as in Plutarch, but the city which he may have loved more than Cleopatra. For Cavafy, in any case, Alexandria is a beloved being. The Parisian's voluptuous enjoyment of Paris, savored, possessed from its outer boulevards to the memories of its Louvre, might be for us the closest equivalent of such a passion. But one difference subsists: despite her upheavals, despite the rage to destroy and the craving to renew, Paris has kept very visible testimonies to her history; Alexandria has retained, of all her remote splendors, no more than a name and a site. Cavafy may have been well served by the luck which granted him a city thus bereft of glamour and the melancholy of ruins. For him the past lives *new*, conjured up from the texts with none of those lovely intermediaries which Baroque painting and Romantic poetry have accustomed us to put between Antiquity and ourselves. The very fact that the break caused by Islam occurred eight centuries earlier in Alexandria than in Athens or Byzantium forces the poet to relate directly to an older, culturally richer Hellenic world anterior to the Orthodox Middle Ages, and thereby saves him from that Byzantine turn of mind which often, and to excess, marks neo-Greek thought. Alexandria in the most cosmopolitan sense, but also in the most provincial, of this misunderstood word: Cavafy passionately loves his great city, noisy and restless, rich and poor, too busy with its commerce and its diversions to brood over a past fallen into dust. Here this exemplary bourgeois has savored his pleasure, known his victories and his failures, run his risks. He steps out onto his balcony to get a breath of air, "watching for a moment the movement of the street and the shops"; merely by living in it he has "impregnated with meaning" the city he adores. Here he has had, in his own fashion, his *inimitable life*. It is himself he admonishes through Mark Antony.

Now let us turn to the domain of the strictly personal poems; more particularly, that of the love poems. We may regret, in passing, that the phrase "erotic poetry" bears such an unfortunate connotation; rinsed of what is worst about it but not entirely scoured of its ordinary acceptation, the expression precisely defines these poems at once so marked by sensual experience and so remote from the excesses of amorous lyricism. The incredible control of expression Cavafy nearly always manifests* derives perhaps, and in part, from their ex-

* I except some ten poems of a slack and self-indulgent sentimentality, while wondering if the modern reader's (and my own) irritation in the

clusively pederastic inspiration—from the fact that the poet, born a Christian and a nineteenth-century man, deals with forbidden or disapproved feelings and actions. Incontrovertible *I*'s, associated with grammatical specifications leaving no doubt as to the gender of the beloved, appear quite rarely in his work and only after 1917, which is, however, *before* the period when such audacities of expression were to become relatively common in Western poetry and prose. The rest of the time, it is the historical poems, the gnomic and impersonal ones which complete for us (and supplemented for him) the more infrequent and almost always more veiled personal avowals. But the interest of these half silences would be slight if they did not ultimately confer upon these deliberately specialized poems something abstract which enhances their beauty, and which, as with certain rubaiyats of Omar Khayyam in Fitzgerald's translation or with Shakespeare's sonnets, makes them, even more than poems to the beloved, poems about love. So much so that poems like "Afternoon Sun" or "On the Deck of a Ship," in which the poet-lover speaks in his own name, seem tainted by weakness, or, let us say, by self-consciousness, compared to those distinct, limpid poems in which the author's presence, recessed from his work, is revealed at most by the shadow it casts. The "I" may burst forth upon an unpremeditated impulse, but the use of "he" presupposes a stage of reflection which reduces the share of the fortuitous and diminishes the risk of exaggeration or of error. Further, the "I" in certain carefully delimited confidences—for example, "Far Away"—ends by acquiring in Cavafy a meaning as naked, as

---

presence of such effusion does not constitute a form of prudery as dangerous as any other. It is a perverse constraint upon passion, our recognition of its right to violence and not to a languishing or tender reverie. Nonetheless, and from a purely literary point of view, a few of Cavafy's poems seem to me of a flat sentimentality which it is hard not to find "indecent."

detached, as the "he" of the impersonal poems, and a kind of admirable extraterritoriality.

> *I should like to tell this memory . . .*
> *but it has faded now . . . almost nothing is left,*
> *it was so far off, in my first years of manhood.*

> *A skin that seemed made of jasmine . . .*
> *August, that night . . . Was it August? I hardly remember*
> *the eyes. I think they were blue.*
> *Oh yes, blue—sapphire blue.*

An essay on Cavafy's love poetry would take into consideration his Greek predecessors, the *Anthology* in particular, of which his own works are after all the latest segment, as well as the fashions in erotic expression prevailing in Europe early in the twentieth century: the latter, ultimately, count much more than the former. Greek poetry, however intellectualized its expression, is always direct: cry, sigh, sensual appeal, spontaneous affirmation born on a man's lips in the presence of his beloved. Such poetry rarely mixes either pathos or realistic elaboration with its almost pure lyricism or obscenity. A Callimachus would never have dreamed of describing the young workman's hands grimy with rust and oil in "Days of 1909, 1910, 1911." A Strato would have seen them at most as no more than an erotic stimulant. Neither, surely, would have made out of such a subject this short, dense meditation on poverty and wear, in which desire is accompanied by muted pity. On the other hand, the sense of a moral constraint, the rigor or hypocrisy of propriety, did not burden those ancient poets as they did the modern one, or rather (for the problem is complex and even in Antiquity was framed differently from country to country, from century to century), did not burden them in the same way, nor above all with the same weight; they did not have to transcend the inevitable first phase of the struggle with oneself.

> *Quite often he promises himself he will reform.*
> *But when night comes with its promptings*
> *and its promises and prospects,*
> *when night comes with its own power*
> *of the body's longings and demands,*
> *he returns, bewildered, to the same fatal pleasure.*

Any concept of sin is distinctly alien to Cavafy's work; on the other hand, and on the social level entirely, it is clear that the risk of scandal and censure mattered to him, and that in a sense he was obsessed by them. At first glance, it is true, all signs of anxiety seem to have been quite rapidly eliminated from this orderly writing: this is because anxiety, in sensual matters, is almost always a phenomenon of youth; either it destroys its victim, or it gradually diminishes with experience, with a more accurate knowledge of the world, and more simply with habit. Cavafy's poetry is that of an old man whose serenity has had time to ripen. But the very slowness of his development proves that such equilibrium was not easily achieved: the interplay of concealment and confidence, of literary masks and avowals mentioned earlier, the curious mixture of rigor and excess at the very heart of this style, and above all the secret bitterness permeating certain poems, testifies to the fact. "The Twenty-fifth Year of His Life," "On the Street," "Days of 1896," "A Young Poet in His Twenty-fourth Year" are so many high-water marks in a field once flooded and allowed to drain. In "Their Beginning," the shame and fear inseparable from any clandestine experience give the poem the beauty of an etching made with the most corrosive acid.

Their forbidden pleasure had been taken.
They get up from the bed and hurriedly
put on their clothes without speaking.
They leave the house furtively, and out
on the street they walk somewhat uneasily,
as if they suspect that something about them
betrays what kind of pleasure they have just taken.
But how much the artist has gained from it!
Tomorrow, the next day, years later, he will write
the powerful poems that had their beginning here.

Like any reflective man, Cavafy varied not only in his degree of adherence to his own actions but also in his moral judgment as to their legitimacy, and his vocabulary preserves the traces of the hesitations he passed through. He seems to have started from what we may call the romantic view of homosexuality, from the idea of an abnormal, morbid experience outside the limits of the usual and the licit, but thereby rewarding in joys and in secret knowledge—an experience that would be the prerogative of natures sufficiently passionate or free to venture beyond what is known and permitted ("Imenos," "In an Old Book"). From this attitude, one conditioned precisely by social repression, he moved on to a more "classical," certainly a less conventional, view of the problem. Notions of happiness, fulfillment, and the validity of pleasure gain ascendancy; he ends by making his sensuality the mainspring of his work ("He Asked about the Quality," "In the Dull Village," "He Came to Read," "Passage," "Very Seldom"). Some poems, dated near the end, are even calmly licentious, though without our being able to determine if the artist has here achieved a total liberation, has reached, so to speak, the comedy of his own drama, or if they simply testify to the gradual weakening of the old man's controls. Whatever the case, and even in the erotic realm, Cavafy's development differs very distinctly from that of the Western writers of his time with whom it first seemed possible to compare him. His exquisite lack of imposture keeps him from yielding, as Proust did, to a grotesque or falsified image of his own inclinations, from seeking a kind of shameful alibi in caricature, or a fictional one in transvestite disguise. On the other hand, the Gidean element of protest, the need to put personal experience in the immediate service of rational reform or of what (it is hoped) will constitute social progress, is incompatible with Cavafy's dry resignation which takes the world as it is and people's ways as they are. Without much concern for being approved or not, the old Greek openly returns to the hedonism of Antiquity. This poignant yet light view, totally free from the delirious pursuit of "interpretation," to which we are accustomed since Freud, ultimately leads him to a kind of pure and simple assertion of all sensual freedom, whatever its form.

> *Joy and fragrance of my life, those moments*
> *when I found pleasure as I desired it.*
> *Joy and fragrance of my life: that distance*
> *from all habitual loves, from all routine pleasures.*

Erotic poems, gnomic poems on erotic themes, as we see, rather than love poems. At first glance, we may even wonder if love for anyone in particular appears in these poems: either Cavafy experienced it very little or he has been discreetly silent in its regard. On a closer look, however, almost nothing is missing: encounter and parting, desire slaked or unappeased, tenderness or satiety—is this not what remains of every erotic life once it has passed into the crucible of memory? Yet it is evident, too, that clarity of vision, refusal to overestimate, hence wisdom, but no less perhaps the differences in condition and age, and probably the venality of certain experiences, afford the lover a kind of retrospective detachment in the course of the hottest pursuits or the most ardent carnal joys.* Doubtless, too, the poem's slow crystallization, in Cavafy's case, tends to distance him from the immediate shock, to confirm presence only in the form of memory, at a distance where the voice, so to speak, no longer carries, for in this poetry where "I" and "he" contend for primacy, "you," the *beloved addressed*, is singularly absent. We are at the antipodes of ardor, of passion, in the realm of the most egocentric concentration and the most avaricious hoarding. Consequently the gesture of the poet and of the lover handling his memories is not so different from that of the collector of precious or fragile objects, shells or gems, or even of the numismatist bending over his handful of pure profiles accompanied by a number or a date, those numbers and dates for which Cavafy's art shows an almost superstitious predilection. Beloved objects.

"Body, remember . . ." This preference for life possessed in the form of memory corresponds, in Cavafy, to a half-expressed mystique. And certainly the problem of memory was "in the air" during the first quarter of the twentieth century; the best minds, in the four corners of Europe, strove to multiply its equations. Proust and Pirandello, Rilke (the

---

* We may also wonder if Cavafy's sensual life was not intermittent or impoverished, especially during just the period when his poetic sensibility was being formed, and if the constant rumination upon past pleasures is not primarily, in his case, the mania of a solitary man. Certain poems sustain this hypothesis, others dispute it. Such secrets are almost always well kept.

Rilke of the *Duino Elegies*, and even more of *Malte Brigge*: "To write good poems, you must have memories . . . And you must forget them . . . And you must have the great patience to wait for them to come back"), and Gide himself, who in *The Immoralist* adopts the extreme solution of instantaneousness and of subsequent oblivion. To these versions of memory, subconscious or quintessentialized, deliberate or involuntary, the Greek poet adds another, born, it would seem, of the mythologies of his country, a Memory-as-Image, a quasi-Parmenidean Memory-as-Idea, incorruptible center of his universe of flesh. We have reached the point where we can say that all of Cavafy's poems are historical poems, and the emotion which re-creates a young face glimpsed on a street corner in no way differs from the emotion which "re-creates" Caesarion from a collection of Ptolemaic inscriptions.

> *Ah, there you are with your indefinable charm!*
> *In history, you rate only a few lines,*
> *so I was free to picture you in my mind.*
> *I made you handsome and sensitive.*
> *My art gives your face*
> *a dreamy, appealing beauty,*
> *and so completely did I imagine you*
> *that late last night,*
> *as my lamp went out—I let it go out on purpose—*
> *I thought you came into my room;*
> *you seemed to stand there in front of me*
> *as you would have stood in conquered Alexandria,*
> *pale and weary, ideal in your grief,*
> *still hoping they would pity you,*
> *those traitors who whispered: "Too many Caesars."*

Now let us compare this son of Cleopatra with a less cele-brated youth, an anonymous figure in the dark streets of modern Alexandria:

> *Looking at an opal with grayish lights in it*
> *I remembered two beautiful gray eyes*
> *I had seen—it must have been twenty years ago . . .*
>
> *For a month we had loved each other.*
> *Then he went away—to Smyrna, I think,*
> *where he had a job, and we never saw each other again.*
>
> *The gray eyes—if he's still alive—will have lost*
> *their luster; the handsome face grown ugly.*
>
> *Memory, show them to me tonight as they once were.*
> *Memory, bring me back tonight all that you can*
> *of this love, all that you can.*

If a modern poet at grips with the past (his own or that of history) almost always ends by rejecting or altogether negating memory, it is because he confronts a Heraclitean image of time, that of the river eating away its own banks, drowning both contemplator and the object contemplated. Proust struggled with this image throughout his work, and only partially escaped it by mooring to the Platonist shores of *The Past Recaptured.* Cavafian time belongs, rather, to the space-time of Eleatic philosophy, "the arrow, flying, that does not fly," identical segments, firm, solid, but infinitely divisible, motionless points constituting a line that seems to us to be moving. Once gone by, each moment of such time is surer, more definite, more accessible to the poet's contemplation and even to his delight than the unstable present, always likely to be still in the future or already in the past. It is fixed, as the present is not. Seen from this perspective, the poet's effort to return to the past is no longer located in the realm of the absurd, though still pathetically situated on the confines of the impossible. In "According to the Formulas of the Ancient Greco-Syrian Magi," the unrealizable demands of memory filter out the sediment of a facile sentimentality:

> *"What magic philter," wondered the lover of perfection,*
> *"what herbs distilled according to the formulas*
> *of the ancient Greco-Syrian magi could give me back*
> *for a day or even for a few hours (if its power*
> *can last no longer) my twenty-third year, or*
> *could give me back my friend when he was twenty-two—*
> *his beauty, his love?*

> *"What herbs distilled according to the formulas*
> *of the ancient Greco-Syrian magi, turning time*
> *backward, would give us back as well*
> *our same little room?"*

This poem is the only one in which Cavafy records a partial failure of memory, due in part to time's irreversibility, in part to the extraordinary complexity of the nature of things. Ordinarily it is not so much the resurrection of the past that he seeks as it is an image of the past, an Idea, perhaps an Essence. His sensuality leads to a mystical sifting of reality, as spirituality would have done in another case. The gaps in history, and consequently the absence of details which for him are superfluous,* help the amorous necromancer evoke Caesarion more effectively; it is because of a twenty-year separation which isolates and definitively seals the memory

---

* It is hardly necessary to remark that Cavafy, "poet-historian," here puts himself at the antipodes of history proper. No serious historian has ever rejoiced at knowing too little.

that the poet conjures up out of the depths of his recollection the image of the young man with gray eyes. In "Days of 1908," the figure of the swimmer standing on the beach, fastidiously scoured of anything incongruous and mediocre, is silhouetted forever against a splendid background of oblivion.

> *Summer days of 1908! that cinnamon-colored suit*
> *has fortunately faded from your image.*
> *All that remains is the moment when he removed,*
> *when he flung from him the worthless clothes,*
> *the mended underwear, and stood there*
> *entirely naked, flawlessly beautiful,*
> *a marvel. His uncombed hair pushed back,*
> *his body slightly tanned by the sun, by going*
> *naked, mornings, to the beach.*

On the other hand, in "To Remain," it seems as if the wish formulated in "According to the Formulas of the Ancient Greco-Syrian Magi" has been granted; the sensual reminiscence brings with it a fringe of banal external references which serve to authenticate it; the work of art receives *as is* the wretched, scandalous, and yet almost sacred memory.

> *It could have been at one in the morning,*
> *or one-thirty.*
> *In a corner of the tavern,*
> *behind the wooden partition . . .*
> *There were only the two of us in the empty room,*
> *dim by the light of one kerosene lamp.*
> *The waiter was dozing on his feet in the doorway.*
>
> *No one could have seen us. But already*
> *passion had robbed us of all precautions.*

Our clothes were unbuttoned—we weren't wearing much,
it was scorching hot that divine July.

Delight of the flesh between the gaping clothes!
Sudden baring of the flesh! That image
has passed over twenty-six years, and now has come
to remain in this poem.

Carnal reminiscence has made the artist master of time;
his loyalty to sensual experience leads to a theory of immortality.

Each poem by Cavafy is a memorial poem; historical or
personal, each poem is at the same time a gnomic poem; such
didacticism, unexpected in a modern poet, constitutes perhaps the boldest aspect of his work. We are so accustomed to
regard wisdom as a residue of extinguished passions that it is
hard for us to recognize it as the toughest and most condensed form of ardor, the gold dust born of fire and not the
ashes. We resist such chilly, entirely allegorical, or exemplary
poems as "Apollonius of Tyana in Rhodes," a lesson in perfection, "Thermopylae," a lesson in constancy, "The First
Step," a lesson in modesty; we accept with difficulty the
abrupt transition from didacticism to lyricism, or vice versa,
in splendid poems like "The City," a lesson in resignation but
even more a lament for the human incapacity to escape
oneself, or "Ithaca," poem of the exoticism and of the quest,
but above all plea in favor of experience, a warning against
what I should call the illusions of disillusionment.

When you set out for Ithaca,
pray that your road is a long one,
full of adventure, full of discovery.

Lestrygonians, Cyclops, angry Poseidon,
don't be afraid of them:
you won't find things like that on your way
as long as your thoughts are exalted,
as long as a high emotion
stirs your spirit and your body.
Lestrygonians, Cyclops, angry Poseidon,
you won't find them

unless you bring them along inside you,
unless your soul raises them up before you.

Pray that your road is a long one.
May there be many a summer morning when—
full of gratitude, full of joy—
you come into harbors seen for the first time;
may you stay at Phoenician trading centers
and buy fine things, mother-of-pearl and coral,
amber and ebony, voluptuous perfumes of every kind,
as many voluptuous perfumes as you can;
may you visit numerous Egyptian cities
to fill yourself with learning from the wise.

Always keep Ithaca in mind.
Getting there is your goal.
But don't hurry the journey at all.
Better if it lasts for years,
so that you're old when you reach the island,
rich with all you've gained on the way,
not expecting Ithaca to make you rich.

Ithaca gave you the wonderful journey.
Without her you would never have set out.
She hasn't anything else to give.

And if you find her poor, Ithaca has not deceived you.
Wise as you have become, with so much experience,
you'll have understood by then what an Ithaca means.

It is eminently worth our while to watch this wisdom
ripen, to see the emotions of anxiety, solitude, separation,
still very apparent in the early poems, give way to a tranquil-
lity deep enough to seem facile. It is always important to
know whether a poet's writings ultimately side with rebellion
or acceptance; in Cavafy's case, a surprising absence of
recrimination and reproach characterizes the work. Along
with the importance assigned to memory, it is undoubtedly
this lucid serenity which gives him his very Greek aspect of
the poet-as-old-man, at the antipodes of the romantic ideal of
the poet-as-child, the poet-as-adolescent; and this precisely
though old age occupies, in his universe, the place almost
everywhere reserved for death or else counts as the one irrep-
arable disaster.

The aging of my body and my face:
wounds from a terrible knife.
I am anything but resigned.
I take refuge in you, Art of Poetry,
who know something about remedies . . .
who try to numb suffering by imagination, by words.

Wounds from a terrible knife . . .
Bring your remedies, Art of Poetry,
they keep us (for a while) from feeling the wound.

We may say without paradox that here rebellion is located
within acquiescence, becoming an inevitable part of the
human condition which the poet acknowledges as his own. In
the same way, the splendid lines inspired by a passage in

Dante, *"Che fece . . il gran rifiuto,"* a poem of revolt and denial, nonetheless remain at the very heart of acceptance, formulating the extreme and personal case in which there is a rebellion in not rebelling. This is because a completely accepting perspective can only be based on the very powerful sense of what is unique, irreducible, and finally valid in each temperament and each destiny.

> *For some people there comes a day*
> *when they must come out with the great Yes*
> *or the great No. It's clear at once*
> *who has the Yes ready in him; and saying it,*
>
> *he goes on to find honor, strong in his conviction.*
> *He who refuses never repents. Asked again,*
> *he'd say No again. Yet that No—the right No—*
> *defeats him the whole of his life.*

Finally, with even more finality than for Mark Antony as cited earlier, everything comes down to a divestment too readily consented to not to be secretly desired:

> *When the Macedonians abandoned him*
> *and showed they preferred Pyrrhus,*
> *King Demetrius (he had a great soul)*
> *didn't behave—so they said—*
> *at all like a king.*
> *He took off his golden robes,*
> *discarded his purple buskins,*
> *and quickly dressing himself*
> *in simple clothes, he slipped out—*
> *just like an actor who,*
> *when the play is over,*
> *removes his costume and goes away.*

The same absence of rebellion allows Cavafy to move easily within his Orthodox heredity, and makes him, ultimately, a Christian. A Christian as remote as possible from torment, outpourings of the heart, or ascetic rigor, but a Christian nonetheless, for *Religio*, in the ancient sense of the word, as well as *Mystica*, belong to the universe of Christianity. The "good death" following—for the Cleon of "The Tomb of Ignatius," for Myris, for Manuel Komninos—upon a sensual existence is another kind of submission to the nature of things; this monastic divestment extends in its own fashion the themes of stoical wisdom, secretly satisfies that Oriental nihilism often infused into Greek thought, which at first appears so contrary to it in every regard. But the Orthodox tradition chiefly remains, in Cavafy, a form of attachment to milieu and atmosphere; it takes, all told, only a secondary role in his poetry. The strictly mystical elements are rather to be found in the pagan part of the poems, in the scrupulous concern not to hamper the demonic or divine endeavor ("it is we who interrupt the task of the gods, we impatient, inexperienced mortals"), and still more in the perpetual equation poem-memory-immortality, *i.e.*, in the intimation of the divine in man. Morality scarcely departs from what a contemporary of Hadrian or Marcus Aurelius might have practiced. Like the flesh bearing within itself an armature of bones and tendons, these poems conceal at their core the vigor necessary to any sensual soul. Everywhere, even in the most deliciously softened forms, we find the hard vertebrae of Stoicism.

This quasi-Goethean mystique is linked, in Cavafy, with the elements of a poetics which at first glance seems to derive from Mallarmé. An aesthetic of secrecy, silence, and transposition.

190 ✣

He wrapped them carefully, methodically
in costly green silk.

Roses of ruby, and lilies of pearl, and violets
of amethyst, beautiful, perfect, the way

he wants them to look, not as he saw them
in nature, or studied them. He leaves them

in the safe, a proof of his bold and cunning art,
and if a customer walks into the shop

he takes from their cases other wares, splendid
jewels, bracelets, chains, necklaces and rings.

But secrecy does not lead to a linguistic or literary hermeticism;* the poet's position remains what it was in the great periods, that of an exquisite artisan; his function is limited to bestowing upon the most ardent and chaotic substances the clearest and smoothest forms. Nowhere is art considered more real or noble than reality, or even transcendentally opposed to notions of sensuality, of fame, even of common sense with which it remains, on the contrary, prudently linked. Art and life assist each other: everything becomes an asset to the writer, sometimes love ("The Silversmith"), sometimes humiliation ("Their Beginning"). Conversely, art enriches life in its turn ("Very Seldom"); it has remedies which, "for a while," heal our wounds ("Melancholy of Jason"); it collects, in the manner of a precious

---

* This is what gives his poetry its strange quality of authentic, *i.e.*, well-hidden, esotericism. Thus in "Evocation" and in "Caesarion," the real or allegorical darkness, the image of the candle and of the extinguished lamp, seem to forsake the realm of literary ornament, or even of erotic fantasy, for that of occultist reference; we are inevitably reminded of the magician's formula: *extinctis luminibus*. The same is true of that enigmatic poem "Chandelier." A subtle light.

vessel, the distillation of memory ("One Night," "An Image Remains"). Further—an avowal made almost accidentally by this poet of the past-as-present—art has means of "combining the days" ("I Brought to Art"). But it achieves its ends only by the most dedicated study. A series of historical or fictive portraits illustrates this art of writing which is also a strict art of living: Aeschylus was wrong to have his tombstone mention his heroism at Marathon, whereby he was a Greek like any other, and not his works, whereby he was irreplaceable ("Young Men of Sidon"); Eumenes will learn to be content with his rank, already a high one, as a secondary poet ("The First Step"); the disasters of war, *i.e.*, reality endured, will not keep Phernazis from concerning himself with his task, which is reality transcribed.

> *The poet Phernazis is composing*
> *the important part of his epic:*
> *How Darius, the son of Hystaspes,*
> *assumed the kingdom of the Persians.*
> *(From him is descended our glorious king,*
> *Mithridates, hailed as Dionysus and Eupator.)*
> *But this calls for serious thought; he has to analyze*
> *the feelings Darius must have had:*
> *arrogance, perhaps, and intoxication? No—more likely*
> *a certain insight into the vanities of greatness.*
> *The poet ponders the matter deeply.*

> *But his servant interrupts, running in*
> *to announce very important news:*
> *the war with the Romans has begun.*
> *Most of our army has crossed the borders.*

> *The poet is dumbfounded. What a disaster!*
> *How can our glorious king,*

Mithridates, Dionysus Eupator,
bother about Greek poems now?
In the middle of a war—just think, Greek poems! . . .

But are we really safe in Amisos?
The town isn't very well fortified . . .
Great gods, protectors of Asia, help us . . .

But through all his distress and agitation
the poetic idea keeps fermenting in him:
arrogance and intoxication—that's most likely, of course:
arrogance and intoxication are what Darius must have felt.

This apparently banal poetics is based on literary methods
which are insidiously, perhaps dangerously simple. The author early renounced the impulse to oratorical amplification,
to lyrical reduplication (of which a poem like "Ithaca" still
affords examples), in favor of the unadorned idea, a kind
of pure prosaism. The dry, flexible style makes no commit-
ments, not even to concision; admirers of ancient Greek will
recognize this smooth surface, without highlights, almost
without accents, which like certain modeling in Hellenistic
statues reveals itself, when seen at close range, to be of an
infinite subtlety and, one may say, mobility. In the best
poems, at least; for there are some in which Cavafy affects a
lyrical or erotic effusiveness ("In the Evening," "In an Old
Book," "In Despair") flavored on occasion with a rosewater
Hellenism ("Tomb of Iases," "Sophist Leaving Syria,"
"Cimon, Son of Learchos," "Kleitos' Illness"), and even
elaborates an occasional scholarly and futile pastiche
("Greek since Ancient Times," "Before the Statue of En-
dymion").* The number of these questionable poems in-

* Critics often dispute the definition of "scholarly pastiche." I use the
term to refer to a work, in the category of an exercise or a game, in which
the author confines himself to imitating, in its every detail, a form of ar-

creases or diminishes, of course, with each reader's severity or good will; however few, they mar this poetry in which nothing has been left to chance, and Cavafy's exegete ends by wondering if these poems tainted with self-indulgence do not represent, somehow, the paradoxical result of the Cavafian *ars poetica*, or if, on the contrary, they should be regarded as the vestiges of bad taste often latent in almost any work of extremely refined sensibility and against which the poet has tried to defend himself by using such means of expression so deliberately discreet, so deliberately chary. As in the *Greek Anthology*, in any case, as in certain productions of Alexandrian or Greco-Roman statuary which also obey aesthetic canons of the same order, a scarcely perceptible demarcation line separates what is exquisite from what is trifling, factitious, or flat.*

---

chaic art, without giving it a new content and without attempting to revive its old content. At least ten of Cavafy's poems, chiefly in the genre of the funerary elegy, tend toward such pastiche in their lack of convincing emotion. Other poems, especially those which present, for all their Grecian drapery, street scenes or low-life studies which might have been (and perhaps were) modern, actually belong to the realm of disguise and concealment.

    * I should add that frequently what first struck me as a defect has, on rereading, seemed an essential characteristic, a bold stroke, perhaps an ultimate strategy. I have come to find in this disconcerting mixture of dryness on the one hand, of pliancy on the other, the equivalent of the two styles of Greek popular music, the facile grace of Ionian island songs, the harsh pathos of those of the Aegean Islands. The undeniable monotony of erotic expression now seems to me a warrant of authenticity in a domain where secret routines almost always prevail. The obvious clumsiness of certain poems prevents one's thinking of Cavafy as a mere virtuoso. What once seemed insipid now seems limpid, what once figured as poverty is now an economy of words. The same is true of the deliberately banal, almost conventional adjectives Cavafy uses in his erotic evocations of youth and beauty. Stendhal, Racine, and the Greeks before them were also content to say "delicate limbs," "fine eyes," or a "charming head."

    Subtlety and clumsiness are not mutually exclusive, quite the contrary. Remoteness from major literary movement, from clans and sects, may account for something dated and yet extraordinarily fresh in Cavafy, something both elaborate and ingenuous, which is often the mark of an artist

But perhaps we should consider, should study Cavafy's poetry as a whole not so much from a stylistic as from a compositional point of view. The typically Alexandrian juxtaposition of erudite poem, popular sketch, and erotic epigram allows the poet to avoid the appearance of striving for effect: such disparity and such continuity are those of life itself. The Alexandrian preference for the minor work, an art which can be controlled down to the last detail, becomes in Cavafy an exclusive system: his longest poems are no more than two pages; his shortest, four or five lines. The passion to elaborate on the one hand, and to simplify, to shorten on the other, produces at the end an extremely curious method which for lack of a better term I should call that of the memorandum or the marginal gloss. A good number of these fastidiously reworked masterpieces are scarcely more than a line of script, at once cursive and cryptic, a slender paraph traced by the pen beneath a known and beloved text, the torn-off leaf from a solitary's engagement book, the code of a secret expenditure, perhaps a riddle. With all their lyricism, they retain the naked beauty of a note jotted down for oneself. His loveliest lines give us only the point of departure or the conclusion of their author's ideas or experiences; they leave aside everything which, even in the most discriminating writers, is evidently addressed to the reader, everything which belongs to the realm of eloquence or explanation. His most moving poems are sometimes confined to a barely annotated quotation. Rarely has so much solicitude been put in the service of so little literature.

---

who works "out of the way." One might take the liberty of saying that "Portrait of a 23-Year-Old Youth Painted by His Friend of the Same Age, an Amateur" irresistibly suggests a Douanier Rousseau; Cavafy himself has his Sunday-painter aspects.

Another specifically Cavafian characteristic, the extraordinary elaboration of monologue, seems to have affinities with both Hellenistic comedy or mime and, more particularly, the old exercises of Greek rhetoric. "The Gods Should Have Bothered" and "From the School of the Renowned Philosopher" suggest the techniques of Herondas's *Mimes*: brief pieces without action in which, for our greater diversion, a character describes himself. "The Battle of Magnesia," "John Kantakuzinos Triumphs," "Demetrius Soter," "In a Large Greek Colony, 200 B.C.," and especially "Demaratos," a masterpiece of the genre, have for their prototypes the schemas of orations, the models of epistles, or the summaries of famous trials dear to the ancient sophist, whose tradition survives so pathetically in our French schools' assignments. These clear and complex poems sometimes suggest Browning's intricate monologues, but a Browning in whom drawing has replaced all the painter's colors and impasto; they permit Cavafy, the potential dramatic poet, to internalize the emotions of others and to externalize his own; they offer this mind so closed and at certain points so fixed upon itself the possibilities of *acting* in every sense of the word. In "The Battle of Magnesia," the indirect presentation and the use of the present tense recapture the past in its weltering actuality; in "In a Large Greek Colony, 200 B.C.," the murmur of Greek voices commenting on an inscription of Alexander's at over a century's remove achieves an effect of choral poetry, helping us by comparison to measure the time which has accumulated between Philip's son and ourselves. In "Demaratos," a dissertation topic sketched by a young sophist of the late Empire summarizes in twenty lines an episode in the Median wars, and with it the eternal drama of the deserter torn between two causes and two camps: the very dryness of the academic exercise safeguards this story of an insulted man from false pathos.* This technique of intermediaries sometimes corresponds to Cavafy's concern for discretion, but more often to his desire to have his own emotions confirmed by another mouth: in "Imenos," for instance, two passionate lines, which might have found a place in any love poem, are given as citations from a letter written by an imaginary or forgotten Byzantine. In the tragic "Aimilianos Monai," Cavafy manages to make the monologue express precisely *what is kept silent*, the shyness, the pathos, the melancholy gaze under the discreetly lowered visor:

> *Out of my talk, appearance, and manners*
> *I shall make an excellent suit of armor;*
> *and in this way I shall face evil men*
> *without fear or weakness.*
>
> *They will try to harm me. But of all*
> *who approach me, none will know*
> *where to find my wounds, my vulnerable places,*
> *under the lies that will cover me . . .*
>
> *So boasted Aimilianos Monai.*
> *Did he ever make that suit of armor?*
> *At all events, he did not wear it long.*
> *At the age of 27, he died in Sicily.*

---

* Not without an obscurity which is one of Cavafy's defects and which derives less from his subjects than from stylistic mannerisms. The shift from direct to indirect discourse within the same short poem often presents the reader (and the translator) with extraordinary obstacles. Of the same order are those breaks within certain gnomic poems at which the poet addresses in turn the reader, himself, and an allegorical character who is only half himself; also in this category is Cavafy's preference for what I should call the indirect title, *i.e.*, one taken from a secondary figure or incident and not from the poem's main theme or its central character. This is an obliquity to be studied on its own.

Thus the study of technique has brought us back to what matters, which is to say, to the human. Whatever we do, we always return to this secret cell of self-knowledge, at once narrow and deep, sealed and translucent, which is often that of the pure sensualist, or of the pure intellectual. The extraordinary multiplicity of intentions and of means ultimately constitutes, in Cavafy, a kind of closed circuit, a labyrinth in which silence and avowal, text and commentary, emotion and irony, voice and echo inextricably mingle, and in which disguise becomes an aspect of nakedness. At last this complex series of mediating personae releases a new entity, the *self*, a kind of imperishable person. We said earlier that all of Cavafy's poems are historical poems; "Temethos of Antioch" warrants the assertion that in the last analysis all of them are personal poems:

> *Verses by young Temethos, the lovelorn poet,*
> *and entitled "Emonides." This Emonides, a very*
> *handsome young man from Samosata, was the beloved*
> *companion of Antiochus Epiphanes. But if*
> *these verses are impassioned, it is because Emonides*
> *(he lived in a very early period, around the year 137*
> *of that Hellenic dynasty, perhaps even a little earlier)*
> *is only a made-up name, though a well-chosen one.*
> *The poem expresses the love felt by Temethos himself,*
> *a beautiful love, and worthy of him. We his friends,*
> *we know for whom these verses were written.*
> *The Antiochians, who do not know, say "Emonides."*

ATHENS, 1939
CIRENCESTER, GLOUCESTERSHIRE, 1953

TRANSLATOR'S NOTE: Though I have consulted and combined the Keeley-Sherrard, Dalven, and Mavrogordato versions of Cavafy, I have relied heavily on Marguerite Yourcenar's own versions to which this study originally served as a preface in 1958.

Humanism and Occultism
in Thomas Mann

THE WORKS OF THOMAS MANN HAVE attained to that very rare category, the modern classic; that is to say, they are among productions still recent and still open to debate, but worthy of being taken up again and again for examination and reconsideration in all their aspects and at every level of their meaning; they serve to nourish the mind, but to test it, as well. Such works appeal to us on a fourth or fifth reading for reasons quite different from what made us like them in the first place, or even for opposite reasons. The non-German reader who approaches *Buddenbrooks* for the first time finds the atmosphere strange and almost exotic; but the strangeness wears off with repeated readings, or with more intimate knowledge of Germany itself, leaving exposed the human document, the drama of a man at grips with those familial and social forces which have formed him, but which are slowly moving to destroy him. What was new and "contemporary" in a novel like *The Magic Mountain*, firmly focused as it is upon a specific time and place, no longer conceals from us the truly a-temporal and cosmic basis of that masterpiece; the sensual element which once proved disquieting in *Death in Venice* does not take the reader now

This English translation is slightly shorter than the original French version.

by surprise; thus he is left wholly free to contemplate at leisure one of the finest allegories of death that the somber spirit of Germany has ever produced.

German works these, without question: German in their resort to hallucination to penetrate outer reality, and likewise in their search for occult wisdom, the secrets of which, whispered or implied, hover between the lines as if intended to remain there virtually undisclosed. German, too, in their feeling for those great entities which have ever haunted Germanic thought, the Earth-Spirit, the Mothers, the Devil, and Death, a death more active and more virulent than elsewhere, mysteriously mingled with life itself, and sometimes endued with attributes of love. And last, these works are German in their strong symphonic structure, in the contrapuntal character of their parts as developed throughout more than half a century. But this Germanic substance has been permeated, like the country itself, with leaven from other lands: the heroes of *Death in Venice* and *The Magic Mountain* both owe their supreme revelation to the Greek mysteries; the learned convolutions of the *Joseph* tetralogy are impregnated with Jewish thought (talmudic, and sometimes cabalistic, even more than biblical), although these volumes were composed at the very time that the German government was decreeing destruction to the Jews; the transcendental eroticism of the story *The Transposed Heads* comes from Hindu philosophy, with which German thinking so often claims affinity; fatidic Asia speaks in *The Magic Mountain*, through the stammering lips of Mynheer Peeperkorn. And frequently in the novels the figure of the beloved is specifically non-Germanic: that typical German matron Frau von Tümmler happens to love an American; Adrian Leverkühn woos, rather feebly, a French girl, improbable though she is;

the phantoms whom Gustav von Aschenbach and Hans Castorp pursue are in both cases Slavs.

Such diverse materials as these are wrought into a solid mass more suggestive of some slow geological stratification than of exactly planned, architectural construction. Mann's rock-crystal structures of allegory only gradually take form in the mother-solution which his meticulous realism provides, that veritably obsessed realism so characteristic of German vision; realism is also the bed for his nearly subterranean stream of myth and of dream. *Death in Venice*, opening with the detailed account of a stroll in suburban Munich and proceeding to give other realistic details (the schedule of trains and steamers, the barber's prattle in full, the conspicuous coloring of a tie), slowly fashions from the vexations and mishaps of a journey an allegoric Dance of Death; far below the surface, burning but inexhaustible, secretly born of some more ancient symbolism, flows the profound meditation of a man in prey of his own death, drawing both his love and his disaster from within. *The Magic Mountain* is a highly accurate description of a sanatorium in German Switzerland about the year 1912; it is also a medieval *summa*, an allegory of the City of the World; and last, it is a mythological epic of a Ulysses of the inner depths, of a voyager bound over to ogres and to larvae but ultimately reaching his modest Ithaca, a certain wisdom within himself. *The Black Swan* portrays a German matron of the 1920s, with all her slightly ridiculous particularities; but this woman is also Germany in allegory; of import deeper still, her stricken body is the cave where Cancer battles Desire and the two, like crabs, devour each other. Possibly Peeperkorn is Gerhart Hauptmann, but at the same time he is some god Pan strangely carved in a crag of the Engadine; he is, above all, life personified, a figure massive and powerful as life itself, and mythically related to the waterfall against which the author silhouettes him shortly before his death. Are Naphta and Settembrini authentic portraits, hardly even caricatural, of originals whose every aspect is noted, their attire, state of health, means of livelihood, their mental twists and peculiar habits of speech? Rather, do they not exist merely to signify what is empty and arrogant in most of our philosophical discussions; have we climbed those glacial heights only to pursue with them *ad absurdum* an endless sophomoric debate? Or do they, on the contrary, embody two governing principles in the world; are they gigantic megaphones through which are voiced, with the clumsiness of mere words, two sides of a problem grotesquely stated because far too vast for words? Actuality, allegory, and myth merge in Mann's works; by some process of continuous circulation all these elements are constantly reabsorbed into life's ebb and flow, from which they are born.

The same complexity obtains in these novels in the matter of time, and of its corollary, place. Time is infinitely varied in Mann, since he draws in great part upon a historic or legendary past, both remote and near, and since whatever was contemporary in his narratives, just because they have been fashioned in the course of a long life, has been caught up in the turning of Time's wheel, and has slipped from the present to the past. His picture of post-1870 Germany in *Buddenbrooks*, and of pre-1914 Germany in "The Blood of the Walsungs" and in *Death in Venice*, the pre-1914 Germany as seen in retrospect in *The Magic Mountain*, the post–World War I Germany of *The Black Swan*, and finally the ravaged Germany of *Doctor Faustus*, at the end of the Second World War, though separated from first to last by scarcely three-quarters of a century, are as remote each from the other as all of them are from the Goethean setting of *The Beloved Returns*. Furthermore, by some process in his thinking, the immediate in Mann enters promptly into the category of the historical; for this analyst of transmutations, and of time in motion, the present has no privileged place in the sequence of centuries; all periods, including this in which we exist, are drifting alike within time itself. Occasionally these novels, though set in the past, have encroached upon the future, as when at the end of *The Magic Mountain* Joachim's ghost appears wearing a helmet from a war which has not yet taken place; the discomfiture of the upper middle class, as represented by the Buddenbrooks family, is more complete today than in the years when it was described; the existence in our world of a mysticism of terror, like that of Naphta in *The Magic Mountain*, worthy of a Grand Inquisitor, has been grimly authenticated by the subsequent course of actual historical events.

Gradually Mann's spatial and temporal conceptions have been enlarged, if not changed, by his progression throughout half a century from realism in the literal sense of the term to realism in its full philosophic implications. The drama of *Buddenbrooks* was still set against a background of urban life, and moved with the town clocks of Lübeck. In *The Magic Mountain*, however, Hans Castorp's evocation of waves and sand along a distant Baltic shore suggests the beat and timeless particles of pure duration. The feverish tempo of the sanatorium, so exactly situated in an hour of universal history (just before the outbreak of the War of 1914), is gauged on the scale of geological time, like that of the mountain itself. The *Joseph* novels have their own, biblical time, running at a mere trickle in the immensity of that Mesopotamian plain immemorially inhabited by man. In *Doctor Faustus* time has been extended, with the Devil's help, to infinity, but at the cost of the hero's life; although the main action is inscribed within the limits of the last years of pre-Hitlerian Germany and is supposedly narrated during the war years which follow, it is wholly unrelated to the visible passage of day and night. Thus, more and more explicitly is historical time assimilated into a cosmic conception of eternity.

"I adore you, phantom of water and albumin, destined for dissection in the tomb." Such, in effect, is Hans Castorp's strange avowal of love to Claudia Chauchat. Mann is only formulating here, in terms of organic chemistry, views akin to those of the great humanist occultists of the Renaissance: man the microcosm, formed of the same substance and governed by the same laws as the cosmos, subject like matter itself to a series of partial or total transmutations, and connected with everything else by some highly developed capillary system. Such basically cosmic humanism is, of course, quite unconcerned with Platonic and Christian ideas of antinomy of soul and body, of the world of the mind and the world of the senses, of God and matter. It admits, therefore, neither of the process of rejection and conversion such as marks an Aldous Huxley's approach to a concept of mystic universality, nor of that asceticism, on aesthetic grounds, which raises a Proust from contemplation of a world of imperfect and transitory reality to the vision of a world which is flawless and pure. Nor does it allow for that identification of the physiological with the repulsive which is so typical of Sartre, and of many other novelists of our time, for whom the Christian concept of the indignity of the flesh persists in a context otherwise shorn of Christian ideals. But the simple and reassuring notions of felicity, good health, and moral equilibrium, so important for the old, traditional humanism, are likewise alien to this humanism, which sounds the abyss. Desire, sickness, death, and evil and, by a bold paradox, thought itself, slowly corroding its bodily support, all are ferments and solvents in a process of alchemical transmutation; they bring the "phantom of water and albumin," whether willing or no, again into contact with its original sphere, which is nothing less than the universe itself.

Mann's attitude in the presence of conclusions to which his own premises have led him (conclusions frequently subversive) is not without suggestion of the cautious deliberation of his hero Hans Castorp. His principal characters differ from many of those presented by the literature of our day in that they do not at first sight appear to be solitary and desocialized, cut off from ideological bases, or even questioning that such bases exist; nor are they launched in the absurd, or comfortably installed in some imaginary world. Instead, his heroes are first portrayed as inseparable from a class or a group, supported but also bound fast by social customs which they believe to be good, and which have been so, perhaps, but which are now no more than sclerotic remains of a life gone by; their initial state is much less one of despair than one of a certain blind complacency. Only belatedly, and in fumbling fashion, will each one in turn try to penetrate beneath that petrified crust, seeking to regain the world of vital energy to which he belongs, but which he cannot rejoin without sacrifice of his external man in actual or symbolic death. Indeed, Mann seems never to have eliminated wholly from his consciousness, and still less from his unconscious mind, some remnant of puritanical reprobation, or bourgeois timidity, in face of that adventure in self-discovery; in a period when the prevalent literary themes inclined more and more toward facile self-liberation, he steadily warned, and with almost comic insistence at times, that gruesome perils beset him who would go beyond familiar and lawful bounds. To the very last this drama of the artist in revolt against his middle-class environment, though the problem is frankly conventional, remains for Mann the symbol of a terrifying choice; his caution, his daring, his slow-paced irony, the winding detours of his very thinking are in direct ratio to the dangers inherent in this most dubious, as it seems to him, of human endeavors.

The heroes of Mann's earlier works fall victim to the abyss; they have not yet ventured to explore it, and only unwittingly do they become its accomplices. In the dull atmosphere of *Buddenbrooks*, against the ominous skies of *Death in Venice*, characters whose virtues are nearly spent are still desperately resisting the solicitations of chaos: Thomas Buddenbrook, drearily confined within his middle-class pattern of propriety, dies in the harness of a social order which is honorable but outworn; Gustav von Aschenbach, though struggling against love's insidious infection, preserves his sad and solitary respectability to the end. The same mixture of apathy and despair prevails in the shorter stories written before 1914 and set in provincial Germany; life is rotting there, under its cover of rigor and decorum; the sole means of escape are through passion or dream, or by flight to another land, and each of these ways leads inevitably to death. The daemonic power of love which Aschenbach comes to know, Albrecht van der Qualen's erotic fantasy in the story called "The Wardrobe," little Herr Friedmann's howl of suppressed desire—these are given vent only at the brink of dissolution, or in the total irresponsibility of dream. When the hero is a man of letters, that renegade in bourgeois society, the author is especially severe, in part, it would seem, playing the conformist, but in part as a form of self-punishment. In *Tonio Kröger*, the one note of sentimental comedy in that series of chiefly tragic conflicts, the hero (through whom Mann doubtless speaks) pleads for compromise between the anarchy of the artist, which he feels within him, and that well-regulated existence which rather naïvely he continues to regard as the symbol of moral rectitude coupled with bodily ease, of reassurance together with physical comfort; paradoxically, it is order, or what is called order, that tempts the faltering Tonio Kröger, not chaos.

Schopenhauerian pessimism and Stoic conformity both give way, at last, in *The Magic Mountain*, where positive and daemonic force triumphs in Mann's thinking for the first time: the young officer Joachim, martyr to rigidity and refusal, yields precedence to his cousin Hans, whose utterly bourgeois qualities are brought into play to investigate the abyss. Here myth dawns, too, upon the snow: that element of the fantastic which appears from time to time in some of the early stories is channeled now in accordance with the laws of primitive, magic epic and of rituals of initiation. With this work Mann reaches what may be called a classic phase in his romanticism, recognizable from the fact that the narrative comes to its close, like all classic achievement, with some slight gain in the realm of knowledge; the novel of the triumph of death has become a novel of education in the vein of *Wilhelm Meister*: Hans Castorp has *learned* to live. That somewhat inept, almost comical young fellow, whom the author dispatches into the battle smoke of the War of 1914 without wishing, or perhaps being able, to tell whether or not he will come out alive, exemplifies a species threatened more and more with extinction, *Homo sapiens*. Such an eternal student is the antithesis of the Sorcerer's Apprentice: for him the study of science, which is too often blamed for dehumanizing, leads only to a more accurate conception of the possibilities and limitations of man's lot, and does so by a method which has ever been that of the true humanist; experimentation with those doubtful sciences, half true, half false, which are called the occult sciences, is no more than a valiant exploration carried on to the farthest point of human understanding. Hermetic wisdom now means simply wisdom to him.

But nothing can truly be called *simple* in the work of Mann: in the final pages of *The Magic Mountain* Hans Castorp is made to turn back to "the flatland," precipitating himself into war almost joyously and with the feeling, apparently, of going back to ordinary reality and to ordinary human fellowship again. Such sentiments were not uncommon in a recruit of the War of 1914, but it is surprising that Mann records them as late as the year 1924 without reservation of any kind. All the indications point to a conclusion wherein the recently liberated Hans, after completion of his long voyage of discovery, falls back into the place of the unenlightened, militaristic Joachim, and does so with the author's approval. More than that, Hans now feels "saved." Thus even in this, the most classical of Mann's works, the free exercise of intelligence is still looked upon as suspect procedure; the call to war provides the exorcism which allows this "delicate child of life" to escape from what is now suddenly termed the "magic mountain of sin." To be sure, great books sometimes have factitious endings which bring them into line, at the last moment, with the current thinking of their readers at the time; but the conception of intelligence as identical with original sin is too prevalent in Mann to allow us to drop these closing pages from consideration: although this long work is devoted to the development and formation of a mind, at the very end the intellectual investigations of honest Hans are explicitly denounced by the author as an excursion into Evil.

The tetralogy *Joseph and His Brothers*, set on the borderland between history and myth, is one of those great humanistic interpretations of the past made possible of accomplishment only because of the slow, careful work of generations of scholars, in this case notably ethnographers, historians of ancient religions, and archaeologists working in the last half century. For the first time a literary work which is intended neither as a defense of the Jewish point of view nor as Christian exegesis shows us both what unites the Jewish race with, and separates it from, the vast world of pagan religion and myth: we are made to witness the almost unnatural birth of the monotheistic notion of God. If of all Mann's great books the *Joseph* novels alone have the erotic interest concentrated almost exclusively upon conjugal love, or rather, upon the procreative forms of sensuality, it is because the entire series is, in a way, the story of a symbolic pregnancy: Jacob-called-Israel gives birth to God much as Rachel brings forth the True Son. The great merit of Mann's descent into these dim recesses of human recollection is that he brings again to light that primitive consciousness which has become for us our unconscious process. Under its appearance of chronicle packed full with men's lives this is a metaphysical work: the characters in this version of the biblical story telescope within themselves whole generations, and live through experiences and emotions of their ancestors as if those adventures were their own; thus they are less individuals than more sacred entities, personages of a mythical drama. Authors and actors each of his own play, they stop short of tragedy partly because of

their comedy of errors, cheating games, and verbal equivocation, and partly because their world is ruled by two conceptions (themselves apparently opposed), the omnipresence of
the present and the eternal recurrence of events; such characters are still, and quite naturally, all of a piece with the universe. Both Ishmael and Esau are alike the Red Spirit, the
simoom, and Set the Murderer; Abraham is both grandfather
to Jacob and his immemorial ancestor, the Moon Wanderer
setting forth to find God beyond Ur (that symbolic archetype
of all cities), a kind of Wandering Jew forever walking anew
the road of Time's beginning. Joseph himself is Tammuz-
Adonis, the Torn and Resurrected; but he is also that character so dear to Mann, less heroic than compliant, the darling
of fate, the artist, the delicate, charming heir of an ancient
race, a less sickly brother to Hanno Buddenbrook, a Tonio
Kröger with more assurance, or a less slow-minded Hans
Castorp. With him the epic of Jacob's search for God is
resolved almost too readily into a *modus vivendi* with God.
After the two first volumes, dominated by the primitive,
majestic figure of Jacob, the story is spun out into something
like a comedy of manners for protohistorical times: the three
volumes dealing with Egypt are encumbered with archaeological details as devoid of vitality as the description of Israel
in the first part of the story is vivid and strong. Such ponderous elaboration of the ways and customs of a vanished society
would be wholly futile did it not suggest the merest corrosive
satire upon all society whatsoever. The human element runs
dry in the monotony of these some thousand pages extending
like the sand, and is lost in the teeming night of myth, in the
mirage-like irony, in the hypnotic modulations, like dunes,
and in the interminably complicated pattern, like designs in
an Oriental carpet.

Humanism and Occultism in Thomas Mann

The element of game, even of equivocation, as distinct from irony or fantasy, develops slowly in Mann as a mode of expressing essentials of his thought. *Royal Highness*, for example, a short novel of 1909, retains the somewhat old-fashioned charm of slight comedy for court theater, and is disturbing only in its very superficiality, as is often the case with Mann. The amusing story *Disorder and Early Sorrow* treats both the annoyances of inflation in Germany and the gulf between parents and children in a period of swift change, but the author maintains a bland tone of mere polite bad-inage, even when he verges upon personal confidences. On the other hand, the picaresque autobiography of Felix Krull is an early attempt at literary game, apparently intended to be as significant in Mann's work as is *Lafcadio's Adventures* in the work of Gide, but the first chapters, published in 1911 and reissued in 1921, were not further developed until the very end of his career. So it is only with the comedy and inter-play of myth which constitute the *Joseph* series that a calm and almost sportive quality enters more and more visibly into Mann's major work, a kind of involuntary scherzo which predominates in certain great writers who have reached a final stage of maturity. *The Transposed Heads*, a mildly liber-tine "legend," treats lightly the Oriental, and Hegelian, motif of perpetual change. That medieval ballad *The Holy Sinner*, through the medium of a thin gothic disguise, presents secret themes of Mann in the freedom of masquerade; the absurd dangers of the adventure in self-discovery are surmounted here with the half-sly facility of the dreamer-who-knows-that-he-dreams: from scandalous love is born sanctified fruit, and the lovers' talk, in their incestuous bed, is turned into a scholarly diversion by the author's shift to Old French. The sensuous themes of *Death in Venice* are resumed, after an

interval of forty years, in the novel *The Black Swan*, but this
time the setting is one of flat domesticity: household inti-
macies and bourgeois comfort veil the horrors of this new
Dance of Death, in which a highly susceptible widow is the
protagonist, instead of a man won over against his will. Thus
these later novels occupy a position in Mann's writings not
unlike that of *The Winter's Tale* and *Cymbeline* in the late
work of Shakespeare: pessimism and optimism alike have been
left behind: the world of fixed forms, and of moving forms,
too, order and disorder, life-in-death and death-in-life, these
have become merely different aspects of a single MYSTERIUM
MAGNUM grown thoroughly familiar now to this wise old
alchemist; the sense of game inherent in the order of things
is gradually supplanting the sense of danger.

To this realm of game are transposed two themes which
have steadily obsessed Mann, the equivocal nature of the
artist and the dubious activity of the intelligence; both appear
in two works which it may, at first sight, seem shocking to
couple, *The Confessions of Felix Krull, Confidence Man*
(the title given in the still incomplete publication of 1954)
and *The Beloved Returns*, published in 1939 between the
last two volumes of the *Joseph* tetralogy. In *The Beloved
Returns* the game is carried on under cover of that most
glorious name in German letters, Goethe, the Olympian
Goethe of the last years, who does indeed seem to represent
the most imposing figure in all literary history, and the greatest professional success as well. In *Felix Krull* the game is
played through the medium of an engaging character, an
artist in every form of imposture, a charming thief akin to
the mythological Hermes; such is the clever protagonist of
the satyrique drama which concludes Mann's graver works.
In *The Beloved Returns* the irony at surface level is directed

against the group surrounding the Master, and the usual malevolence and pettiness to be found there; but at more profound depths the irony plays upon the position of the "great man" himself, upon the subtle difference between the stereotyped conception of him, commonly held, and his inner reality, so utterly incommensurable with any social pattern, or even with any human pattern whatsoever, least of all with the romantic picture of the lover which Goethe himself had drawn. By a series of changes in the stylistic level we are led from the honored sage, decorously playing his role of celebrity in the small circle at Weimar, to the old sorcerer intent upon some process within, the mysterious operations of the chemistry of genius secreting thoughts which will never be wholly divulged. The extraordinary lyric outburst at the end of the book, highly rhetorical, sweeps us still farther along, to the edge of a veritable volcano of daemoniac forces no longer limited by human form.

The almost morbid tendency on Mann's part to view the artist as basically abject is held in check in *The Beloved Returns* by the very fact of Goethe's great prestige, but in *Felix Krull*, on the contrary, it inspires some rather virulent pages, retained intact from the early version of the book. A visit backstage to an actor whom the public adores for his elegant ease as a man of fashion reveals him as a low, vulgar fellow in a dirty dressing room, still sweating under his remaining makeup; his skin, which had seemed so fine and fair, is covered with disgusting sores. The author's preoccupation with this element of imposture which he finds inherent in every artistic realization is equally apparent in the passage where Krull, as a small boy, mounts the podium with his little violin and acquires a reputation as an infant prodigy by merely pretending to play the brilliant selection which the orchestra is rendering. Here we have again the darling of fate, the delicate heir of a bankrupt papa, a young Joseph who no longer resists the advances of middle-aged women, a master of disguise and of double-dealing, a tourist who goes around the world and is attentive auditor to the cosmological ramblings of a Professor Kuckuck: this Felix Krull is the amiable caricature of Mann's great heroes and, in a sense, their comic residue. Life turns into farce in this last product of an octogenerian author: the portrayal of Frankfurt is still allegorical, like some fair German city in a medieval painting, but it is followed by a "gay Paree" reconstructed from memories of musical comedy and vaudeville of 1910; an indistinct Lisbon is the next scene of this unfinished work, which closes rather lamely without indication of how Mann intended to bring his comic chronicle eventually to an end.

Doctor Faustus stands apart from the other works of Mann's late years, the one lofty peak to appear after the great mountain systems which we recognize in *Buddenbrooks, The Magic Mountain*, and the *Joseph* tetralogy. Game and its ambiguities prevail here, too, but, like the music of irony and terror in the *Apocalypse* composed by Adrian Leverkühn, hero of this somber book, the scherzo characteristic of the author's last manner turns strident, with frantic undertones. Game and danger meet face to face here, like two monsters carved above a cathedral door. Never has Mann exhibited more consummate craftsmanship than in this novel where, in a fugue-like progression, three separate themes, political, theological, and ethical (specifically, that of involvement in magic), make way for and then sustain the discussion of music itself; in turn the musical problem is fused into the more general problem of the Understanding, what its scope and its limits are, and the price to be paid for overstepping its bounds. The will to learn how to live, and the individual's accord with life's very rhythm, themes of such import in *The Magic Mountain*, have ominously disappeared; the hero of this work achieves his full stature by means of slow self-destruction, in the course of what amounts to total imprisonment within himself. Hans Castorp, withdrawn into his sanatorium room, has already provided an example of this type of reclusion, but Hans's windows open out upon the whole universe while those of Leverkühn give on an alarming void. The initiate of the earlier works has now become the damned. The extraordinary lack of all concern for spirituality in the work of Mann, in spite of his bent for esoteric matter, leaves the field free, so to speak, for the transcendence of Evil in *Doctor Faustus*. Goethe's Faust finally gains salvation before he dies; the humanist whose Renaissance heritage had been filtered through the rationalism of the era of enlightenment could hardly have admitted that it might be otherwise, or that the infinite aspiring of mankind could in itself be a sin against the Spirit. In Mann's *Faustus*, on the contrary, the musician belongs to the Devil, irrevocably, even before receiving the fatal visit. Weird misfortune overtakes those he loves: Rudi, a mediocre young man, is the victim of a sensational, almost grotesque society murder; the child Nepomuk, who is the one incarnation of innocence and Grace, is caught in the same diabolic machinery that has trapped Leverkühn and dies in the convulsions of spinal meningitis, which ironically imprint upon his small angelic face the horrid grimace of the damned. Art has become a pursuit apart, strangely separated from life; but it nevertheless anticipates life's course, in that the voluntary destruction of form in music seems to prophesy cataclysms to come; the composer's productivity is enormous, but resembles only the strange, inorganic increase of the crystals which his father liked to start in a chemical solution, and which reappear more than once in the book as a symbol of illusory growth.

With the sinuosity characteristic of his literary game the author interposes a narrator between us and the hero of *Doctor Faustus*, allowing the grim tragedy of the ailing genius to be reported in uninspired and platitudinous terms, thus reducing it to about what Faust's story would be if recounted by the scholar Wagner, or Hamlet's story, if told by some Horatio who is perhaps half Polonius. The virtuous sentiments of this good Dr. Zeitblom provide something like a neutralizing agent between the accursed musician and the legitimate apprehension of the reader. So grave are the implications of Leverkühn's problem that we understand why Mann has resorted to prudent circumlocution; for this ambiguous work tends, on the whole, to indicate that Satan's collaboration is inevitable, and for that reason almost justifiable, in every human achievement. The reader is made the more uneasy by the fact that this novel, intermingling as it does incidents drawn from the personal lives of Nietzsche and Tchaikovsky with portraits à clef and autobiographical suggestion, seems to mirror Mann himself in its Faustus-Leverkühn, who is supposed to have treated in music subjects which Mann has treated in literature, including even a *Lamentation of Doctor Faustus*; and it seems, furthermore, to make a formidable echo, after an interval of nearly half a century, to the complaints of Tonio Kröger bemoaning the equivocal condition of the artist and the sinister nature of artistic creation. We begin to ask ourselves if the somber grandeur of this product of old age is not due simply to a return to the views of traditional morality, warning men against all dealing with the powers of evil; or if instead, under the appearance of tragic denunciation of daemoniac power, a

strangely subversive daemonism has not secretly won the
day.

It would be easy to compile from Mann's writings a list of
hermetic themes or incidents somewhat similar to the symbols
of Goethe's *Fairy Tale* or of the second part of *Faust*, or to
Masonic allegories in the story of *The Magic Flute*, showing
the marked influence upon his work of ancient occult tradition. It would be less easy, however, to determine when the
novelist has deliberately drawn upon a common store of magic
symbols and when symbolic images or myth-type episodes are
born spontaneously from the inner chemistry of his composition. The grotesque incident of Castorp's uncontrollable laughter, at the beginning of *The Magic Mountain*, is a typically
esoteric motif, the first effect of a cure for all set habit. Toward
the middle of the same book the description of an evening at
the cinema, so closely related to Plato's image of the Cave of
Shadows, likewise introduces an initiatory theme, which re-
curs later on in the account of necromantic séances held in
the unspectacular setting of the sanatorium basement. The
typically symbolic episode of "descent into the tomb" is represented in the *Joseph* sequence by the casting into the pit and
into the prison, in *The Magic Mountain* by burial in the
snow. Initiatory, too, near the opening of the latter novel is
the conversation in the dark between Settembrini and Hans
Castorp, during which the older man tries to dissuade the
younger from his plan for installing himself in the sanatorium,
an episode which sets forth in semirealistic, semisymbolic
terms the occult theme of the threatening guardian at the gate.
In *Doctor Faustus* the imagined descent by diving bell among
the creatures of the deep is a variant of the Hebraic vision of
the abyss; a feebler echo of this theme in *Felix Krull* is the

descent to the basement of the museum, to the awesome collection of anthropology. The prevalence of disguise in the
Joseph narratives has esoteric significance; Jacob-in-Esau,
Leah-in-Rachel, brother-in-stranger. Still more esoteric is the
conception of separation from one's self, that almost sinister
game of the man-who-knows-more-than-he-knows, played by
Joachim and by the young dressmaker in *The Magic Mountain* as each one faces his death. Again suggesting initiation,
in this same novel, is the imagery of parturition in the scene
where the young medium "gives birth" to a phantom, and her
convulsions are compared to those of eclampsia. Finally, the
role assigned to physical suffering is hermetic: in these non-
Christian works suffering is not bound up with the concept of
salvation but with that of decomposition and change. In *Buddenbrooks* illness is as yet only a refuge in which little Hanno
escapes the burden of existence. In later novels, however, illness will signify a secret means of entry into the Mysteries:
the moist spot on Hans Castorp's lung, Adrian Leverkühn's
syphilis, these are symbols of accession into dangerous knowledge; both are parts of the initiatory themes of the tollgate and
the pact.

Intimately allied to the conception of change-sickness-death
in Mann is the insidious quality of his eroticism; he treats
love as one more aspect of the physiological serving as channel
to the universal, and thus it is related to initiatory themes.
The loved ones, Frau von Rinnlingen, Tadzio, Claudia Chauchat, Esmeralda, and Ken, are little more than conductors of
souls, divinities in Hermes' role; they disappear as soon as
they have led the living, or the dying, to the edge of the inner
abyss. Even the most fully embodied of these loves are hardly
more tangible than the bizarre entities in "The Wardrobe"
and in *Doctor Faustus*, the naked storyteller and the little sea-

maid (both of autoerotic origin, perhaps). Identity of sex in lovers or disparity in their race or age, the conjunction of beauty and disease within the same body, the lack or rarity of physical possession, such are essential ingredients of the potion which carries us far beyond all that is habitual or licit or known. Sometimes it takes us far from probability itself. Nothing is more unlikely, from the angle of physiology and psychology alone, than the representation of young Hans's sexual life, limited throughout his seven long years in the sanatorium first to a single night with Claudia Chauchat, just before her departure, and then to the peculiar Platonic relationship established between these one-time lovers after her return. Only because in matters of sensual experience there is nothing wholly impossible do we accept the narrative of Leverkühn's love life as it is presented to us, severe continence over thirty years' time interrupted once in his student days for brief, intentional contacts with a prostitute whom he knows to be diseased, and later on, when he is approaching middle age, for a liaison hardly less brief, this time with a youth. One may well ask if there is not something equally incredible in *The Black Swan*, not, of course, in the fact that the mature Frau von Tümmler is in love with young Ken, but in the intellectual, almost virile attitude of this woman, who is otherwise so feminine, toward her passion; and especially in her obsession with the decline of sensuality as inevitably coinciding with the arrival of the menopause, an idea which is closer to Peeperkorn's fixation, in *The Magic Mountain*, on the "cosmic cataclysm" of impotency than to a woman's usual anguish about growing old, and no longer being loved or desired.

Whatever the degree of probability in such portrayals, it seems clear that Mann, like Balzac and Proust, is of the type of novelist who, though unquestionably a master of realistic detail, superposes upon that realism an irrational, dreamlike sequence of events whenever the element of love or sexuality enters in, and once within this state of dream the rules of verisimilitude no longer obtain. Actuality undergoes a change: from the moment that Frau von Tümmler steps with Ken into the motor launch for what will prove to be her last outing the story unfolds on a rhythm which is that of dream; nightmare forms people the Carnival during which Hans finally approaches Claudia; it is at night and in sleep that Gustav von Aschenbach consummates his impossible passion, a climax achieved only in dream and under the transparent symbol of a Dionysiac orgy. In *Doctor Faustus* everything pertaining to the lowly Esmeralda takes place in another dimension: the minor happenings of everyday life occur in an order different from before, and under a new light, from the time of Leverkühn's accidental visit to the brothel to the macabre comedy of the two physicians, one suddenly found dead and the other arrested by the police. In *Joseph and His Brothers* even within the edifying framework of conjugal love the stress is placed upon the passing strange: the long delays before Jacob and Rachel are united, the confusions of disguise, Rachel's thirteen years of sterility, placing her in the ambiguous position of the best beloved and, at the same time, destitute young wife; legitimate love is here surrounded by an atmosphere of hidden threat and interdiction wholly unexplained. Only under some such constraints as these, apparently, is erotic emotion released in Mann's work.

Quite without paradox we may include within the category of the occult the theme of incest as it is treated in "The Blood of the Walsungs" and *The Holy Sinner*. For incest, which in the last analysis amounts to a retreat of the individual back upon himself and his family group, thus sealing in their unique aspect, as it were, while breaking violently with the mores of this group, tends to constitute for at least a part of mankind both the supreme sexual crime and the supreme magic act, and is consequently imbued with both horror and prestige. "The Blood of the Walsungs" transposes to a wealthy Jewish setting in Berlin of the early 1900s the Wagnerian theme of incest between the mythical Siegmund and Sieglinde; what seems to interest Mann most here is the perfect isolation of the identical couple, the exquisite and luxurious flower of a civilization and a race which are closing jealously in upon themselves. The subject of *The Holy Sinner*, in which the union of a twin brother and sister is complicated by a further union of *their* son with his own mother, already haunted Mann at the time that he was writing *Doctor Faustus*, and to the extent that he represents his musician-Faust as composing an opera upon this very story. Although the immediate source of *The Holy Sinner* is an old German poem of the twelfth century, this legend of a holy Pope Gregory of scandalous origin goes back farther still to a type of more ancient folk narrative wherein the hero, or predestined one, is a son born of incest.*

The recurring theme of incest is closely bound up in Mann's work with the theme of the Gemini of myth, with the virtually androgynous figure of an indivisible pair formed by two persons of different sex but of equal beauty. Even in the comic *Felix Krull* Mann cannot keep from introducing into the background the twin silhouettes of a brother and sister endowed with exotic charm, and luxuriously attired, who are together the object of an ambivalent love. In the *Joseph* series,

---

* It might be added here also that the metaphor of incest, the mysterious *nuptiae chymicae*, the traditional chemical union of elements in alchemical vocabulary, appears also in *The Magic Mountain*, and is implied in some other works.

in addition to mention of incestuous play between the young Ishmael and young Isaac, incest reappears in caricatural form: the aged twins Tua and Hua, wedded brother and sister (in accordance with ancient Egyptian custom), are grotesquely portrayed as living out their well-padded existence in the lap of luxury. Unlike the tragic twins of *The Holy Sinner*, whose guilty issue later becomes a saint, this correct, conventional couple produce a Potiphar; and since they always conform to the best current practice, they have had him castrated in infancy in order to assure his eligibility for the highest posts in the royal household. The tradition of Potiphar as a eunuch comes down from Jewish and Islamic legends of Joseph, but the episode of the old couple representing a brother-sister marriage, Egyptian fashion, is of Mann's own invention; it allows him to offer a ludicrous variation on one of his favorite themes, freed of religious interdiction and therefore deprived of human drama, a picture of legitimate, and accordingly desacralized, incest.

As he does for eroticism, Mann treats music as if magic in essence: in the Wagner-dominated world of *Buddenbrooks*, *Tristan*, and "The Blood of the Walsungs," music is strangely destructive, and already working evil; in *The Magic Mountain* it becomes frankly necromantic, and at last is truly daemoniac in *Doctor Faustus*, where Arnold Schönberg's well-known experiments are made the final symbol of the breaking up and renewal of forms. One might be tempted to consider this stress upon the significance of music a wholly German trait, but the fact is that Proust, a writer so typically French, is almost as much concerned with the mystery of music as is Mann. "More extraordinary than table-turning . . .": Proust, too, had felt that by some admirable black magic each virtuoso who executed Vinteuil's Sonata was reverently bringing the composer back to life. Still, for the author of *Remembrance of Things Past* music is less a ritual incantation than an intimation of immortality: Swann does not descend, as Hans does, into the realm of Death, hypnotically entrained by arias from popular opera caught in the whirling grooves of a gramophone disk. Notwithstanding the continuous, and almost excessive, use of technical terminology in Mann's discussions of music, it is Proust, perhaps, who is the more musically aware of the two, more sensitive to the mathematical beauty of musical structure and not to its hypnotic power alone, or to its somber, visceral compulsion. For him this art is bounded firmly by aesthetic limits; only through perfection of form does it rise above the purely sensory, and thence to that world of Platonic recollection to which all his work finally attains. For Mann, on the contrary, music opens the portals of night. It plunges the human creature once more into secret depths of the universe, into the heart of a telluric world both above and below man's sphere, like the Goethean world of the Mothers. The concept of immortality recedes for him in the presence of the concept of eternity.

Reflections of a Non-Political Man: this title given by the novelist to a collection of essays* published in 1918 is still wholly applicable, regardless of appearances, to all the rest of his work. It would be idle to seek for explanation of his novels in his successive reactions to the political tragedies of the day, for it can even be said that Mann adopted the same semi-detached attitude toward events of his century as did both

---

* We are concerned here only with Mann as novelist, so this is not the place to discuss the content of these essays in particular, in which he undertook, like so many German writers of his time, to defend Germany's imperial policy during the War of 1914. Mention need be made of them only to show that in the interminable dialogue between Joachim and Hans Castorp the author was slow to break with Joachim's point of view.

Goethe and Erasmus for their respective times. If his books, like convex mirrors, reflect a condensed image of Germany over some sixty years, it is precisely because the author has refused to combine techniques of fiction with those of journalism. The pessimism of the works which he published between the years 1898 and 1914 translates a normal reaction of a German sensibility in presence of the gross optimism of the period, its smug materialism and rigid militarism, all doomed to a bad end; his later absorption in daemonic power strangely anticipates that violent release of elemental forces and deadly ideologies which have swept over Germany, and the world, for more than thirty years. His conception of illness, so important in his work, has been imposed upon him in part by his study of these great ailing bodies. But when Mann does describe morbid symptoms in the body politic, he sees them only as the most conspicuous and most external indications of an evil inherent, first of all, in Being itself. The feeling for biological fact, on the one hand, and the obsession with metaphysical problems, on the other, which together have protected him in his novels from mere psychologizing, where so many of his contemporaries have been content to dwell, have likewise kept him from errors of purely political perspective. The political movements which so profoundly transformed nineteenth-century Germany have only a muffled repercussion in *Buddenbrooks*, or are limited there to minor local incidents; the War of 1870 is but mentioned in passing, in the course of a conversation about the improved market for wheat. In *The Magic Mountain* the state of mind which led to the War of 1914, "acute irritability," as Mann dubs it, is perceived much as is some barometric phenomenon preceding a cyclone, and is described in terms more cosmic than human. The satire on Fascism in *Mario and the Magician* is submerged early in the story in grim fantasy, indeed is quite covered up in a Hoffmannesque portrayal of the grotesque and horrible. The massive *Joseph* series, though in composition over the period between 1930 and 1943, does not turn, as might have been expected, into a protest against the atrocious destruction of a race; neither does it exalt the Children of Israel. In *Doctor Faustus* the summary of events of the fatal year 1944 forms a rumbling base to the posthumous account of the musician's life, and doubtless more or less reproduces Mann's own voice in his role of *praeceptor Germaniae* over the radio from America; but this commentary on the German catastrophe is merely secondary to the inner drama, to the tragedy of the man of genius bound over irrevocably to Evil.

Certainly it seems sometimes as if the ambiguous *Doctor Faustus* can be reduced to a relatively simple allegory of the political condition of contemporary Germany, since at the end of the book the central character is almost explicitly identified with the German Fatherland, at the point of death in consequence of the Nazi adventure. Furthermore, we are tempted to think of Hitler, and of the millennium which he promised to National Socialism in its hour of triumph, from the moment that the vulgar, petty little man who incarnates the Spirit of Evil proposes to the tragic hero a pact assuring him almost superhuman development of his genius, and guaranteeing him an adequate portion of time before the infernal settlement falls due. Possibly, too, the author may have intended to present in his two principal characters, the somber and solitary Leverkühn and the benevolent, ever-fluent Zeitblom, two aspects of German civilization, the man of intuition and the man of bookish learning. But, as is almost always the case with Mann's symbols, the circle which they purport to form around reality is never quite closed, and seems to let something escape, as if by design. For, after all, the Devil keeps his promise to the composer, who becomes by such means a musical genius of Beethoven's stature, gloriously fulfilling his life as an artist, even though at the cost of his life as a man. It is hardly necessary to indicate where we should end if we were to pursue this parallel into the actual political world. To read *Doctor Faustus* purely as partisan allegory would be to judge it in the first place as a didactic piece of propaganda, and in the second as internally contradictory.

Other great writers in the German language of the same generation as Mann, or of the generation immediately following his own, have tried to fuse into one whole the secrets of magic and those hardly less dangerous secrets of wisdom; others have looked, like him, to some half-esoteric theory of knowledge for an explanation of the universe which neither the bourgeois nor the revolutionary materialism of their time seems to afford; others, too, have opposed the principle of contradiction. Allegory or myth may serve as common denominator for minds wholly unlike in other respects and completely foreign to each other: Spengler and Kassner, Gundolf and Jung, Rilke and George, Kafka, Jünger, and Kayserling show traces here and there of the vitalism of Paracelsus, the Orphism of Goethe's last years, the Titanism of Hölderlin, Novalis's angelic theurgy, or the subversive Zoroastrianism of Nietzsche. All have to some extent inherited views which are humanistic in part, and in part hermetic, passed down from the German Renaissance to German Romanticism: all have tried to transcend human destiny in terms of universal destiny; all have followed, or caught some glimpse of, methods for developing knowledge which engage the will or the imagination; all have sought for a truth too near the center of things not to be also subterranean.

But Mann is closer to Goethe in line of descent than any of these great contemporaries, possibly for the reason that merely in following his vocation as novelist he has found a counterbalance both to pure dream and to dogmatic systematization in the study and description of the individual, and decidedly average, man. The result is that often, even in the highly metaphysical aspects of his novels, a kind of pragmatism appears, not unlike that to which Goethe's Faust turns (in the second part of *Faust*) shortly before his death. Like Goethe, too, in his commentaries on his own Orphic poems, reducing almost ineffable truths expressed there to somewhat prosy exhortations toward a good life, Mann tends to exalt the homeliest and most exoteric virtues in that central massif of his work, *The Magic Mountain*. Honesty, modesty, and kindness are the qualities with which the hero Hans Castorp is endowed, with only enough courage and common sense added to keep those virtues from falling, as they so often do, into the service of existing prejudice or new and dangerous error. Even in *Doctor Faustus*, where the emphasis is placed upon excess inherent in the nature of genius, to the exclusion of every average virtue or vice, that weird adventure, pitched like Leverkühn's music itself at the furthest limits perceptible to human ears, is reported to us by the very commonplace character who serves as narrator. The merits of humdrum humanity must apparently be defended by Mann in the presence of genius: this pedestrian Dr. Zeitblom is not afraid to analyze what is subject for terror, to love what lies beyond his grasp, and to serve his appalling hero as confidant, counselor, and collaborator. Nothing is more like Goethe than this use of the middle position to comment upon extremes. We are given a somewhat pedagogical presentation of madness by reason, of the unconscious, or rather the supraconscious, by the conscious, of the wizard by the professor; of the eternal Luther (incarnated in the ex-theologian Leverkühn, devil-haunted like the man of the Wartburg) by the eternal Goethe, or rather, by the eternal Eckermann, represented here at a wholly bourgeois level by the academic Zeitblom. It is as though the impossible or inexpressible could not be brought to realization in action or in words by Mann except through the filter of prosaic, heavy good sense, of something almost gross, or, in any case, flatly human.

Even the style of Mann, somewhat slow in pace and at times heavily descriptive, carrying over into the dialogue the paraphrasis and courteous formulas of a bygone age, is less hermetic than exegetic. That cautious advance which takes up no new point until the preceding has been properly exhausted, that thesis which perpetually produces its own antithesis, reminds us of medieval scholasticism but also of Renaissance scholia. The ponderous, interpretative dialectic in *Doctor Faustus*, the half-frenzied proliferation of analysis in the *Joseph* volumes (where among other such arguments are set forth with rabbinic meticulosity Joseph's seven reasons for resisting Potiphar's wife) belong historically to a type of devious thinking which Mann inherits; his purpose is not to offer a rational explanation of a world too vast and complex for human categories, but to scrutinize it with what help our reason affords. As is to be expected, therefore, he tends in his writing to conserve the logical structure of language in its strictest form even at the sacrifice of realism in dialogue, and to preserve for discourse its classical role of intellectual rather than emotional medium of expression. At certain strategic points of his work, in passages where something unutterable or inadmissible is concerned, he chooses not to break explosively with syntax, in the fashion of the modern poet, but to change from customary speech into more secret language, which is sometimes a learned language as well. Examples of such indirect, protective devices are the virtual parody of archaic style in *The Holy Sinner*, the lovers' extraordinary French in *The Magic Mountain*, dream-like and slightly distorted by these foreigners, and that German of Luther's time which Leverkühn employs in his confession, and in his heightened states of delirium. At a less intellectual level, the lisping of Potiphar's wife and the relapse into dialect on the part of Frau von Tümmler serve the author also as rudimentary forms of stylistic circumlocution, the equivalent of half-conscious, thinly veiled expressions of desire.

The long, circuitous course of Mann's writing is in keeping with the cautious deliberation of his approach to reality; he sees to it that the reader, like the character, advances gradually, and not on the surface level alone. Such skillfully delayed exposition is very different from the haughty obscurity of a poet like George, where half-revealed meanings flash with a diamond's fire, or from the triple-locked allegory of a Kafka. Carried one step further, Mann's discursive commentary would be downright didacticism; he stops just short of that error by introducing myth; in myth, by its very nature, are fused all the complex elements which didactic explication would detail. Imbedded in the heavy ore of everyday existence, to be perceived there by none but watchful eyes, myth is for Mann only a more hidden, but more final, form of explanation.

Accustomed as we are to an almost academic definition of the term "humanism," we may ask whether or not a mind so concerned with the irrational, and sometimes with the occult, so open to change and indeed almost to chaos, can still be called "humanist." Assuredly it could not if we were to retain without qualification the old, strictly limited definition of a humanist, that is to say, of a scholar well versed in classical literature, with its central focus on the study of man. Nor even if we were to enlarge that definition to make it include, as is often done nowadays, the concept of a philosophy which is based on the worth and dignity of the human being (on what Shakespeare calls the infinite faculty of this masterpiece, man) would the appellation apply. For both these views suggest an element of optimism with regard to humankind, and possibly even an overvaluation of the species, which can scarcely be attributed to a writer so obsessed by the dubious aspects of the human personality, so concerned to portray man as a mere particle of the universe and a refraction of the whole. But Shakespeare's phrase "how infinite in faculty" suggests still another form of humanism, one alert to what lies deeper within the human being than his ordinary deportment may betray; whether we will or no, those words lead us to depths in which we come into contact with forces stranger than are dreamt of in a philosophy where Nature is regarded as a simple entity. A humanism directed thus toward the shadowy and unexplained, even toward the occult, seems at first view opposed to traditional humanism, but it is rather the extreme extension of the latter, a kind of left-wing humanism. Mann rightly belongs to that small, somewhat isolated group of thinkers who are cautious and tortuous by nature, and often are cryptic by necessity; once emboldened they seem to venture in spite of themselves, as if moved by some inner compulsion; though conservative in letting nothing be lost from the accumulated cultural riches of thousands of years, they tend nevertheless to the subversive in their continual reinterpretation of human thought and behavior. For such minds all arts and science, myth and dream, the known and the unknown, and human substance itself are objects of an investigation which will go on as long as mankind endures. In their company the student of "humane letters," to employ a term dear to Hans Castorp, approaches to the very edge of the ultimate abyss.

In an essay devoted to the scope of the work of Sigmund Freud, Mann seems more or less consciously to have defined the nature of his own attempts and aims when he speaks of "a humanism of the future which will recognize truths about mankind quite unknown to the humanism of the past." The hypothesis of a humanism of the future seems more hazardous today, when the very word "future" tends to take on apocalyptic significance, like the music of Leverkühn. Mann himself, in his very last essays, expressed fear of total collapse for the human race, which would bring with it, of course, total loss of all that we have gained in our knowledge about man. Even if these anticipated catastrophes do not take place, or if they are retarded, man turned robot, lowered in his value as an individual by his species' terrifying numerical increase, cut off from his normal environment by too rapid and too dangerous acquisition, cut off, too, from the past, but threatened with extinction at each further step, stuffed with machine-made ideas distributed gratis for propagandistic ends, such a man offers little as a subject for future humanism; and should such a humanism come into existence it would doubtless prove to be more than ever a subversive pursuit. Thomas Mann's vast, labyrinthine works are already in danger of being buried in the ruins of twentieth-century culture.

Indeed, we cannot endow Mann with clear intentions to set before us more or less dogmatic views on the nature of man and man's knowledge. It is nevertheless striking that his great novels, like those of Proust and of Joyce, also composed during the first half of the twentieth century, are built up of notions very different from those we now call (and which were already called then) "modern" or "contemporary." Of these great works, those of Mann may be the most difficult, since his involved hermeneutics hide under a bourgeois realism which may be already outmoded, and obey the rules of a literary game which the modern reader follows less and less. They probably contain, however, the best analysis of the latent powers of man, and of their formidable and secret dangers. In our time, when both these powers and dangers seem to have acquired an evidence unknown until now, we are perhaps better able to follow his inquiries—psychological and physiological, certainly, but also those in which theology and alchemy are uppermost—on the nature of man considered at the same time *sub specie saeculi* and *sub specie aeternitatis*.

FAYENCE, VAR, 1955
MOUNT DESERT ISLAND, 1956